SHERLOCK HOLMES

The Vanishing Man

ALSO AVAILABLE FROM TITAN BOOKS

COMING SOON FROM TITAN BOOKS

SHERLOCK HOLMES

The Vanishing Man

PHILIP PURSER-HALLARD

TITAN BOOKS

Sherlock Holmes: The Vanishing Man
Print edition ISBN: 9781785658426
Electronic edition ISBN: 9781785658433

Published by Titan Books
A division of Titan Publishing Group Ltd
144 Southwark St, London SE1 0UP

First edition: June 2019
2 4 6 8 10 9 7 5 3 1

A CIP catalogue record for this title is available from the British Library.

Printed and bound in the United States.

Did you enjoy this book?
We love to hear from our readers. Please email us at:
readerfeedback@titanemail.com, or write to us at Reader Feedback
at the above address.

To receive advance information, news, competitions, and exclusive offers
online, please sign up for the Titan newsletter on our website:
www.titanbooks.com

To all those who have preceded me in John Watson's footsteps, but especially Stuart Douglas, Kelly Hale and George Mann.

FOREWORD

I recently received through the post a package sent from my friend Sherlock Holmes's retirement retreat in Sussex, which upon inspection proved to contain a bundle of papers relating to an investigation that occupied Holmes and myself during part of the September of 1896. Some of them I remember my friend showing me at the time; others are new to me. Though Holmes has made occasional annotations, there was no letter accompanying the enclosed material. I have nevertheless taken this as conveying his view that the time has come for the story of the case to be told.

In preparing this account for publication, I have remained faithful to my contemporary impressions, resisting the temptation, beyond some necessary tidying and polishing and the checking and correction of certain facts, to elaborate upon the notes I set down shortly afterwards. However, some of those papers which Holmes must have acquired in the years since demonstrate that the incident of the Evolved Man was one with ramifications that I at least, and perhaps even he, did not fully grasp at the time.

Although their relevance is sometimes tangential, it is clear that Holmes considers all these documents to be of potential interest. I have therefore interspersed them between the chapters of my own account, to provide the reader with a more complete understanding than was available to us then.

John H. Watson, MD, 1928

CHAPTER ONE

'In the space of an hour's walk this afternoon,' Sherlock Holmes told me, 'I have observed three pickpockets, a housebreaker and a man who disappeared.'

I stared at him, a little befuddled. He had returned from his constitutional, to all appearances energised and invigorated, to find me in the chair by the fire in the cosy fug of our rooms. I had earlier declined to join him on his perambulations on the grounds that the afternoon was wet and chilly, and my old war-wound had been troubling me. Though I had certainly been reading the newspaper when he left, I confess that I might have fallen into a light doze during his absence.

'Disappeared?' I asked, struggling to think of an intelligent reply. 'That hardly seems possible on a London street in daylight, even when the sky is so dark with cloud. But what,' I added, 'do you mean about the pickpockets and housebreaker? I can't believe you've seen four crimes committed during one short walk.'

The time was, I noted with a surreptitious glance at the clock, about five-thirty in the afternoon. The day was a damp Tuesday in September. After a sunny morning, heavy clouds had swept in over London during lunch, surrendering a burden of water which had had our window-panes resounding like a drum – albeit a peculiarly soothing one – all afternoon. Outside, I saw as I opened the window for a breath of air, the gutters still flowed murkily. Cabmen and their horses grumbled beneath their oilskins, while pedestrians jostled their way through the puddles under umbrellas, or with droplets cascading from their hats. It seemed an inauspicious day for crime, let alone for unnatural disappearances.

'Alas,' said Holmes, vigorously stoking the fire, 'I saw none of them breaking the law. I merely inferred their intentions from their behaviour and manner. The pickpockets were fleet-footed, nimble-fingered fellows, walking briskly at the side of the pavement nearest the road, unencumbered by umbrellas. Their coats were too light for the weather, short in the arm and tight-fitting about the cuffs, with deep pockets. Their eyes darted about as they walked, sizing up each person they passed.'

He threw himself down into his armchair and continued. 'The housebreaker was a different specimen, thin as a wire with large, strong hands. Though he could have moved as quickly as any of the pickpockets, he instead trudged slowly through the rain, gazing up at the buildings around him with a rustic's curiosity. He lingered for a while on Baker Street, lit a cigarette, took in his surroundings along with his leisurely smoke, then trampled the cigarette-end and went his way.'

As I re-seated myself I wondered, not for the first time, how Holmes could be certain of such firm convictions based on what were surely mundane observations. 'Anyone might take an interest in his surroundings while enjoying a quiet smoke in the street,' I admonished him. 'I'm sure I've done it myself.'

Holmes smiled. 'I would venture, Watson, that you have not chosen to linger opposite a bathroom window which hangs ajar on a broken catch, and which might with judicious footwork be reached from the street at dead of night.'

'Not chosen, no.' I added obstinately, 'But I might happen to.'

'Perhaps, Watson, perhaps. By that time I was wanting the comforts of home, or I should have followed the man and seen whether the coincidence repeated itself further down the street. In any case, Mrs Hudson must advise her counterpart at Number 213 to have that catch mended with all haste.'

I recalled the rest of his peculiar statement. 'But what did you mean about the other man?' I asked, allowing a note of amusement to enter my voice. 'Did he fade away before your eyes, or did you merely infer from his manner an intention to disappear at some time in the future?'

Holmes said good-naturedly, 'Ah, but that case was different again. I confess that the man I speak of did not vanish in front of me. I could discern, though, that he had recently disappeared from his previous life. The number who do so might surprise you, Watson, steadfast and reliable as your own presence is.' He stood again and paced across the room, to gaze out of the window into the Baker Street drizzle. 'Some leave wives and families, of course, whether for some new infatuation or simply because they feel oppressed by their obligations. Others flee the consequences of a crime or scandal, or from debt. And where better to remain invisible than in a city of so many million souls?

'The man I saw was dressed like a workman and his hands bore cuts and the beginnings of calluses, of the kind one sees on operators of machinery – but all were recent, while the shape of the same digits showed the deep groove of a pen, telling of years spent as an office clerk. His chin was raw from unaccustomed shaving, and he sported whiskers of perhaps a month's growth, inexpertly kempt although they were the kind in which the wearer normally takes some pride. He doffed his cap to ladies, but with a sense of novelty to the movement, as if used to wearing a different kind of hat entirely.'

I remained sceptical. 'It seems a rather flimsy chain of

reasoning on which to base such a conclusion. Perhaps the man had simply suffered a recent change of circumstances.'

Holmes continued. 'As he passed beneath a clock I saw him absent-mindedly reach to his midriff, thinking to take out a pocket-watch and set it, before recalling that he wore no waistcoat and carried no watch. He glanced nervously at the faces of those around him to see whether he had been observed. When he saw my eye on him he blanched and hastened away. He had become visible again, and that is what a vanished man fears the most.'

Holmes turned to me and smiled again. 'But here we are, Watson, discussing the disappeared when we are about to be favoured with an unexpected appearance.'

I went to the window. In the street beneath were two figures, picking the way through the puddles to our doorstep. The rain persisted still, and all we could see of them were their legs and the black domes of their umbrellas.

'There's not a lot you can deduce from that,' I observed, knowing as I said it that I was in all likelihood handing Holmes another opportunity to prove me wrong. He barked an amused 'Ha!' and, shutting the window against the cold, crossed the room to stand before the fire.

A few moments later the sitting-room door opened and Mrs Hudson ushered in two gentlemen, now divested of their outer garments. The senior of the two was a handsome man of about sixty, clean-shaven, with bright eyes and swan-white hair flowing from a high, intelligent forehead. His companion was under thirty years of age, tall and slight, with dark curly hair and large eyes.

'Ah, Sir Newnham Speight,' said Sherlock Holmes at once, before Mrs Hudson could introduce them. 'May I present my associate, Dr Watson?'

The older man nodded politely to me and said, 'But I

wasn't aware we'd met, Mr Holmes. I'd have thought I would have remembered.'

I recognised Sir Newnham's name, of course. The reader will doubtless recall him too, as the inventor lauded by a grateful nation for such practical boons as Speight's Self-Igniting Tinder-Pipe, Speight's Doubly-Adjustable Bedstead with Integrated Mattress, Speight's Rotary Clothes-Press Wardrobe, and Speight's Miniature Bedside Tea-Urn with Integrated Alarm Clock. I owned one of the last myself, a present given in gratitude by an eccentric patient, which I had never yet used.

'No more we have,' Holmes replied, gratified by the man's perplexity. 'But I had the opportunity to observe your umbrellas as you arrived outside. Each is unmistakeably a Speight's Super-Collapsible Pocket model, but with certain ingenious adjustments. I take it that today's inclement weather has been an opportunity for you to test out a prototype for a more advanced design?'

'Two different prototypes, in fact,' the younger man said in a light, musical voice. He seemed amused by Holmes's odd manners, and introduced himself as Talbot Rhyne, Sir Newnham's assistant. 'Sir Newnham has the brolly with my improvements, and I the one with his. We're carrying out a comparative field-test.'

'Capital!' cried Holmes. 'Do you hear that, Watson? The perfect marriage of the entrepreneurial and the empirical spirit.'

'You chose a day that suited the experiment, anyway,' I said. 'Won't you sit down and take some tea?'

'Tut, Watson,' insisted Holmes, 'they haven't come for tea.' My view was that given their chilly journey they might welcome it nonetheless, but Holmes was unlikely to succumb to persuasion when gripped by such an enthusiastic mood. 'Take a seat, gentlemen, and tell Dr Watson and myself what is on your minds this sodden evening.'

'It's a very peculiar affair, Mr Holmes,' said Sir Newnham as they both settled into chairs. Though perfectly articulate, his voice retained echoes of the working-class Londoners outside on the street, and I recalled reading that Speight, a millionaire several times over and knighted by the Queen to boot, was a self-made man of humble origins. 'I fear it's not really in your usual line, but if there's a man in London who can explain it to me, it's yourself.'

'I am already intrigued,' said Holmes. 'If there is one thing guaranteed to endear a case to me, it is that it should be peculiar. Pray proceed.'

'Well, that's part of the question,' Sir Newnham Speight said. 'It may not even be a "case" in the criminal sense. *Something* has happened, certainly – something decidedly out of the ordinary – and the explanation may well involve a crime of some sort. But at the moment it's impossible to say whether Thomas Kellway is missing or dead.'

'That is distressing,' I suggested sympathetically, remembering Holmes's earlier comments about men who abandon their positions in life, 'but perhaps not so very unusual.'

'It's the possibilities that make it so, Dr Watson,' Talbot Rhyne put in eagerly. 'You see, it may be that Kellway is one of the greatest hoaxers in history, or it may be that he has somehow managed to transport himself to the planet Venus. I think that puts it in the realm of the remarkable, at least.'

'The planet Venus?' I repeated in astonishment.

Holmes smiled tightly. 'In principle, gentlemen, it is a trivial matter to guess which of your alternatives is the more likely. I have known a considerable number of hoaxers during my career, but am yet to meet a single interplanetary traveller. I imagine, though, that you have more to tell me. Watson, I believe we may after all benefit from some tea, while Sir Newnham recounts this surprising story to us from the beginning.'

Our guests settled themselves while I rang for Mrs Hudson and outlined our requirements. As she departed, Sir Newnham began his tale.

'Among my other interests, I am the Chairman of the Society for the Scientific Investigation of Psychical Phenomena. Our aim is to investigate through experiment and observation those phenomena commonly ascribed the label "psychic" – thought-transference, mental action at a distance, clairvoyance, et cetera – with a view to either proving or disproving their existence.

'I see you frown, but you must understand that my own interest isn't in the mystical mumbo-jumbo with which imaginative people so often surround such claims – the spirit world and Druids from Atlantis and the like. I'm a scientist, not a metaphysician. My interest lies in research, and that obliges me to be as open-minded on this question as on any other.

'I will admit that the Society attracts members of various types, with varying philosophical and even religious persuasions. Provided they pay their dues and don't interfere with the experiments, they're all welcome. My own view is not fixed as to the veracity of those exceptional phenomena that witnesses in history have from time to time reported – levitation, precognition, bilocation and what-have-you. So far I haven't seen compelling evidence one way or the other.

'I am firm, though, that if such things exist then they are neither magical nor miraculous, but can be measured and observed like everything else in the universe, and on that basis analysed, predicted and eventually reproduced. If ever that were done successfully, then the potential contribution to future science would be incalculable. Alternatively, there may be nothing at all to measure – but to the scientist a discovery of truth is never truly a failure.

'Over the years I have found it helpful to set up the facilities for my researches in the more conventional sciences at my home, Parapluvium House in Richmond, and among these I've constructed an annexe where claims of extraordinary phenomena may be tested under a variety of controlled conditions. Its most salient feature is a set of three Experiment Rooms in which subjects may be isolated from one another, and from any necessary experimental materials, so that we may be sure that any interaction between the rooms is exclusively mental.

'For such trials we need subjects, and it is necessary to encourage those who believe themselves to be gifted in the psychical arena to come forward. Such persons are generally reluctant to subject themselves to a full scientific investigation, but this is not always because they are dishonest. Many may be quite sincere in their claims, but mistrust our motives, or lack the education to understand our aims, or fear that the experiments will be invasive or painful.

'To overcome such reluctance, I have made a standing offer of a reward of ten thousand pounds to any claimant who can successfully convince the Committee of the Society, in a simple test, of a psychic ability or corresponding phenomenon.

'Such an outcome would be merely the start of the process, of course – the condition for the reward is the Committee's satisfaction, whereas the criteria for scientific proof would be a great deal more rigorous, and could take months of repeated experiments. If any trial subject were to pass the first test, we would naturally offer all possible inducements to persuade them to stay on. However, in the three years since the reward was first offered, several dozen claimants have come forward, and none have satisfied the Committee's credulity, let alone the strictures of experimental proof.

'At least – that was certainly the case last night. It may no longer be possible to say so this morning.'

Sir Newnham fell broodingly silent for a few moments before continuing. 'Ten thousand is a very substantial sum, of course,' he said. 'It has attracted a few subjects who came close enough in the experiments to persuade some of the Committee that they were genuinely gifted. It has brought us many who are sincerely deluded, and a few overconfident fraudsters. The latter group have sometimes been remarkably ingenious. So far we've found out all their deceptions, but it remains a fear of mine that one day I will be taken in by some hoax.

'That, then, is the background to our current quandary. I shall proceed to the more immediate events.

'A little over two months ago I received a letter from a man named Thomas Kellway, who informed me that he had psychic abilities. He prefaced it with a lot of waffle, as they generally do. In any case, while Kellway's spiel may have been about how interplanetary etheric influences had boosted certain abilities in him that are latent in all of us, his gist was that he could make an object move some distance away using the power of his mind – the technical term is "telekinesis". Our experimental facilities can certainly put such phenomena to the test, so I invited him to come and meet me.

'My first impressions of the man were favourable enough. He is a soft-spoken Yorkshireman, a fine physical specimen, perhaps fifty years old but hale and strong. Intelligent too, and articulate, with a calm, persuasive way about him. His most remarkable characteristic, though, was that he was entirely bald – not a hair on his head, not even an eyebrow, nor yet on his hands.

'I found him eccentric, to be sure, but no more so than many who come our way. No more so than some in our Society, if truth be told. We encounter freemasons, theosophists, spiritualists, vegetarians – all sorts. He attended last month's meeting of the Society, and many of them were quite taken with him. He has called at several of our houses, including mine, on a number of occasions since.

'As I have said, Kellway's particular fancies are in the cosmological line. He believes – or perhaps I should only say that he claims – that he has been remotely influenced since before his birth by superior intelligences from the second planet in our solar system.

'These Venusians supposedly established a form of pre-natal psychical communion with Kellway, and under their influence he has become a more highly developed form of human being, mentally and physically superior to the rest of us – although he insists that anyone can become such with the proper discipline. An "Evolved Man" is what he calls himself – the next stage of human development – although I have also heard him use the term "Interplanetary Man". He told me that he was born bald, hair being a useless vestige of mankind's evolutionary past. He maintains that for similar reasons he lacks the normal vermiform appendix, though I am of course in no position to confirm that statement and I cannot imagine how he can be certain of it either.

'According to Kellway, the goal of the Venusians, having raised all life on their planet to the peak of its evolutionary potential, is to assist those of us here on Earth to perfect ourselves likewise, becoming angelic paragons like the Venusians themselves. To do him justice, Kellway claims merely to be a step along that road rather than its final destination. Supposedly the Venusians were blessed in this way aeons ago by beings from Mercury, and intend that we in turn shall show the same favour to the inhabitants of Mars, each world bestowing enlightenment on the next one out from the Sun, which is the original source of these emanations of divinity.

'His cosmology is rather primitive, you see, despite its modern veneer. He speaks with an occasional rather biblical turn of phrase, which I might have put down to a non-conformist upbringing were it not for these messianic pretensions of his.

'It was decided early in our Society's existence, however, that we would judge our subjects on the practical results of our experiments, not on their own beliefs. I agreed with Kellway that we would conduct a trial to prove or disprove his ability. We agreed the form that this experiment would take, which is our standard one for telekinesis, though with a few modifications. The date was set for yesterday.

'Kellway would be locked in an otherwise empty room, next to another, similar room, also locked, which would also be empty but for three things: a table, a closed wooden box on top of it, and an ordinary billiard ball placed inside the box. The intervening wall would mean that Kellway would be unable even to see the experimental materials. His task would be to open the box in the next-door room and remove the ball, using nothing but the power of his mind.

'The Experimental Annexe was built to my own specifications, two years ago. I hope you will take the opportunity to inspect it yourself, Mr Holmes. In the meantime, allow me to describe it to you.

'It is reached from the house via a passage from my chemical laboratories, or from the grounds through an external door. Both of these doors are located in the antechamber which adjoins the three Experiment Rooms, which are in a row next to one another and are designated A, B and C. The experiment required that Kellway occupy Room A, with the experimental materials in Room B. Each room is a cube, eight feet by eight feet by eight feet, with a large glass panel in the door and a window at the top of the far wall. The windows can be opened for comfort during hot weather, but they are narrow and barred, as well as high. A cat might squeeze through one of them perhaps, but not a man. The doors are of a design normally used in store-rooms, which can only be locked and unlocked from the outside, and the lock's manufacturers advertise it as unpickable. There are no connecting doors between the three rooms, of course – that would hardly serve the purposes of the experiment. Have I been clear enough, Mr Holmes?'

Holmes said, 'I believe I can visualise the arrangement. I, too, hope that I will be able to examine it in person before long. Pray continue.'

'Well, Kellway told me that he could accomplish the task, but he had certain stipulations. He spoke of charging up his psychical energy like a battery, until he had a sufficiency of it to perform the task – those may not have been his precise words, but that was his drift. This would, he insisted, take many hours of meditation to do. This process would have to begin at sunset, with Venus still visible in the sky. He added that experience had shown him that direct artificial light would interfere with the frequency of his psychic vibrations, and would render the experiment futile.

'I need not say that this rang alarm bells for me – in my experience, a subject who prefers to work in the dark has something to hide. However, it transpired that Kellway had no objection to Room B being well lit, nor the anteroom, merely his own room. Each has its own independent electric light, so the box on its table would be illuminated clearly throughout, while Kellway himself would be visible, though not strongly lit, by the brightness from the anteroom. Given the aim of the experiment, I felt that, provided we could observe the experimental materials, it would be less important to see exactly what Kellway was doing. After some consultation with the members of the Society Committee, I agreed to his stipulations.

'Last evening, therefore, at seven o'clock, nine members of the Society, including the two of us, assembled in the Experimental Annexe at my house, along with Mr Kellway and a couple of attendants. We all observed as the experimental materials were placed in Room B, the middle room. I locked the door, leaving the light on. The table and closed box were clearly visible through the glass of the door. At half-past seven, with Venus twenty minutes away from setting by the almanac, Kellway entered the unlit Room A. Again I locked him in myself. Room C was to play no part in the experiment and was never unlocked, or for that matter lit.

'Kellway took off his shoes and jacket and began his meditations. We could see him dimly in the light from the antechamber, sitting in what is called the lotus position. From the moment I turned the key he could not have escaped the room by normal means – he would have needed to slither under the door or float through solid brick. Even the window was locked shut, it being a cold night.

'At eight o'clock, as we had arranged, we all left the room except the first pair of observers. Our standard practice for protracted sessions such as these is that Rhyne here, who serves as secretary to the Committee, draws up a rota of such observers. As I say, it is less usual for such events to occur overnight, but fortunately my house is large and I have no family, so my staff were able to arrange accommodation for those who needed it.

'The reason for using two observers at a time is of course to reduce the risk of human error or collusion with the subject. As a general rule in such cases, the observers are not constantly peering through the glass at the subject, as naturally this tends to distract them. Our normal approach is that the observers look through the doors at timed intervals of five minutes, one checking on the subject while the other confirms the status of the experimental materials. Nobody enters the rooms, of course – they remain locked.

'On this occasion the first two observers were Dr Peter Kingsley – a gentleman of your profession, Dr Watson, who is my neighbour in Richmond – and Professor Elias Scaverson, one of our more distinguished scientific members. Between observations they spent most of the time playing cribbage, and they reported nothing unusual or amiss. At ten o'clock Rhyne here relieved them, along with Major Bradbury; and so we continued throughout the night, with pairs of individuals taking two-hour shifts, until the four to six o'clock shift this morning.

'The observers at that time were Frederick Garforth, the artist, and my butler, Anderton. Unlike myself and Rhyne, Anderton is an honorary rather than a full member of the Society, as, if truth be told, he has little interest in scientific matters, but he has helped make up our numbers on several past occasions, and I would trust him as an impartial observer above a number of our regular members. At a little before ten to five Major Bradbury, having woken early in a companionable mood, joined them once again. At ten minutes to five, five to five and five o'clock, Garforth and Anderton looked into the rooms as usual and saw, as before, the box sitting undisturbed upon the table in Room B, and Kellway meditating with great concentration in Room A.

'At five minutes past five they checked again, and Garforth cried out that Kellway had vanished. Bradbury and Anderton immediately checked his observation and confirmed it. Thomas Kellway had disappeared, Mr Holmes, from a locked room, leaving behind him not a trace of his passing.'

Schedule and Plan for an Experimental Test of Telekinesis
The Psychic Experimental Annexe, Parapluvium House,
14th & 15th September 1896

SUBJECT: Thos. Kellway

SCHEDULE:

7 p.m. to 8 p.m. START OF EXPERIMENT.
Setting-Up and Locking of Experiment Rooms. All Society Members welcome to attend. *NB: Venus sets 7.49 p.m.*

8 p.m. to 10 p.m. FIRST OBSERVATION:
Dr Kingsley, Prof. Scaverson.

10 p.m. to 12 p.m. SECOND OBSERVATION:
Major Bradbury, Mr Rhyne.

12 p.m. to 2 a.m. THIRD OBSERVATION:
Revd Small, Mr Beech.

2 a.m. to 4 a.m. FOURTH OBSERVATION:
Lord Jermaine, Mr McInnery.

4 a.m. to 6 a.m. FIFTH OBSERVATION:
Mr Garforth, Wm. Anderton.

6 a.m. to 8 a.m. SIXTH OBSERVATION:
Sir Newnham Speight, Hon. Mr Floke.

8 a.m. onwards END OF EXPERIMENT.

Release of Mr Kellway, followed by Breakfast and Discussion of Results. All Society Members welcome to attend.

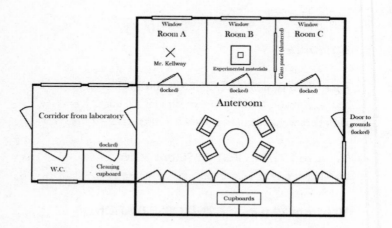

CHAPTER TWO

I whistled, and Holmes, who had been listening intently throughout all of this, was equally impressed. He said, 'I had hopes that you were leading up to some spectacular revelation, Sir Newnham, and you have not disappointed me. Please tell us the rest. What happened next?'

'Well,' said Speight. 'After Bradbury and Anderton had reassured Garforth that his eyes were not deceiving him, Anderton came to find me at once.

'I was already awake and mostly dressed, as I was to take the sixth and final shift. I sent Anderton to knock up Rhyne, and went down to the Annexe straight away. I would have been there by ten past five. Bradbury and Garforth were waiting for us in the anteroom, and had nothing new to report. When we arrived I unlocked the door to Room A and the three of us searched it together – not that there's anywhere in that bare space where Kellway could possibly have concealed himself. We also checked on Room B, but found the billiard ball still inside the box.'

'Did you check the third room?' Holmes asked.

'For form's sake, yes. It was perfectly empty. There are also some cupboards in the anteroom where experimental equipment is stored, and when Rhyne joined us he suggested searching those as well, in case Kellway had somehow... Well, we were all at a loss for an explanation, and by now I'm afraid we were clutching at straws. Nothing had been disturbed in any case, and of course there was no sign of Kellway.

'We roused the rest of the household, and assembled the Society members in the Experimental Annexe. Nobody could explain how Kellway had left a room that was, for all reasonable purposes, sealed tight, nor where he might be now. Of course, by that I mean that nobody was able to offer a conventional explanation. Inevitably, several of those present were inclined to take a supernatural view of the affair.

'For my own part I am sceptical enough to believe for now that this is an unprecedented hoax, though as to its mechanics I am just as much perplexed as everybody else. In fact I have been half-expecting Kellway to stroll in and claim the reward, but when I left Richmond this afternoon he had not yet reappeared.

'This, then, is the problem I came to put before you, Mr Holmes. How did Thomas Kellway escape from that room, where is he now, and does the Society for the Scientific Investigation of Psychical Phenomena owe him ten thousand pounds?'

'A most attractive problem, indeed,' Holmes said. 'Although I fear the possibilities that Mr Rhyne outlined at first are extreme ones. If Kellway has indeed vanished away, there is no more reason to suppose him on Venus than anywhere else – indeed, I venture to suggest that the feat of transporting oneself instantaneously and intangibly from one place to another would be no less marvellous if one's destination were Putney Common. And if Kellway is a hoaxer, I venture that he is more liable to prove a talented practitioner than an unprecedented genius, though I admit the effect he has produced is an exceptional one.

'I have a few questions, Sir Newnham, if I may. To begin with, where were the keys to the Experiment Rooms kept during the procedure? I mean the keys to the windows as well as the doors.'

'My housekeeper, Mrs Catton, keeps one set,' Speight said, 'which she is meticulous in locking away when they are out of use. The other was on my key-chain, which I keep on my person. When the Annexe is not in use, that set remains in the safe in my study, to which only Rhyne and myself have the combination. The windows all use the same key, and that is on a ring with the three door-keys.'

'Was your key-chain on your person while you were asleep?' Holmes asked, somewhat sceptically.

'No – it was not, of course,' agreed Sir Newnham. 'It was on my night-stand in my room – I always place it there at night, and I remember seizing it in haste on my way down to the Annexe. It was, however, within two feet of me, and I am an unusually light sleeper, as my manservant will be able to confirm. I tend to wake several times during the night, and last night was no exception. I cannot see that anyone could have entered my room and borrowed the chain without my being aware of it.'

Holmes proceeded with his questioning. 'You said that the experiment rooms were empty other than Kellway and the table, box and ball, but you then told us that Kellway took his shoes and jacket in with him. Precisely, please, what was in Room A?'

'Precisely? Well, Kellway himself, of course. The light bulb and a coat-hook are the only fixtures. Normally we provide a chair for the subjects, but Kellway insisted he had no need of that. He took in the clothes he was wearing, naturally, including his jacket and shoes. I believe he also had with him a walking-cane.'

'What was in his jacket?' I asked.

'A highly pertinent point,' said Holmes. 'I trust that you at least searched his pockets for suspicious items.'

'We do so as a matter of routine,' Sir Newnham said, seeming a little hurt. 'As I said, we have been troubled by pranksters in the past. I don't believe we found anything out of the ordinary, though. What did he have on him, Rhyne?'

His secretary said, 'A pocket book containing cards and notes, some loose change, a handkerchief, a door-key. That's all.'

'No cigarettes or tobacco?' Holmes asked. 'No matches?'

'Kellway's a strict non-smoker,' Rhyne said. 'It's one of his fads. But, gentlemen, if you know of something a chap could hide in his clothes that would let him disappear from a locked room – or to move an object in an adjacent room, for that matter, since that's what we were expecting – I'll be astonished to hear of it.'

Holmes nodded thoughtfully. 'I will need to examine the items even so, assuming they are still in his jacket. I take it he spent the night in shirtsleeves and socks?'

'He took off his socks as well,' said Rhyne. 'I didn't see him do it, but he was certainly meditating barefoot by the time I came on watch.'

'You said that one reason for pairing observers together was to prevent collusion,' Holmes said to Speight. 'But it is surely conceivable that two men might collude together with a third.'

'I said it reduced the risk,' Sir Newnham corrected him. 'It is impossible to rule it out altogether. We do our best to avoid pairing together relatives, business partners or close friends. In this instance, of course, Major Bradbury was unexpectedly also present at the time of the disappearance. Of course many of our members come to know one another through the Society itself, but I know of no particular connection between Bradbury and Garforth, and I most certainly trust Anderton. He has been with me for nearly thirty years, first as my manservant and then as my butler, and is an intelligent man of shrewd judgement and great loyalty.'

'And Garforth and Bradbury? What can you tell us of them?'

'Both good men, as far as my knowledge goes,' Speight said. 'Major Bradbury I have known since he retired from service in India, seven years ago. He's quite the enthusiast for Eastern religion, but keeps a level head in everyday matters, though I believe he was quite charmed by Kellway. Garforth has been with the Society for a year or so. I don't know him as well as the others, but I believe he's a friend of Rhyne's family.'

'Oh yes, I've known Garforth since I was a boy,' Rhyne confirmed, in his boyish tones. 'I called him Uncle Freddie as a lad. He's a very sound fellow.'

'You stood Major Bradbury's own watch with him, Mr Rhyne,' Holmes said. 'Did he strike you as especially interested in Kellway at the time?'

'Well, not especially,' the young secretary said. 'He takes an interest in all our subjects – he seems to have seen a lot of mystical stuff that impressed him out in India, and he lives in hopes of seeing the same thing reproduced scientifically here. I'm not surprised he was interested in how things were proceeding, come the morning.'

'And what did you make of Kellway?' I asked him. Rhyne hesitated.

'You may as well tell them, Rhyne,' Sir Newnham said with a sigh. 'You know I can't stand intellectual dishonesty.'

'Well.' Rhyne shrugged. 'He's a remarkable fellow, forceful and charismatic. I'm not so fond of his esoteric cosmology; as Sir Newnham says, it's more like some superstitious hangover from medieval astrology than anything scientific. But it's not so hard to believe that, if anyone had extraordinary mental powers, it would be a man like Kellway. And… well, look, a chap doesn't just disappear, not in the natural course of events. As you say, it's not so very important whether he went to Venus, just that he went *somewhere* – and, to be frank, I believe he did. He might be waiting for the right conditions for his return, or... well, he might not even have survived the journey. Or the destination, if it were the South Pole or the bottom of the ocean. He might not have had control of the process, you see.'

Sir Newnham sighed expressively. 'And there you have it – Rhyne is a rational man, or I would never have employed him as my secretary, and *he* is convinced. Oh, don't fret, Rhyne, I don't take it personally. Mr Holmes, I don't care at all about the money – ten thousand's nothing to me. But if we hand Kellway the reward and he turns out to be a fraud, the Society will become a laughing-stock and my reputation will be ruined. I am not just an inventor, Mr Holmes, I am a scientist, and I rely on my standing among others of that profession. It would be a grave blow to me, a grave blow indeed.'

Holmes said, 'If Kellway should reappear to claim the reward, how will the matter be decided?'

'The Society Committee must agree it. That's myself, Dr Kingsley as Vice-Chairman, Professor Scaverson, the Reverend Small, the Honourable Gerald Floke and the Countess Irina Brusilova – and Mr Gideon Beech, who is our Treasurer. Rhyne acts as secretary to the Committee but does not have a vote.'

'Gideon Beech?' I asked in surprise. 'The playwright?' The author of a number of scandalous plays that had outraged the morals of society, Beech was considered an *enfant terrible* of the theatre; but he had also been canny enough to write *The Man for Wisdom*, a popular light comedy that had won him financial success and acclaim from the masses of less highbrow theatregoers who remained untroubled by his more challenging works. Beech was forever penning articles and letters to the press, their primary subject, whatever their ostensible topic, always seeming to be himself. From them I knew that he was a ferocious Fabian, a teetotaller, an advocate of spelling reform and numerous other enthusiasms, but this was the first I had heard of his having more esoteric leanings.

Speight nodded. 'He was one of our earliest members, as a matter of fact. As I was saying, I would call an extraordinary meeting of the Committee and there would be a vote on the matter. As Chairman, I would only cast my own vote in the event of a tie. In the current situation, I'm not sure I would get the chance. Floke is young and rather impressionable, and admires Kellway greatly. The Countess is an inveterate advocate of outlandish phenomena of all kinds, so I fear she would take little persuasion to go along with him. And Kellway's cosmic mumbo-jumbo has a very particular appeal to Beech, as it supports his own idiosyncratic views on evolution. Beech won't hear a word against him, in fact. Since this morning he's been quite convinced the wretched man has been spirited away to Venus.'

'Much, then, would depend on the votes of Professor Scaverson, the Reverend Small and Dr Kingsley,' Holmes observed.

'Indeed,' agreed Speight. 'Kingsley and Scaverson are men of science, and reliable. But Mr Small is not only a believer in the supernatural by profession, but a man of a rather... individual bent. I understand some of his own parishioners view him as a troublemaker, in fact. I fear that Small might vote to endorse Kellway purely for his own amusement, and that would be the Committee won over.'

'Well, I shall hope to speak to them all in due course,' said Holmes. 'In the meantime you may perhaps take comfort in the fact that Kellway has not yet reappeared to cash in on his remarkable *coup de théâtre*. Sir Newnham, if I accept this case, it will be with one stipulation. My primary interest will be in establishing how this person vanished, and you may decide about the reward accordingly. His current whereabouts, unless they prove germane to his method, will be of lesser importance to me.'

'Well, I won't object to that,' Sir Newnham said. 'I hope the fellow's safe, of course, but I admit it would spare us some trouble if we never saw him again. My hope, though, is that you will uncover the truth, whatever it may be.'

'What's your view of the case, Mr Holmes?' Talbot Rhyne asked.

'I always try to avoid theorising without sufficient data, Mr Rhyne. I hope to have a clearer picture once I have inspected the scene of the disappearance itself. I fear I have some business to attend to this evening which cannot wait, but if you are agreeable, Sir Newnham, Watson and I will call upon you in the morning.'

'Of course, Mr Holmes,' said Speight. 'But, like Rhyne, I'd appreciate hearing any thoughts you may have at this point, however unformed.'

Holmes sighed. 'At present I have little beyond the obvious. You tell me that Kellway was visible in the room at five o'clock, and visibly absent five minutes later, and that in the meantime he could neither have hidden himself in the room nor left it by natural means. As it is unlikely that Kellway has performed a feat that all prior scientific thought tells us is impossible, my first hypothesis must be that you are mistaken in some aspect of the story you have presented to me.

'I hope to make my own assessment of the escapability of the room when I inspect it tomorrow, but if what you have told me holds then I shall be left with the likelihood that you have been lied to. Several witnesses including yourself saw Kellway enter the room and stay there; multiple pairs of observers testify to his presence throughout the night; and you affirm that you found him absent from the locked room at ten past five. Since I have no choice but to trust your own account, the point where the story is weakest is at the time when Garforth,

Bradbury and Anderton attest that the vanishing took place, and you have their word alone for what happened.

'The case thus becomes a question of conspiracy to defraud, involving a mere picked lock or copied key, rather than anything supernatural. Our working hypothesis must be that these three witnesses colluded to let Kellway escape, and all of them have lied to you about it.'

But the great inventor had been shaking his head for some time. Now he said, 'I've read Dr Watson's case-studies, sir, and I'm familiar with your maxim about eliminating the truly impossible and accepting any remaining improbabilities. But to apply it, one must first draw the line between the impossible and the improbable, and where *that* line lies can be partly a matter of personal judgement. I don't know Garforth well, and I could perhaps believe that Bradbury had somehow been compromised, but Anderton is as loyal to me as my right arm. I have known him since we were boys. If he needed money, or were being blackmailed, or compelled in any way, I am certain he would have come to me at once.

'It seems to me, Mr Holmes, that your dictum fails to account for different types of impossibility. I might well be persuaded that the continuum of phenomena allowed for by our current science is incomplete, but I could never believe that William Anderton would conspire to defraud me.'

Holmes nodded. 'I had rather supposed that you might say that. It certainly serves to make the case more interesting,' he said. 'Good evening, gentlemen, and I look forward to furthering our acquaintance on the morrow.'

The Chiswick Weekly Parish Examiner

Friday 7th August 1896

IT MUST BE APPREHENDED that the Editors of this Organ have no truck with anti-clerical sentiment with which our Mighty and Venerable Nation, built upon the Piety of those simple souls who make up the greatest portion of Her Majesty's subjects, has of late been plagued. The English Church is a Pillar of our Nation, and in its awful Majesty, the indispensable foundation of Her Majesty's own.

It is for this very reason that the Church's peerless Reputation among the general populace must be safeguarded, at All Costs, and that those Individuals who bring this Holy Institution into vile Disrepute must not be acquiesced to, even when they hide their wolfish Predilections in a Shepherd's Garb, but must instead stand Challenged with all the forcefulness that a humble yet locally respected Publication such as our own may bring to bear.

It has been made known to us, by some with some reasons for Concern, that one in a Position of Authority in this Parish has sanctioned with his presence a body going by the ungodly name of The Society for the Scientific Investiture of Psychic Phenomenon. This nice Gathering unites Devil-Worshippers, Hindoos and other Cursed Heathens with the most Atheistical and Nihilistic of our Nation's Scientific Unbelievers, with the aim of creating Marvels without the intercession of Our LORD.

The Editors understand that these purported Prodigies include the Tricks of knowing the Thoughts of Others, of Moving Objects without touching them, of Foretelling the Future and of Flying through the Air. We need not inflict upon your ears, tender Reader, the name to which such Vile Practices would have been given in simpler Times (*Exod. Ch. 22 v. 18*).

We have had Cause to

complain before of how this same Pernicious Individual has written in his learned books for Atheistical Professors in Universities and Libraries up and down our fair land, denying the Divinity of our Saviour and the reality of the Hereafter (wherein, as its reality will never be questioned by the Faithful, he can surely look for a Warm Welcome indeed! (*Matt. Ch. 25 v. 46*), but we feel it our Godly duty now to make the Reader aware, having been ignorant ourselves before, that such Company is being kept, by one into whose Hands those, doubtless Deceived by his Wiles, have Misguidedly placed the cure of the Souls of this parish.

As to the name of this person, let it merely be said that, though we are Greatly Distressed by this news, yet our Concern is SMALL.

'He who has ears, let him hear' – *Matt. Ch. 11 v. 15.*

CHAPTER THREE

The following day dawned fine and fresh, as bright as the latter days of summer had been, but cooler. When I awoke I learned, to my surprise, that Holmes had spent half the night watching out for the housebreaker whom he had spotted lurking in the street the previous day, eventually apprehending the man with the help of a passing constable as he scaled the wall of Number 213 Baker Street at half-past two in the morning.

'In such a trivial matter I hardly had need of your assistance, Watson,' he told me cheerfully, apparently invigorated by his night's work. 'Given your sluggishness of yesterday, I hoped you might appreciate the chance to refresh yourself fully.'

Rhyne had told us the night before that he and his employer had travelled from Richmond to Baker Street on the underground. It seemed that Sir Newnham had created a prototype, now nearly ready for factory production, for a form of motorised transport which might navigate ordinary city and country roads rather than requiring a system of rails, and that in the meantime he scorned cabs and carriages as outdated. Holmes and I did not share the inventor's scruples, and followed our usual custom of travelling by hansom cab.

By ten o'clock in the morning, when the cabman deposited

us at Sir Newnham's house in Richmond, the only signs of the previous day's downpour were diminishing puddles lurking in the shade of walls and trees.

An odd encounter occurred as we arrived. Just as I finished paying our cabman, a stranger rushed from a leafy recess in the hedge surrounding Sir Newnham's property, and ran around to the other side of the hansom. Climbing aboard, he shouted some urgent directions to the driver, and the cabman cracked his whip and drove away at speed. The moment's glimpse I had of the man left me with the impression of a quantity of flowing silver hair over a dark-grey cape, and the glint of a monocle.

'Someone is in a hurry,' I observed to Holmes.

'And there is a story behind it, no doubt,' he said, 'though perhaps it is nothing more interesting than an urgent appointment. In any case, while we have no means of pursuing the man, we know his destination. He asked the cabby to take him to an address in Camden.'

We turned our attention to Sir Newnham Speight's house. Some years before, what was now Parapluvium House must have been a handsome Georgian mansion set in a large acreage of garden, but in recent times it had acquired so many excrescences, extensions and annexes in a more modern style that it reminded me of those zoological hybrids showmen display at vulgar fairs, monsters sewn together by taxidermic Frankensteins from the anatomies of diverse species. Sir Newnham's view of architecture was evidently a purely utilitarian one. Holmes was delighted by the place.

We were met by Anderton the butler, a man only a little younger than Speight whose accent suggested a similar background unrefined by his master's education, and whose contented demeanour and generous girth attested to the millionaire's indulgent treatment of his servants. He showed us first to Sir Newnham's study, a well-appointed modern room on the first floor of the main house, with a view over the grounds crowded with their occupying structures.

Sir Newnham and Rhyne were in attendance, and greeted us warmly. At Holmes's suggestion they took us on a tour of the facilities, many of them manned by technicians or other staff in Speight's employ. We were shown a large, well-fitted workshop with a forge and a glassblower's kiln; a photographic studio and darkroom; a room housing a mathematical calculating engine of Speight's own devising; a huge storeroom where his larger prototypes were housed; a heated greenhouse where he was experimenting with growing tropical fruit; a large glass tank for testing prototype boat-hulls; a rooftop eyrie containing an astronomical observatory, a weather observatory and a camera obscura commanding a fine view over the grounds; a tall and echoingly empty tower for testing the dynamics of falling objects; a substantial technical library; a generator-house supplying the electrical needs of the mansion and all its satellites; and an extravagantly appointed chemistry lab, which Holmes particularly coveted.

From this last location, a short passage led us to where our business lay, in the Psychic Experimental Annexe. We found it laid out exactly as Sir Newnham had described the night before. To our right as we entered were the cupboards; to our left, the doors to the three Experiment Rooms stood open for our inspection, each with its glass panel and a brass plaque bearing a large capital A, B or C. At the far end a further door gave directly onto the grounds, although for all I knew Sir Newnham had plans to build an experimental cinematograph theatre or dentist's surgery the other side of it.

The anteroom was comfortably carpeted, wooden-panelled to waist height and wallpapered above, and furnished with armchairs and a low round table for the comfort of the observers. This had a shelf beneath, holding some books and magazines, a chess-set and a deck of playing cards. By contrast the Experiment Rooms were stark: their floors were tiled, and their walls whitewashed, but otherwise bare.

'There's no fireplace in any of these rooms,' I noted. 'Kellway must have been rather chilly, sitting on a tiled floor.'

'And yet I find myself feeling perfectly comfortable,' Holmes noted, bending to press a palm against the floor. 'Indeed, the tiles are pleasantly warm. Your doing, I suppose, Sir Newnham?'

Speight explained proudly that the Annexe, like much of the rest of the house's labyrinthine addenda, was heated from beneath using a system of his own devising, based on the Roman hypocaust. Holmes's ears pricked up at learning that there was a space a mere few feet beneath us that was large enough for a man to crawl through, but Speight assured us that there was no way of entering it from the Annexe without first taking a sledgehammer to the floor.

'Besides,' he added, 'the hypocaust would have been hot enough to roast a hog. Kellway would hardly have been comfortable there.'

'Perhaps he added fire-walking to his miraculous abilities.' Holmes smiled. 'But no, on the whole that is not an assumption that the facts will support.'

He inspected the floor of Room A nonetheless, and found no sign that any of the tiles had been prised up or otherwise interfered with. He examined the walls, tapping them at intervals to assure himself of their solidity, then stood on tiptoe to look at the far window. The bars were set approximately two inches apart, cemented firmly into the wall, and, despite Sir Newnham's comments of the previous evening, I had trouble imagining a full-grown cat making its way through. When the inventor unlocked it for us, the window swung open only a few inches on its catch.

'Certainly no-one could have left that way. Unless he was cut into small pieces,' Holmes added macabrely. 'But that would have left traces it would be hard for anyone to ignore. Is there attic space above us?'

We had seen the Annexe from the outside when visiting the generator-house, and we knew that it was only a single storey high, with a low-sloping roof. Speight assured us that the hollow roof space was negligible, inaccessible, and led nowhere. The room's ceiling was as evidently unbroken as its floor.

Finally Holmes looked at the door itself, paying especial attention to the glass panel. Leading us all outside, he closed the door and invited me to peer through. I said, 'This window distorts everything. It makes things look smaller near the edges.'

'And thus almost the whole room may be seen through a single panel,' Sir Newnham said. 'A process for thickening the glass gives it lens-like properties. My own invention, of course. The glass is also extremely tough, thanks to the same manufacturing technique. These panels are practically unbreakable.'

'This one was recently refitted, though,' Holmes noted, peering at the putty around its edges.

Rhyne looked rather impressed. 'Around a month ago, yes. One of our subjects had a rather disagreeable reaction to being locked in, and while I was fetching the keys from Sir Newnham he tried to smash the door down with a chair. As Sir Newnham says, these windows are hard to break, but it was rather badly scratched. Why the chap didn't mention his claustrophobia beforehand, I can't imagine.'

By shutting one of us at a time in the room and trying out different positions, we confirmed that there was no space in the room, even in the nearest corners, where a person might stand altogether unobserved. The special properties of the glass meant that even when lying along the floor at the bottom of the doorframe, a person's body could still be seen from above.

'From the point of view of a smaller man,' Holmes told me as I emerged from taking my turn lying on the floor, 'you might perhaps have been foreshortened to the point of invisibility, but we could all see you perfectly. How tall are Garforth and Bradbury?'

'Not short,' said Rhyne. 'Bradbury's a little below average, Garforth slightly above. But only by an inch or so.'

'And as I understand it Kellway is bulkier than Watson, so more difficult to hide. In any case,' Holmes added, 'it would be easy to confirm whether a body was lying next to the door by looking underneath. There is an unusual depth of clearance, I see, almost an inch. What is the reason for that?'

'A rather awkward mistake,' Rhyne admitted. 'We had to dismiss the original builders when their work was nearly done. There was some trouble with supplies going missing, and we came to feel they couldn't be trusted. The replacement company we got in finished the job, but there was some sort of mix-up over the height of the doors. I can dig up the details if you need them.'

'Never mind a cat – Kellway would have had to turn into a mouse or beetle to crawl under there,' I joked.

A jacket of heather-coloured tweed still hung on the coat-hook by the door, above a pair of sturdy black shoes and a malacca cane. Holmes gathered them all up and placed them on the table in the anteroom before proceeding into Room B, which still held Speight's 'experimental materials'.

The table was an ordinary baize-covered card-table, and the box a brass-hinged rosewood one without additional decoration. With Speight's permission I opened it to see the billiard ball, which was white and seemed to be made of the usual ivory, although knowing Sir Newnham it could well be some clever artificial material designed to mimic the effect.

Holmes paid these objects only cursory attention, preferring to examine a pair of shutters in the wall adjoining Room C. He ran a finger along the top of the shutters. 'How often are these rooms cleaned?'

'Once a week on a Friday,' Rhyne said. 'So, not since the experiment. The annexes are too much for the household staff to manage, of course, but there's a small army of cleaners who come in from nearby and deal with them all in rotation. They're paid to be exceedingly thorough.'

'Please do not allow them in again until this matter is settled,' said Holmes. 'We cannot afford to miss any potential evidence.'

He opened the shutters between Rooms B and C to reveal another glass panel. This one was a plain window, with no special optical properties. 'We use that in experiments where a line of sight is needed,' Speight explained. 'Some of our trial subjects claim to need to see the objects, or each other in the case of experiments in telepathy. That's thought transference, you know,' he added, seeing my incomprehension.

In other respects, Rooms B and C were identical with Room A, even down to the coat-hook in the wall. Holmes led us all back into the anteroom. 'Did your subject also arrive with a coat and hat?' he asked as he picked up Kellway's shoes.

'They'll still be in the vestibule by the front door. I'll have Anderton fetch them.' Rhyne hurried off.

Holmes sat down at the round table, with the items in front of him. 'The shoes are cheap but sturdy,' he said, taking out his magnifying glass to peer closer. 'They have been well worn, by a man with a healthy stride and an even gait. They have been resoled twice, but are in a serviceable condition. I can see no signs of any hidden compartments, or any other kind of tampering.

'We turn to the jacket. It too is inexpensive, and is somewhat the worse for wear. A button is missing from the left sleeve and there is a tear in the lining, running nearly all the way up the seam of the back. In the pockets we have – a handkerchief, a pocket book and nothing else. Presumably his keys and coins were in his trousers pockets?'

Rhyne confirmed that they were.

'No socks,' said Holmes. 'Neither in the jacket nor balled up in his shoes. What do you make of that, Watson?'

I made very little of it. 'Perhaps he put them in his trousers pocket too?' I speculated.

'They would be rather bulky there, perhaps,' said Holmes. 'Somewhat uncomfortable while meditating. But perhaps that would not trouble an Evolved Man. And so we come to the cane,' said Holmes, swinging it from left to right by its rounded metal handle. 'Like the other items, it has seen better days, but retains its utility. The shaft is battered and the handle – hello, what have we here?'

Gripping the body of the stick with his other hand, he gave the handle a twist and a sharp pull, and it came away. 'A sword-stick, I declare! Perhaps our Mr Kellway had enemies. But – ah. Here, I fear, we meet the limits of its functionality.'

The stick had indeed been a sword-stick at one time, that much was obvious. It had once had a blade mounted on a short length of cane used as a grip, which would have fitted snugly into the hollow body of the stick's remaining wooden length, to be drawn by the bearer with a twist. That blade, though, had been broken off a mere half-inch from the hilt, leaving behind an ugly stump. With the hilt screwed into place it remained a perfectly serviceable walking stick, but as a weapon the worst it could inflict would be a shallow, jagged cut.

'An old break, I think,' said Holmes. 'See how dull the exposed metal has become. Most likely Kellway bought it in its current state.'

Holmes placed it with the shoes and jacket on the anteroom table, and sat to go through Kellway's pocket book. 'A few coins,' he said. 'No notes. A clip of calling cards: Thomas Kellway, The Evolved Man. There is an address in Chiswick. The cards of others – our host, Rhyne, Mr Beech, Mr Garforth, the Reverend Small… Countess Brusilova's is in its small way a rococo masterpiece. Do these belong to other members of your Society, Sir Newnham?'

They did, apart from one from an esoteric bookseller in the Charing Cross Road and one, rather shoddily printed, from a traveller in gentlemen's accessories. The pocket book was otherwise empty.

The coat and hat were brought in by Anderton, but Holmes's examination of them yielded little of further interest. Their quality and age were of a piece with Kellway's other belongings, and the pockets of the coat contained only gloves and the cheapest model of Speight's Super-Collapsible Pocket Umbrella.

'It seems little enough,' I mused, 'to be left behind by a man capable of miracles.'

'And yet suggestive,' Holmes replied. 'What do you conclude from it all, Watson?'

I considered. 'The impression it gives is of a frugal man, but a prudent one. Where a repair was necessary he seems to have made it, but otherwise he didn't consider it a priority. Someone might wear a jacket with a torn lining for years, for instance, but worn-down shoes can be disastrous for the feet. It doesn't look as if he intended to use the sword-stick as a weapon – if so, he would have replaced the blade. Presumably he bought it because it was cheap and still functioned as a walking stick. Perhaps some of the other items are also second-hand. His belongings show him as a man of limited means, then, whose professional asceticism made a virtue out of necessity.'

Rather pleased with myself for thinking of all of this, I finished, 'That isn't to say that the picture they paint is an accurate one, of course. If Kellway is a fraudster, all of this might be the impression he hoped to cultivate.'

'Persuasive, Watson,' Holmes said, 'quite persuasive. And yet I wonder. You called Kellway a fine physical specimen, Sir Newnham. Would he have needed a walking stick?'

'Now you put it that way, it does seem a bit odd,' Sir Newnham agreed. 'And he's not the sort of fellow to carry one for appearance's sake.'

'Even if he did,' said Holmes, 'it is unusual that he would take it with him after surrendering his coat and hat, when embarking on an activity for which even shoes were superfluous. Sir Newnham, with your permission I will take these items back with me to Baker Street for further consideration.'

'By all means,' Speight said. 'If you're finished here, I'll have Anderton lock up the Annexe.'

'Please leave it open for the time being,' said Holmes. 'With your permission I may wish to return later. In fact, may I see outside?'

Anderton unlocked the external door and we stepped outside, to see the nearby flotation tanks and farther away a summerhouse, a remnant of the time when the grounds were laid out for pleasure rather than for Speight's work. Not far beyond it lay the high wall that surrounded the grounds. In answer to a question from Holmes, Rhyne named the street that lay beyond it.

We returned to the main house along the narrow corridors of lawn. Back in his study, Sir Newnham filled a Speight's Self-Igniting Tinder-Pipe, and Holmes and I took out our regular models. Rhyne smoked a cigarette.

Rhyne showed Holmes the rota for observation of the experiment on Thomas Kellway, which he studied carefully. 'Who would have been aware of the information on this paper?' he asked.

'It was distributed to all the members of the Society, whether or not they were to take part,' Rhyne confirmed. 'Oh, and Kellway had a copy, of course.'

'Commendably well-organised,' said Holmes. 'And who in fact attended the grand locking-in of Mr Kellway?'

Rhyne took the list from him and peered at it. 'Everyone named here, apart from Lord Jermaine, Giles McInnery and Freddie Garforth. Countess Brusilova was there, too, with her companion Miss Casimir – they'd taken rooms for the night at the Star and Garter Hotel, to avoid sleeping in a houseful of gentlemen. The Countess has views on such things, or at least Miss Casimir maintains that she has. The Countess is not an easy person to communicate with, unless one is a spirit of some kind.'

'So these other observers arrived at the house later?'

'Yes. Jermaine and McInnery turned up together at around ten o'clock – they'd shared a cab from town – and Garforth later still, I think.'

'And in the morning? Who else arrived for breakfast to discover that the experiment had had no definite conclusion?'

'Let me see… Dr Kingsley spent the night at his own house, and in the morning he was called out to attend a patient, but all the other observers stayed the night. The Countess and Miss Casimir rejoined us, and Mr Felix Herrisham and Lord St Andrews came too. They're newish members who Mr Floke introduced.'

'A full house for breakfast, then,' I said. 'I hope Anderton was not too tired from his nocturnal observations.'

'We were all rather in shock, Anderton included,' Sir Newnham replied gravely, 'but I have a large and competent staff and they were able to take care of the matter.'

'What is the full membership of the Society?' Holmes asked.

Rhyne said readily, 'We have seventy-eight members at present, but about half of those are members primarily by correspondence. Some live abroad. Others are rarely in town.'

'I shall need to speak to Major Bradbury, Mr Garforth and Anderton, of course,' Holmes noted. 'Also, I think, to the other members of your Committee, particularly Mr Beech.'

'And what do you mean to say to Mr Beech, you impertinent dabbler?' asked a new voice from the doorway, one with an Irish brogue and a distinctly confrontational tone.

At the same moment Anderton announced, in an apologetic voice, 'Mr Beech is here, Sir Newnham.'

The Daily Gazette

5th March 1894

THE OLD BAILEY: The third day of the trial of Mabel Garman, on the charge of the murder of her husband, Alfred, saw the calling of the celebrated inventor Sir Newnham Speight as a witness.

Sir Newnham's polymathic expertise has been of service to the courts on many similar occasions in the past, in both criminal trials and civil cases, and on subjects as diverse as chemistry, ballistics, optics, telegraphy and maritime navigation. On this occasion he was required to give an account of the operation of the Speight's Original Automated Steam-Mangle which Garman had bought for his wife, and by which he met his grisly end.

With the aid of a Mangle of his own, which required several strong men to manhandle into the court, Sir Newnham first explained the principles by which the device works, which are hydraulic in nature, and then demonstrated the workings of the mechanism.

Asked whether such a machine could cause a person's death, the witness replied, 'Oh, certainly. The forces involved are sufficient to crush the human frame.'

COUNSEL FOR THE DEFENCE (Sir Joseph Garville, Q.C.): You do not consider it irresponsible to manufacture and sell a device that can end the life of a fellow human being?

WITNESS: No more so in this case than in that of a kitchen knife or a croquet mallet. There are very few items that may not be used as a weapon if one is sufficiently ingenious.

COUNSEL: But you will allow that the scope for accident is greater in the case of an item that can exert crushing forces?

WITNESS: I believe not, provided the device is used wisely and responsibly. As with a knife or mallet, the user has a duty to be aware of the risk of harm and to modify their practices accordingly.

COUNSEL: Sir Newnham, you have heard my client's testimony. She contends that, being naturally concerned that the new acquisition might leak oil onto her clean linen, she asked her husband to check the rollers; following which, the mangle unexpectedly started working, trapping his hand and eventually crushing him to death. Would that not qualify as an accident for which the manufacturer might accept a share of responsibility?

WITNESS: It would indeed, which is why the Automated Steam-Mangle is designed to prevent all possibility of such an accident. The operator must simultaneously press upon a pedal and pull a lever to begin the working of the mechanism; if the pedal is released it ceases at once. This causes some restriction of movement when feeding items into the machine, but we considered this preferable to compromising the safety of the operator. Furthermore, the boiler must have been set to warm for at least ten minutes before it builds up a sufficient head of steam to turn the rollers. If somebody meets their death in one of my mangles, it requires careful forethought on the part of another.

A sensation ensued in the court, and several members of the public had to be removed. The witness was dismissed without further questions. The trial continues.

CHAPTER FOUR

'Mr Gideon Beech, I presume,' said Holmes calmly.

'A staggering conclusion, laddie,' Beech smirked, 'given that Anderton there just told you my name. I expect you'll be astounding us all with your deduction that I'm a celebrated playwright next. I must say this is the first I've heard of you taking an interest in psychic phenomena, Mr Holmes.'

The famed controversialist was a tweed-suited man, thin as a sapling, with dark, intense eyes, a sardonic mouth and a somewhat Mephistophelean beard. He was perhaps forty years of age, and certainly had no business to be calling Holmes 'laddie'. Behind him stood another, paler and younger man, with an obstinate set to his chin and green, haunted eyes.

'I confess I could say the same to you, Mr Beech,' Holmes replied. 'Evidently we both have unexpected depths. I look forward to our interview with some anticipation. In the meantime—'

'Hold your horses, Mr Holmes. By what right do you expect to interview me at all?'

'Really, Beech, is this fuss necessary?' Sir Newnham sighed. 'As Chairman of the Society I have engaged Mr Holmes to look into the matter of Kellway's disappearance. He is more than competent to do so, and I would ask you to please cooperate with him.'

'Ah, so you've gone behind the Committee's back,' Beech observed. 'Well, perhaps it's for the best. It gives me the licence to bring in my own man – one whose competencies are rather better suited to the job in hand.'

He gestured at the pallid youth behind him, who rolled his eyes nervously.

Holmes said, 'Is this gentleman known to you, Sir Newnham?'

'We have had some dealings,' Speight replied uneasily. 'His name is Constantine Skinner. He calls himself…'

'I'm an occult detective, Mr Holmes,' said Skinner, proffering a limp hand. 'I specialise in these kinds of cases. It's why Mr Beech has called me in.'

'I see,' Holmes replied, with a wolfish smile. 'I can only express my admiration at so brave a choice of career.' Though he was rarely short of a jibe at the failings of Scotland Yard, my friend's feelings towards the constabulary were positively comradely compared with his view of those investigators, so called, whose faddish and ineffective techniques he believed existed only to gull the public out of their money. 'Tell me, Mr Skinner, how many banshees have you caught in the act of haunting? How many will-o'-the-wisps have you brought to trial? How many boggarts are now securely under lock and key because of your—'

'You may entertain yourself at my expense,' said Skinner defiantly, 'but I've seen things you couldn't dream of.'

Holmes drawled, 'I fear *you underestimate the phantasmagorical effects of cocaine.'

'I shall be fascinated to see you gentlemen match your wits in the face of our current little mystery,' Beech told them both with a broad smile. 'It will be quite the little experiment. But I'm afraid, Mr Holmes, that a career spent tracking down absconding aristocrats and restoring missing gemstones to wealthy owners will help you very little in this case.'

Sir Newnham was beginning to look annoyed. 'Beech, I must ask you to be more polite to my guests.'

'Guests?' Beech made a show of looking around, and then smiled maliciously at me. 'Oh, I'm sorry, Dr Watson. I didn't see you there in Mr Holmes's shadow.'

I contained my temper, without very much difficulty. Beech was hardly the first person who had so misjudged my friendship with Holmes as to attempt to bait me with his deservedly greater fame.

'So now you are here to solve the mystery, Mr Skinner, what shall be your first move?' Holmes asked. 'I am agog to learn from watching your techniques.'

Skinner swallowed, and licked his lips. 'First, I shall visit the site of the disappearance, and inspect the aura the Evolved Man has left behind.'

'The aura?' Holmes echoed. 'This is a wholly new branch of criminology to me. Pray allow me to observe this fascinating new investigative technique.'

My friend was notorious for never suffering fools gladly, but in this instance his mockery of the young man seemed to me excessive. The glint in Beech's eye had made me wonder whether he had enlisted the unfortunate Skinner as a deliberate provocation to Holmes – either for mischief's sake or to distract his attention from the proper conduct of the investigation.

Rhyne led us down to the Annexe, and Anderton unlocked it once more. With Holmes and the others I watched from beside the doorway as Skinner moved the round table with some effort from the centre of the anteroom and stood there himself. He closed his eyes, breathed deeply and slowly raised his arms until his fingers were outstretched on either side of him. Then he began, very slowly, to revolve on the spot.

'What is he doing?' I whispered to Rhyne.

'His technique is based on the idea that everyone carries an aura about with them,' Rhyne said. 'It's field of psychical energy with a pattern unique to the person, whose qualities gifted individuals can sense. In extreme experiences such as injury or emotional trauma, it leaves traces behind. Skinner has learned to read such traces, as Mr Holmes might a set of physical clues.'

'How fortunate that he is so dedicated to his noble calling,' Holmes observed, altogether too loudly. 'With such a readily demonstrated talent a lesser man would long ago have claimed Sir Newnham's ten-thousand-pound reward and retired wealthy.'

Skinner opened his eyes and glared at Holmes, before striding across the room and into Experiment Room A, and taking up his stance once more.

I took my friend aside. 'Really, Holmes,' I whispered, 'is it necessary to harry him so? He does not strike me as a man whose sanity is altogether secure. What he says is absurd, to be sure, but he seems to mean it all. If these "readings" of his represent a genuine delusion on his part, then I fear for his mental stability if you chip too persistently at its foundations.'

Holmes looked very slightly abashed. 'Then I bow to your medical judgement, my dear doctor. It simply galls me that such people—'

He was interrupted by a bloodcurdling screech from the Experiment Room, and the crash of a body hitting the floor.

Holmes and I were nearest, and he allowed me to reach Skinner first. I quickly confirmed that the young man was suffering a seizure, his limbs spasming as he writhed upon the tiled floor. I swiftly turned him on his side, removed his belt and placed it in his mouth.

'My God, what can we do?' Sir Newnham was asking.

'If you have any potassium bromide in your laboratory,' I said, 'I suggest you fetch it at once, with a beaker of water and a pipette.'

Speight hurried away.

'The lad'll be fine in a moment,' Beech said easily, setting himself down in an armchair in the anteroom. 'It's all part of his *modus operandi*.'

I am afraid I snapped at him: 'Be quiet, you fool.' His smile did not waver.

Working as quickly and calmly as I could I made up a dose of the bromide, and had Rhyne hold Skinner tightly while I poured it between his lips. He began to quieten immediately, and within ten minutes, with the help of some smelling salts, he had recovered enough to be moved to a chair and speak to us, though weakly.

'I saw... an echo,' said Skinner, sipping a glass of brandy provided by the redoubtable Anderton. 'A hollow, flapping shape, a pale imitation of what was once alive. The image of a person without the essence. I saw it folding, crumpling and collapsing in upon itself, and being drawn away through the void.'

Beech said, 'What are you saying, Skinner?'

'I don't know.' Skinner shook his head, so violently I feared another convulsion. 'It's as if Thomas Kellway became a ghost, a mere echo of himself, his substance leaching away from him where he sat. As if somebody drew the very life out of him.'

Beech looked more intrigued than appalled, but he placed a hand on Skinner's shoulder and told him, 'You've done well, lad.'

'So you contend that Kellway is dead?' Holmes asked him. Skinner nodded an equally violent assent. 'Well, it may be so. But I fear your insight is unlikely to stand up in a court of law.'

Despite his words, Holmes's voice was gentler now, no longer derisory. Nevertheless Skinner rounded on him, with all the anger and humiliation he must have felt at my friend's earlier barbs, and at his own physical humiliation.

'I will not have this, Mr Holmes! I cannot work – you *see* how difficult my work is for me – I cannot do it with your constant mockery! Sir Newnham, Mr Beech, I implore you – can you not keep this man's superciliousness in check?'

'My dear Skinner,' began Holmes in a conciliatory tone, but Beech interrupted again.

'You see the kinds of men we have each engaged, Speight. Skinner's methods may not be those employed by Scotland Yard to keep the peasants in their place, but you see how deep is his commitment to his work, even at the expense of his own health. Your man, meanwhile, has no regard for the feelings of an invalid, or for anything other than his own grossly inflated self-esteem. Why, even his best friend's accounts of him show him to be arrogant and conceited, treating the lives of others as a game to be played, a problem to be solved. Is he really the one you would prefer to have investigating such a sensitive affair as this?'

I was amazed at Beech's gall in accusing somebody else of excessive self-regard, but Holmes responded haughtily. 'Watson and I are here at your invitation, Sir Newnham, and if we are not welcome, we shall leave. You may rely on Mr Skinner to come up with some imaginative answers to your questions, I feel sure. Come, Watson.'

We got nearly all the way along the corridor without anybody begging us to remain, and I feared that my friend's acerbity had so soured the company's view of him that they would indeed allow him to walk away.

Then Sir Newnham was bustling after us, calling Holmes's name. I saw a moment's satisfaction on my friend's face, soon obscured by stern impatience as he turned.

'I confess I am disappointed by your conduct, Holmes,' Speight said, 'but my reasons for engaging you remain.' More quietly he added, 'I would never have employed Constantine Skinner myself, but we must allow Beech his legitimate interest as a member of the Committee. He is no less entitled than I to appoint an investigator in this matter.' More loudly, for the benefit of those behind us in the Annexe, he declared, 'I will not allow either you or Mr Skinner to interfere with the other's work or to jeopardise its results. Is that understood?'

'An admirable compromise,' my friend said, 'and one to which I am willing to accede.' I wondered whether Speight, who seemed a generous and kind-hearted man, had seen as I had how disappointed Holmes would have been to give up this case.

'Mr Skinner?' Talbot Rhyne asked the younger investigator.

'Oh, I suppose,' Skinner muttered with ill grace. 'I suppose it's all right, as long as he keeps out of my way.'

'Splendid.' Holmes beamed, apparently putting the acrimony completely behind him. 'In that case, Mr Beech, perhaps we might hold that interview now?'

Beech conceded that we might. We placed Skinner in the care of the housekeeper, and made our way to Sir Newnham's drawing room. Holmes asked Anderton to ensure that if any of the other observers of the experiment were to call on Sir Newnham in the meantime they should be asked to wait.

'Of course, sir,' Anderton replied. 'What a pity you missed Mr Garforth this morning.'

'Oh, so Garforth was here?' Holmes asked. 'Nobody has mentioned this to us.'

'I was unaware, too.' Sir Newnham frowned. 'Who did he come to see, Anderton?'

'He was seeing me, Sir Newnham,' Rhyne interjected quickly. He flushed a little as he said it, and for the first time I wondered whether Sir Newnham might be a harder taskmaster than he appeared to be in public. 'It was a flying visit, to find out whether there was any news of Kellway. When I told him there wasn't, he left, being urgently required elsewhere. I'm afraid he didn't tell me where.'

'It is a pity you did not detain him nonetheless,' Holmes observed. 'I have a particular wish to talk to Mr Garforth. Tell me, is he a man of late middle age, with long grey hair, bushy eyebrows and muttonchop whiskers, sporting an ebony cane and a monocle, and wearing an Inverness cape?'

'Well, yes,' said Rhyne, surprised. 'At least – I don't know what coat he was wearing.'

'It was an Inverness, sir,' Anderton confirmed.

Holmes said, 'We saw him as he left, I fancy. He seemed in a great hurry to take our cab. What was his other pressing engagement, I wonder? Well, no matter, I'm sure we will have another opportunity to speak to him.'

'I'll send a message to his studio, if you like,' Rhyne said, 'and have him call back this afternoon.'

Speight and his employees withdrew, leaving Holmes and myself to speak with Beech.

'Now, sir,' said Holmes in what for him was a conciliatory tone. 'It is plain that you are as eager as I to understand the truth of what took place in Sir Newnham's Experimental Annexe last night. In the interests of uncovering that truth, therefore, I beg your indulgence in answering a few simple questions. You stood the third watch with the Reverend Small, I believe?'

'I did,' said Beech, 'and a very tedious time it was too. That parson strives to escape the limitations of his dogma, but the inside of his mind remains a very circumscribed place. Not for him the joys of unrestrained spiritual thought, I am afraid. I pointed out to him that he was privileged to share with me the chance to witness in Kellway the vindication of the supreme universal force that is the Will of Life, and of Her self-expression in mankind through the medium of evolution – meditated, it would now seem, through the benign guidance of Her earlier children, the enlightened beings from that celestial sphere which the ancients in their simple and perhaps unconscious wisdom named after the goddess of the erotic drive, which is to say after Life Herself. He replied in terms so redolent of guilty obeisance to a tyrannical tribal deity that I stopped listening after the first few words. To such people as the aptly named Mr Small, such contemplations of the absolute are, I fear—'

'Mr Beech,' interrupted Holmes drily, 'I find your metaphysical speculations boundlessly fascinating, and shall be sure to buy Watson one of your books so that he can summarise them pithily for me. Meanwhile, if you would be so good as to confine yourself to the matter in hand…?'

'But isn't that what I'm telling you already? The session was a washout. Mr Vortigern Small took no interest whatsoever in discussing our sacred purpose there, blast his short-sighted eyes, and Kellway spent the whole time sitting alone in the dark doing nothing. The experimental materials didn't move. Kellway didn't move. Small would only make small talk. The whole experience was thoroughly vexing – especially in hindsight, given that a few hours later I might have been in a position to witness what ultimately happened to Kellway, as that ass Bradbury, that dauber Garforth and that sycophant Anderton so signally failed to do.'

'And do you agree with Mr Skinner that Mr Kellway was somehow extinguished by supernatural means, or is your view still that he has ascended to a higher plane?' Holmes smirked slightly.

'For pity's sake, man,' Beech barked, 'who mentioned a *plane*? Kellway was very precise about the source of his extraordinary development, and the science of celestial geometry is every bit as clear that Venus is a *sphere*. I realise that this information may be new to you, Mr Holmes, which is why I impart it so patiently. I understand from Dr Watson's jottings that knowledge of astronomy is one of those areas in which your own so widely vaunted polymathy founders.'

I rather regretted, now, committing that particular observation to paper early in our acquaintance, and still more allowing it to reach my publishers intact. Holmes was quite unperturbed, however.

He said, 'When specific knowledge is required of me, I am quite capable of acquiring it from the available sources. I would have been unable yesterday to tell you with any great certainty whether Venus was a planet, a comet or a star, but today I have at my fingertips such facts as are known about its magnitude, its periods of rotation and orbit, its atmosphere and its surface, in case these data should become relevant to the matter at hand. Among other things, I have learned that Venus is judged by astronomers to be a younger world than our own, on the basis of its greater proximity to the sun, just as Mars is supposed to be older. That being the case,' he noted languidly, 'the superior development that Kellway ascribes to its inhabitants appears to me rather anomalous.'

Beech beamed. 'I put just that point to him when we first met. He replied that a five-hundred-year-old tree is not so advanced an expression of the Will of Life as a five-day-old human child – a most profound observation, as I think you'll agree.'

I could see that Holmes did not, but he refrained from saying so, instead returning to the events of the previous night. 'I take it that there was nothing in Kellway's manner, either when you saw him locked inside the Experiment Room or during the time when you were observing him, that suggested anything unusual to you?'

Beech shook his head. 'I saw nothing of the kind. He was both calm and cheerful as we locked him in, and I believe he was perfectly confident that he would leave that room having demonstrated the ability of telekinesis in the dreary manner the Society so inflexibly prescribes. Whenever I looked in on him during my watch he seemed quite serene, with that impassive stillness that comes from prolonged meditation. I freely admit that the curtailment of his night's labours made for as great a shock to me as it did for everyone else. It's my belief that Kellway, too, was taken completely by surprise.'

'Curtailment?' I said. 'So you believe that Kellway was interrupted by some external force?'

'The two of you heard what Skinner said as well as I did,' said Beech tartly. 'If you choose to reject his evidence then you are working with an incomplete model of events. That said, to my ears his description was likely that of a man being twisted through some fourth dimension of space before being translocated and rotated back into normality elsewhere – if existence on the second sphere of our Sun's retinue can be considered normality, of course. Still, if Skinner believes there's been murder done we shouldn't rule it out altogether.'

'That seems a somewhat extreme conclusion for him to have formed on the basis of such flimsy data,' Holmes opined.

'Aye, maybe.' Beech looked uncharacteristically dubious for a moment. 'I'll be honest with you, though, and admit there's something that's been troubling to me. I said before that Mr Small had no wish to discuss any matters of true significance, and nor had I any desire whatsoever for a conversation on the prosaic and puerile topics in which he professed to be interested. Naturally, after a while, we ignored each other, except at the five-minute intervals when we were obliged to coordinate our observations.

'Towards the middle of the second hour, however, I became aware of a low, dull moan emanating from my observation partner. I thought at first that he might be in pain, and thought to offer some of the information I've gleaned over the years regarding herbal remedies and the like, on the charitable assumption that his mind was not yet so firmly wedged shut as to reject such simple forms of wisdom. But then I realised that the noise was rhythmic in nature, the same outlandish syllables repeated over and over.

'You realise, I hope, that I have no interest in or sympathy with the abject and self-destructive tenets of the Christian religion,' Beech said, 'but my parents were so wantonly irresponsible as to bring me up in the Church, and I have since made a certain study of its superfluous rituals. That pastor was chanting under his breath outside Kellway's room in the dead of night, and it was like no Christian prayer that I have ever heard.'

Excerpt from *The Brotherhood of Motley Men, and Other True Accounts of Experiences with the Paranormal* (1909) by Athanasius Larkin

It was during my first meeting with the man who would become my brother-in-law that the topic of the occult was first raised between us; a subject to which our discourse would return on many an occasion during our acquaintance, and which would become a very practical preoccupation of my own during our later adventures together.

'I say, Larkin,' he asked me that day, 'do you ever give any thought to matters of the supernatural?'

'Not overmuch,' I admitted, 'except when I am in church. Pray, why do you ask?'

'Well, it's rather in my line,' he replied, with a modest air. 'I thought you should know that, if you're to marry my sister.'

'Well, that isn't altogether settled, you know,' I responded, rather affronted. 'What do you mean, "your line"? Are you training to be a priest, Skinner?'

'No, nothing so responsible, I'm afraid,' Constantine Skinner replied, with a self-deprecating chuckle. 'I'm an occult detective.'

I stared. 'And what, if I may ask, does an occult detective do?'

'Oh, well as to that,' he said airily, 'I solve occult crimes, of course. Did you hear of the case of the St Pancras Hauntings?'

'I do recall reading about the matter.' If I remembered correctly, it had rendered an entire platform of the railway station unusable for weeks as luggage and, occasionally, passengers were placed in great danger of being propelled onto the tracks, supposedly kicked by unseen feet.

He smiled modestly. 'I laid the ghost there. It turned out to be a workman who had been run over by a faulty engine before the station was even opened. He was cut quite in half, poor fellow, and due to a terrific mix-up at the mortuary his head and chest were buried in a different grave from his legs and middle. It was his lower half that was besetting the platform, you see – the rest of him haunted the engine that ran him over, but as it had been put out of use nobody had noticed. He soon calmed down once I had his parts exhumed and reburied together.'

'What an extraordinary story!' I exclaimed.

He gave a self-deprecating smile. 'There are others where that came from. You may remember reading in the spring of a man savaged to death by a wild animal in Regent's Park? Nobody could determine what it was that killed him, until I realised that one of the tigers at the zoo had been sending out its spirit body at nights – it turned out to be the reincarnation of a Buddhist monk, and had inherited the extraordinary ability from him.

'And then there was the Perfidious Tower at Carrefour Castle, which drove thirteen servants to suicide, and the river-monster that attacked the Hampton Ferry... Oh yes, I've had a few encounters with the Other Side in my time.'

It would not be very much later in our acquaintance that I had the first of my own such stories to tell, as Constantine Skinner enlisted me to help him in the terrifying case of the Motley Men...

It seems there is an entire series of these yarns about Skinner's exploits — it is quite extraordinary. Frankly, Watson, I blame the influence of your own writings. —
S.H.

CHAPTER FIVE

Smirking at our discomfiture, Gideon Beech left us to contemplate his disconcerting suggestion that the Reverend Vortigern Small had performed some occult ritual which had resulted in the destruction of the unfortunate Mr Kellway.

Naturally Holmes dismissed it the moment we were alone as mere malicious troublemaking on Beech's part, but I was surprised to find that I was less sanguine. I admit that the possibilities presented by this extraordinary case were beginning to trouble me.

Though I lack Holmes's exceptional skill in ratiocination, I pride myself that I am nevertheless a man of reason. Like any medical man I am familiar with the principles of scientific philosophy as they apply to my profession, and aware of the great benefits they have brought to that profession's practices. Normally I would expect that such a stance would insulate me from the excesses of superstition. Yet I found that the proximity of serious scientists like Speight and Rhyne, who not only entertained but embraced the idea of the transcendental as a branch of science itself, was having an unsettling effect on my prior certainties.

The idea of a respectable minister of the Church making a man vanish with some kind of malediction was of course ludicrous. Yet Kellway's disappearance was, after all, inexplicable except either by a deception that flew in the face of human nature, at least as Sir Newnham Speight understood it, or else by some equally outlandish behaviour on the part of the universe itself.

Our conversation with Anderton, who we spoke to next, made me even more sceptical of his perpetrating a fraud upon his employer. The butler seemed eminently sensible for a servant, with a touching devotion to his employer. Their families had, it seemed, been neighbours when the two of them were boys. In Anderton's youth, when his father had been driven by debt to kill himself, leaving his family to face the burden in his stead, the young Newnham Speight, just beginning to make his mark as an inventor, had taken pity on his old associates. He had taken William, the only son of the family, into his service – first as his man-of-all-work and later, as Speight's fortune grew and the arrangements of his household became more regular, his manservant, before promoting him to his current position some fifteen years previously.

'I never had much of a head for science or machines, sirs,' Anderton told us earnestly, 'not like Sir Newnham has. Maybe I could have run a factory as well as a household if he'd set me to it, but my old ma was in service before she married my dad, and I suppose it runs in the family. It always seemed the best way I could be useful to him.'

'As I am sure you have been,' Holmes agreed. 'Although it occurs to me that some men might resent an arrangement which placed a person born their equal in such a position of authority over them.'

'I dare say some would, sir,' Anderton agreed cheerfully. 'There's no accounting for how some folk think, is there? But hand on heart, I've never felt anything but grateful to Sir Newnham for how he helped my family out of that spot. Thanks to him my ma lived out her days in peace, and my sisters are respectable women with situations of their own. You can't put a price on that.'

Either his words were heartfelt, or else he was an exceptional liar. Looking at his round, smiling face, I found the second possibility as hard to countenance as Sir Newnham did.

'Now then, Anderton,' said Holmes, 'you were in the Experimental Annexe, I believe, at the time when Mr Kellway made his disappearance. You stood the four o'clock watch with Mr Garforth, is that correct?'

'That's right, sir,' Anderton confirmed. 'I was there at five before four, and Mr Garforth arrived a few minutes later. We exchanged a few words with Lord Jermaine and Mr McInnery, and then they went upstairs to get some sleep.'

'They had nothing to report?'

'No, sir. Mr Kellway had been sitting quiet all the time since two, just as before, and there'd been no change in the other room. Both gentlemen thought Mr Kellway was looking a little tired, but it seemed like the experiment was a wash-out. His lordship said how it was rotten luck, because he'd thought Mr Kellway was the real thing.'

I said, 'And what did you think, Anderton?'

A concerned look crossed Anderton's chubby face. 'It's not my place to think about such matters, sir. I help out when Sir Newnham requires it. My eyes are as good as anybody's if I'm told what to look out for.'

Holmes said, 'It was an early start for you both. Was Mr Garforth in good spirits?'

'He was quieter than usual. Normally he's friendly, and very ready with his jokes. But he'd turned up late the night before, having been out with friends.'

'What time was that?'

'About half-past eleven. Truth be told, sir, I thought he was a little tipsy when I showed him to his room. Not that I suppose painters are early risers generally, unless they're the sort that like painting sunrises.'

'Mr Garforth is not that kind of painter?'

'No, sir. Young ladies is his line, from what I've seen – and not overburdened by clothes, if you take my meaning.'

'I see, yes. So the pair of you remained there for the next hour?'

'Yes, sir. Mr Garforth spent most of the time walking up and down, sir – to keep him awake, he said, and I could see what he meant. That under-floor heating does make the room warm, and of course there'd been gentlemen smoking in there all night, so there was a bit of a fug.'

'Did either of you leave the room at any time?'

'Oh no. Mr Garforth had his jacket slung over a chair, sir, and he kept going back to it and taking things out of the pockets and fiddling with them. Paintbrushes and matchboxes and such, and his cigarettes of course. Mr Garforth's a keen smoker; you almost never see him without his holder. As for me, after I'd made sure Mr Garforth didn't mind, I sat quiet and read my book. I'm a great believer in reading, sir, when I've the opportunity for it. There's nothing like a good book.'

'Did you converse with Mr Garforth?'

'He told me a joke or two, though his heart wasn't really in it. Then of course we had the stop-watch, and every five minutes we'd check up on Mr Kellway and the things in the other room, and I dare say we talked about that a bit.'

'Did you talk about Mr Kellway himself?'

'Well, there might have been a remark or two. It's an odd feeling, sir, when you're watching someone like that. It's like you're spying on them, and yet at the same time you sort of forget they're there when it comes to talking about them. When

Mr Garforth first looked in on Mr Kellway he said he'd thought he was taller, though of course Mr Kellway was sitting down. He's tall enough when he's standing up, to my mind.'

'Had the two of them met before?' I asked, remembering Garforth's card in Kellway's pocket book.

'Just the once, Mr Garforth said – he was leaving here with Mr Rhyne one day just as Mr Kellway turned up, and they ran into each other in the street outside. He'd missed the locking-in that evening, of course, on account of his other engagement. As for me, I think I only said something like, "He surely can't be comfortable sitting like that so long, can he?" and perhaps wondered that he didn't seem to be hungry or thirsty.'

This point had occurred to me also. 'Is it normal for the subjects to go without food and drink?'

'They're not usually in there for so long, sir. And Mr Kellway said he wouldn't need anything like that while he was meditating. I suppose I was more marvelling at it than wondering, if you follow me.'

'Quite so,' said Holmes. 'Did anything else of note happen before Major Bradbury's arrival?'

'Not really, sir. Ah, well, there was one thing. Sir Newnham may not be best pleased when he finds out, but it's only a small thing really, and Mr Garforth did ask me.'

Holmes steepled his fingers. 'Pray tell.'

'Well, sir, I'm afraid we opened the door to the outside for a short while, because it really was very close in the Annexe, and I happened to have that key with me – I carry keys to all the outside doors. It was a relief to us both to get some cool fresh air for a few minutes. But then the cat got in and started scratching to be let through into the laboratory, where she mustn't go on account of how she sheds her fur all over the equipment, so I had to put her out and lock it up again.'

'A night of incident indeed,' said Holmes. 'You are certain that you locked the door, I suppose?'

'Quite sure, sir. I wanted to be sure nobody found it had been open, because, as I say, Sir Newnham wouldn't approve. These experiments are supposed to happen in complete isolation from the outside world.'

'And no other persons entered the Annexe during that time?'

'No persons at all, sir, only the cat. The door was only open for a few minutes, and of course we could see it all the time.'

'Did you leave the Annexe when you put the cat out?'

'No, I knew that wouldn't do. I sort of tossed her out, but quite gently. They land on their feet, sir, you know. Then Mr Garforth shut the door quick, before she could dash back in. And a moment later Major Bradbury came through from the laboratory and left *that* door open behind him. What Sir Newnham would have said if that animal had got in there I don't like to contemplate, gentlemen.'

'So this would have happened between a quarter and ten minutes before five?' Holmes asked.

'Yes, sir. I opened the door just after the four-forty observation, then the cat came in while we were doing the four-forty-five. By the time we'd got rid of her and Major Bradbury arrived, we were about to make the four-fifty. He told us not to mind him, so I looked in at Mr Kellway and Mr Garforth looked at the experimental materials, and we both agreed there was no change.'

'Was Major Bradbury disappointed by that?' I asked. 'Mr Rhyne said he was hoping Kellway would deliver results.'

'He did seem a bit put out by it. He told us he'd had trouble sleeping – he was in his dressing gown, in fact – and since he was awake he thought he'd come and see what was happening. He seemed quite excited about it, until we told him nothing had happened at all. He sat down, a bit gloomy, and lit his pipe. Then he seemed to cheer up again, and was kind enough to talk to me a bit about the book I'm reading. It's an Arthur Morrison one, sir, about a private detective.'

Holmes smiled. 'An improving volume, I have no doubt. Please go on.'

'Well, sir, then we made the four-fifty-five observation and Major Bradbury suggested a game, but he and Mr Garforth couldn't agree on cards or chess. They argued about it until five o'clock, and we made the check again, and found no change – I saw to Mr Kellway that time, and he was sitting just the same as before. So I read, and the Major smoked, and Mr Garforth paced some more. Then the stopwatch chimed again for the five past five, and... Well, sir, you know what happened after that.'

Holmes said wryly, 'If I knew that, Anderton, Dr Watson and I could go home happy with the service we had rendered Sir Newnham. Please tell us in your own words what you observed.'

'Well, that was my turn to look at the materials again, and of course *they* hadn't moved. But just as I was looking Mr Garforth cried out, "My God, but he's gone!" or something like that. He tried the door, then stood aside so Major Bradbury could see. Then the Major said, "Great Scott!" and went a bit pale and sat down. So then I looked too, and saw that the room was completely empty.'

'You could see that clearly?' Holmes asked. 'The room was not lit.'

'There was enough light to see. You've seen the room yourself, sir – the door's got a big window in it, and the shadows weren't anything like deep enough to hide in. I said something like, "Let's look underneath the door – maybe he's fainted from the hunger," and Mr Garforth got down on his hands and knees and looked and said, "No, no, the cove's gone – God alone knows how. Run and get Sir Newnham at once, and make sure he brings the key." And so I did.'

'You found Sir Newnham awake?'

'Yes, sir, and nearly dressed. He sent me to wake Mr Rhyne while he finished, then he and I went down together.'

'Was all as you left it when you returned?'

'Mostly, sir. Major Bradbury was sitting in another chair – I think he'd sat down first on the one where Mr Garforth had hung his jacket. Mr Garforth had put it back on, and I didn't blame him, sirs, I can tell you. That room was warm, but I was feeling the chill myself; it seemed so unnatural what had happened. Of course when I thought about it later I realised it had to have been a trick of some kind, but at the time it properly gave me the shivers.'

'Did any of the other observers join you then?' Holmes asked.

'Only Mr Rhyne, sir, none of the others – not till later, after we'd done a thorough check of the Annexe. That we did without delay, and found nothing else out of the ordinary, and of course no sign of Mr Kellway. I think that's all I can tell you, sirs.'

'Thank you, Anderton,' Holmes said. 'You've given us a very thorough account. Forgive me, but I must ask – you have told us that you were reading, and also that the room was warm and stuffy. I know the effect those circumstances can have on people' – here he glanced at me – 'and this was very early in the morning. Is it possible, Anderton, that your attention might have… lapsed for a moment or two? Long enough, say, for Kellway to have left Room A without your being aware of it and slipped out, either through the open back door or through the laboratory?'

Anderton's chubby forehead wrinkled. 'Well, I can't see how, sir. His room was locked, as you know.'

'But if that difficulty were somehow overcome? And that of his being seen by the other observers?'

'I saw him in the room myself at five, sir, and the outside

door was locked by then. But even so, sir, having it open had cooled the room down a little, and freshened the air. If I'd been going to doze off – which I wouldn't have anyway, sir, seeing as Sir Newnham was trusting me not to – it would have been earlier on, when it was closer in there.'

'Indeed,' said Holmes. 'I see you are a clear thinker, Anderton, head for science or no. Tell me, what do you think happened to Thomas Kellway?'

'Well, sir,' Anderton said again. 'Since you ask… I trust you won't think the worse of me, but I'm not a believer in these psychical phenomena Sir Newnham's Society's been looking into. Sir Newnham's entitled to his hobbies, of course, as all wealthy men are, and I've no objection to helping him out where I can, but… Well, it stands to reason, as I see it, that if such things really existed they'd have found some sign of it by now. Three years it's been, sir, and scores of experiments they've run, and never a success.'

'Unless this is the first such,' I suggested.

'Well, that's as may be, sir,' said Anderton dubiously, 'but seeing as you're asking for my opinion, it's this. I think Mr Kellway would be marvellous doing conjuring tricks up on the stage, and I'd love to know how he did this one.'

Holmes nodded slowly. 'I am inclined to agree,' he said. 'At present, though, my most pressing opinion is that I would very much like to speak to Mr Garforth and to Major Bradbury.'

The Daily Gazette

18th June 1889

England has welcomed back a loyal son in the person of Major Clement Bradbury, late of Calcutta, who returns from twenty-one years' patriotic service in Her Majesty's Eastern dominions with the Duke of Greyminster's Lancers, the 1st Bangalore Pioneers and the Queen's Own Fusiliers. He served under commanding officers including Lord Montrevor, General Pangthorpe of Afghan fame, and the noted big-game hunter Col. Sebastian Moran; and distinguished himself in campaigns in Lucknow, Sind and Bangalore, where he developed an enthusiastic interest in Eastern religion. He is a noted collector of the religious art and statuary of the subcontinent. The younger brother of the late Sir Adelbert Bradbury of North Devon, Maj. Bradbury resides when in London at the Oriental Club.

CHAPTER SIX

'Well, it now seems obvious what happened,' I observed to Holmes with some relief after Anderton left us. Garforth had not replied to the message Rhyne had sent to his studio, but Anderton had told us we would have our opportunity to meet with him and Bradbury that evening. Sir Newnham had invited the artist, Major Bradbury and various other members of the Society to join us for a light supper. Beech was to be there, as was Constantine Skinner, in deference to his equal involvement in investigating the case.

I continued, 'Anderton didn't look underneath the door himself – he just accepted Garforth's word. Kellway must have been lying down there. While Anderton went to wake Sir Newnham, Garforth let him out.'

'With Bradbury's connivance?' Holmes asked. 'Well, perhaps. But we found it impossible to hide beneath the door with that lenticular window in place. You were fully visible when you tried.'

'That was in daylight,' I reminded him. 'And Anderton isn't a tall man. Kellway would have had nearly ten minutes in which to secrete himself somewhere, either in the laboratory or elsewhere in the house, and could have slipped out after the doors were unlocked for the day. That would explain why he insisted the room should be dark during the experiment,' I added, in sudden inspiration. 'With the bulb on, some of the light would have escaped beneath the crack, and Kellway's body would have blocked it. Anderton might well have noticed that change.'

'Your theory has the merit of being founded in everyday phenomena,' Holmes admitted. 'And yet I suspect a man of Kellway's bulk would have been visible though the magnifying panel to a man of medium height, even in the dark. It must also be observed that by this hypothesis Kellway's accomplices have made themselves rather conspicuous, as our suspicions have inevitably fallen on Bradbury and Garforth – despite the fact that it would not have taken two men to release Kellway, and Bradbury was not even supposed to be there at that time. Both would be taking a large and for one of them an unnecessary risk, for a notional third share of ten thousand pounds, which still lie unclaimed.'

'Three-and-a-third thousand pounds is still a great deal of money,' I pointed out.

'That is true. Yet even so, there is the question of how they obtained a copy of the key,' Holmes continued. 'Despite what I said to Sir Newnham last night, that is not a trivial question. Aside from Sir Newnham himself, the most likely persons to have been able to lay hands on his copy would be Anderton and Talbot Rhyne. Anderton would also have been in the best position to extract the housekeeper's keys from her room, though Mrs Catton is a formidable and unbending woman and I find it difficult to credit that she would be so lax. And indeed, if Anderton is involved, why is he not telling us a simple story that exonerates Garforth and Bradbury, rather than this rigmarole of cats and card-games which leaves room for the very doubts you were just expressing? And if the man inside the Speight household is Rhyne, since he was also the man responsible for drawing up the rota he could simply have arranged for himself and one of the others to stand a watch together, and not involved Anderton at all.'

'Still,' I suggested, 'perhaps we should try pushing blankets or something up against that door to see how big a pile it takes to be seen from above. Perhaps Kellway is some sort of contortionist who can make himself seem thinner.'

I was aware that my explanation was once again straying away from the realms of the probable, although a circus performer was surely a less implausible prodigy than a translocating wizard.

'I shall enlist the thinnest servant I can find,' Holmes promised, 'and essay the experiment again. Meanwhile, my dear fellow, I have an errand for you.'

It seemed I was to visit the address given on Kellway's business card, to find out what I could from his living quarters. Rhyne, who had sent several messengers the previous day but had not attended the premises himself, offered to accompany me, and we hailed a cab in the High Street.

We agreed to stop for luncheon at a public house in Chiswick, where it took Rhyne very little time to work the conversation around to the case. 'And how is Mr Holmes's investigation progressing, Doctor?' he asked me. 'Has he discovered some cunning escape route from the room, or does he still suspect conspiracy? I presume he hasn't yet come round to a supernatural view of the matter.'

Though Rhyne was an appealing young fellow, and seemed to me an honest one, I reasoned that, as Holmes had not altogether eliminated him from his list of suspects, I should not be too forthcoming about the progress of our thinking. I offered Holmes's usual platitude about theorising with insufficient data, and Rhyne took the hint. For the remainder of the meal he talked with great enthusiasm about his work with Sir Newnham and the luck he had had in finding his present position. I felt that he was emphasising how much he would have had to lose from engaging in any such conspiracy, though whether from a position of innocence or guilt I was not a precise enough judge of human nature to say.

After lunch we found Kellway's address. It proved to be a rather poky boarding house owned and managed by an elderly widow named Edna Rust.

'Mr Kellway's a peculiar-looking gentleman, that's for sure,' Mrs Rust told us over a cup of tea in her sitting room. 'You don't need eyes as good as mine to see *that*.' I had already surmised from the narrow frown with which she had greeted us at the door that Kellway's landlady was somewhat myopic. 'But what *I* says is, a man can't help his looks, not what with his alopecia and all, and I can't complain of his habits, not really. He don't have visitors, not mostly, not till these last few days, excepting as it's that niece of his, and he'll always take her out for a stroll instead of sitting with her in his room, because you know how tongues wag, seeing the sorts of minds some people have. Some gentlemen have "nieces" what aren't nothing of the kind, as *I* should know, Dr Watson, after running boarding houses these thirty years, but not Mr Kellway, leastways not as *I* ever knew of.'

I had wondered whether it might take some persuasion to entice Kellway's landlady to give an account of his habits. Evidently, though, discretion and reserve were not among Mrs Rust's characteristic qualities.

'So he's mostly been a good tenant?' Rhyne asked her.

She pursed her lips. 'The worst I'll say is as he comes and goes as he pleases, any hour of the day or night. But he's always quiet and considerate with it, and he's friendly and clean, and on time with the rent every Friday evening regular.'

'How long has Mr Kellway been lodging with you?' I asked.

'Ten weeks this Monday just gone,' she replied promptly. 'He came to me with references from his last landlady in Sheffield. Very prettily wrote, they was,' she added.

'And when did you see him most recently?' I asked.

'Well now,' she said, a little dubiously. 'I've so many things to remember, running a place like this, I don't know as I could tell you, not for sure. I remember he said something to me about a job he had to do this week. Sunday evening, that was, because Mr Brightlea was there with his prayer book, just ready to go out to service at the Baptist chapel. He's my oldest tenant, Mr Brightlea is, and he never misses his evening service.'

'A job?' I echoed. 'Did Kellway use that exact term?' It would be an odd way to describe having an experiment conducted on oneself, I thought, but a criminal might well have applied it to a fraud.

'Well, I couldn't rightly say, I'm sure,' she said. '*I* wasn't taking it all down, if that's what you mean. Come to think of it, I'm not sure Mr Brightlea *was* there. I might be getting mixed up with last Sunday.'

'Is he away from home a lot?' I wondered. 'Mr Kellway, I mean.'

Mrs Rust was looking rather affronted now. 'Well, I'm sure *I* couldn't say. *I* don't keep a diary of his comings and goings. Like I said already, he can keep his irregular hours for all I'm concerned. As long as he pays his rent, it's all the same to me.'

Rhyne nodded sympathetically. 'I suppose it works out rather nicely, in fact. I mean, I suppose there are days when you don't have to do his laundry or make his breakfast or clean his room, but get your rent-money all the same.'

It would not have taken Holmes to deduce from the state of the sitting room that Mrs Rust was more lax about her cleaning duties than even poor eyesight could justify, but I could not help feeling that Rhyne's comment was less than tactful. Seeing the landlady open her mouth for an indignant retort, I resorted to a compliment, which I have found is often the best way to gain the trust of witnesses of the fair sex.

With this stern, portly, elderly cockney widow, my choice of compliments was limited. 'This is an excellent pot of tea, Mrs Rust,' I ventured.

She sniffed. 'I should think it might be, seeing as how I've been making it day in and day out these forty years and more.' I thought I detected some slight mellowing in her manner, nonetheless.

She had some justification for being suspicious, as Rhyne and I had been deliberately vague about our intentions. This was partly because we had no official status in the case, there being in fact no official case at all. Had there been any clear evidence that a crime had taken place, Holmes would naturally have contacted our friends at Scotland Yard, but in the absence of such evidence he had respected Sir Newnham's preference for keeping the matter within the purview of his household, the Society and those they had, wisely or otherwise, chosen to investigate the matter.

Mrs Rust peered narrowly at us now, first at me and then at Rhyne. 'Are you his family too, then?' she asked, calculatingly.

'If I may confide in you, Mrs Rust,' I said, 'we're all rather worried about him. He hasn't been seen since early Tuesday morning, as far as we know. So if you could see your way to helping us out a little, we'd be very appreciative.' Seeing her hesitation, I added, 'We might even be able to arrange for his rent to be covered, perhaps for the next month, in case he's somehow prevented from returning.' I hoped that Sir Newnham would consider this an acceptable expense, for it would have made an unpleasant dent in my own pocket.

I could see her lips moving as she calculated the sum involved. 'Well,' she said, finally. 'I suppose if you reckon as some harm might've come to the poor gentleman, I should do my best to help.'

'I knew we could count on you,' I told her warmly. 'We would like to see Mr Kellway's room, if you please. There might be some indication there of where he's gone.'

She showed us up to Kellway's room on the first floor, unlocking it with a key she kept on a stout ring clipped to her waist. The room was cramped, the bed jostling with the wardrobe on one side, while the washstand rubbed shoulders with a bureau close by at the other end. The windows were small and faced north. I had to persuade Mrs Rust to light the gas-lamp before we could examine the room properly.

It was, at least, tidier than the rest of the house, though the furniture and windowsill had not been well dusted. The bed was neatly made; the floor and other surfaces were free of clutter. An embroidered biblical text and a rudimentary print of a bucolic scene, both framed, were the room's only extraneous decoration. Both of them spoke of Mrs Rust's taste, or perhaps that of her late husband. The bureau seemed to double as a writing desk and dressing table, for it held both an inkstand and a mirror.

To do Mrs Rust justice, the room was neither draughty nor damp, and I had certainly seen far worse during my association with Holmes. 'Do all the furnishings come with the room?' I asked.

Mrs Rust peered around as if assessing whether Kellway had left behind anything she might sell. 'He brought that looking-glass with him,' she said finally.

I examined the mirror more closely. It was of reasonable size but inexpensive: an inelegant rectangle without a stand, clearly second-hand and much-handled, the metal peeling from the glass in places. I doubted Kellway's landlady would get very much for it, were he not to return. I asked her for a moment's privacy, and she tutted and withdrew, though I suspected she would remain in earshot.

I opened the drawers in the bureau and found little that seemed personal. There were handkerchiefs and other linens, a soap-dish, another clip of cards, blank sheets of writing paper with envelopes, a cheap pen, candles, a box of Speight's Self-Igniting Wonder Matches (for the candles, I assumed, as there was no sign of tobacco and we had been told Kellway was a non-smoker). Aside from a copy of the schedule we had seen for the Society's experiment on Kellway, the drawers' contents could have belonged to anybody.

Looking at the wardrobe, Rhyne made similar observations. The state of the few shirts and the pair of trousers hanging there was consistent with the well-mended wear Holmes had observed in the clothing Kellway had left behind at Sir Newnham's, but they had nothing else distinctive about them. A second jacket hung at the back, in slightly better condition than the one Kellway had worn. While shabby, its lining at least was intact.

In fact, I reflected, the lack of personality in the room was itself remarkable, given that Kellway had been described to us as a unique and forceful character. In particular, there were no books. To be sure there was no bookshelf to keep them on, but the windowsill, the bureau or even the top of the wardrobe would have served the purpose if called upon to do so. Even given the existence of public libraries, I wondered how a man would develop a philosophy, whether sincere or not, involving etheric vibrations and the planet Venus, without actually owning at least some books on the subject.

Nothing else in the room suggested esoteric or psychical interests, although I was not altogether sure what other form I might have expected them to take – a chalk pentacle beneath the rug, perhaps? I lifted it, justifying this to Rhyne on the somewhat more rational grounds that Kellway might have used it as a hiding-place for letters or other papers, but the floorboards beneath were unmarked and fixed firmly in place.

More for the sake of thoroughness than because I expected it to yield results, I lifted the inkstand. It revealed nothing but a circle of dust and an eyelash.

That left only the print and the sampler. The former was an inferior reproduction of a poor etching of a not-especially-scenic hill with a wooded crest and some sheep; the latter read 'LOVE THY NEIGHBOUR' – excellent advice for boarding-house life, I had no doubt, but suggesting nothing by way of occult significance.

'Rhyne,' I said, 'could you ask Mrs Rust if we may take these pictures down and check the frames for any hidden items?'

While he went to ask, I picked the eyelash up with a pair of tweezers and sealed it in one of Kellway's envelopes, thanking providence for Mrs Rust's indolence. I remembered Holmes remarking once that, should either of us be murdered at home, Mrs Hudson's zealotry for household cleanliness would ensure that the police would never find a clue to the culprit's identity. He had jocularly suggested to her that she might find employment in a freelance capacity among the criminal underworld, ridding crime scenes of their traces. While no crime had been committed in this room as far as I knew, the general point remained.

Rhyne and the landlady returned shortly, and we set about carefully removing the items from their frames. As I had by now expected, there was nothing unusual to be found behind them, and we replaced and rehung them with equal care.

'Did Mr Kellway tell you he had alopecia, Mrs Rust, or was it a guess?' I asked, as idly as I could.

She stared at me. 'Stands to reason, don't it? He's got no hair at all. My auntie had a friend as was the same way, from when she was a little girl. It's crueller for a woman than a man.' I tried to probe further, but quickly realised that on this point Mrs

Rust's rather fallible memory once again had nothing to offer.

'What work does Mr Kellway do?' I asked her, as we reconvened for tea. 'He mentioned having a particular job in progress, but I presume you established that he had a steady income when you took him on as a tenant?'

'He's a commercial traveller,' she said, 'and that's why he's away so much. But,' she added slyly, 'as you're his family you'll know that at least.'

'We're good friends of his, Mrs Rust,' Rhyne interjected, 'and I can assure you we have his best interests very much at heart.'

Further questioning elicited that Mrs Rust had no idea in what commodity Kellway travelled. Plainly there were no samples in his room, but I supposed it was possible that they were held at his employers' office. In any case, the man must make a living somehow. The philosophy he propounded might appeal to a certain type of rich and gullible enquirer, but as far as I knew he had authored no books, conducted no lecture tours, nor purported to offer supernatural services like the wretched Constantine Skinner. Even if he could attract the charitable interest of men of substance like Beech and Speight, that could hardly equate to a regular income, and Mrs Rust had found him to be wholly reliable in that regard.

'Do you still have the letter of recommendation from his Sheffield landlady?' I asked, but as I had by now come to expect Mrs Rust could not put her hands on it amongst her other papers. She promised to send it to me care of Sir Newnham if it resurfaced.

As Rust and I were taking our leave, she unexpectedly said, 'He said he was family too, you know, that first one what came.'

Rhyne and I stopped in our tracks. 'The first who?' Rhyne asked.

I added, 'I thought you said that Mr Kellway had had no visitors except for a young lady.'

'I said as he hadn't till these last few days,' Mrs Rust said. 'This one called around late Monday, before them lot from Richmond what came asking for him all day yesterday. I knows as it was Monday because I was washing Mr Brightlea's best shirt what he wears to church. He said he was looking for Mr Kellway urgent, the man, I mean, not Mr Brightlea, he was at the Working Men's Club with his darts team. He's an abstainer, Mr Brightlea, but he does like his game of darts. He says as there's no harm in it just so long as no money changes hands. Well, there wasn't nothing I could tell him, was there, that man I mean, not Mr Brightlea, I don't keep a record of where Mr Kellway says he is from day to day, I'm sure. He wasn't polite like you gentlemen, though. I said if he was family he should go and talk to Mr Kellway's niece.'

'That was very sensible of you, Mrs Rust,' I said. 'Could you describe this man for us?'

She thought that he was youngish, or at least not especially elderly; large, or at least larger than her late husband, who had been a remarkably small man; not bald like Kellway, but otherwise of no noticeable hair colour; and wearing clothes, she was certain, but ones that had left no firm impression on her mind. Her description was, in short, as useless as anything else she had given us.

Our cab took us back to Speight's house, where Rhyne went to find his employer and I set out to locate Holmes. I tracked him down some time later, in the camera obscura which formed part of Sir Newnham's rooftop observatory.

As I entered the cupola where the device was situated, I found myself in a space that seemed pitch dark after the moderate afternoon sunlight of the rooftop. As I stood, blinking stupidly, I gradually detected a dim glow filling the middle of a round, dark room, and in its centre the slim silhouette of Holmes, sitting cross-legged and gazing at the floor around him.

He was surrounded by a dim pattern of coloured light, mostly green and grey, which it took me several seconds to resolve as a projection of the grounds beneath us. I could see the chemical laboratory and the Experimental Annexe, with an area of unspoiled garden beyond, then a hedge and even further on a section of the street where minuscule pedestrians and carriages could be seen hurrying by. In the green space, next to a small brown shape I supposed must be the summerhouse we had seen earlier, two tiny gardeners were engaged in digging a flowerbed, their industrious activity reminding me of beetles. It felt as if I were on a distant planet, staring at this tiny portion of England through some inconceivably powerful telescope.

I stared entranced until Holmes's sardonic voice aroused me from my reverie. 'A positively godlike perspective, is it not, Watson? The light is fading now, but at noon on a sunny day the world would be one's chessboard.'

I said, 'What does Sir Newnham use it for? Spying on his gardeners?'

'Oh, it is little more than an expensive toy,' said Holmes. 'Its scientific value is chiefly as an illustration of a principle, and even for that purpose a simpler device would make the matter clearer. A tiny aperture in a flat surface can be used to project an image horizontally, but for such an angel's-eye view as this one needs a complex arrangement of mirrors and lenses. It is housed in the canopy above us. See, it can be rotated to show any part of the grounds.'

He demonstrated this, and as the field of view moved the light swirled around our feet until I could see the gables at the front of the house, and the drive beneath, where a carriage no bigger than a child's wooden engine was being welcomed by a footman the size of a tin soldier.

'I believe that is the Countess Brusilova arriving,' Holmes

observed as a tiny figure hesitantly emerged, accompanied by a taller, stronger woman.

'It's a shame the contraption does not work at night,' I observed. 'Somebody might have seen Kellway making his escape.'

'The moon was half-full that night,' said Holmes. 'If someone had sufficiently sharp eyes, and had accustomed himself to the dimness... But no, as far as we know nobody was up here at the time, though we might make discreet enquiries just in case. I have said such devices have limited scientific usefulness, Watson, but imagine their application to law enforcement. A network of towers built across London, their summits bearing chambers like this one, each with its own policeman watching the world beneath... What a deterrent such an arrangement would be to crime! Though also, I dare say, to any amount of legitimate business for which a person might desire privacy.'

I could see that the peculiar sensation of omniscience the camera obscura created had brought on one of Holmes's whimsically philosophical moods. I brought him down to earth with a brisk account of Rhyne's and my observations at Kellway's lodgings.

'So by his landlady's account Kellway has relatives and a job,' Holmes observed. 'Not to mention a harmless skin condition. It is not what I expected of an Evolved Man.'

'He seems to have precious little else to his name,' I said. 'No esoteric texts or magical paraphernalia. No shaving apparatus, for that matter, which supports the alopecia idea. But I did find this.'

We had to step out onto the leads for me to show him the eyelash, which I did once I had ensured that nobody else was around on the roof. 'Come, Watson,' he said after he had examined it, 'I want to look at that summerhouse.'

An iron fire-escape staircase led down from the roof, and

we descended by that route. I said, 'Alopecia takes time to render a person entirely bald, but it does not discriminate between eyelashes and other hair. If Kellway has eyelashes, then his baldness is not due to alopecia.'

'If a man told me that he was hairless all over, it is the first thing I should look at, after his scalp and eyebrows,' Holmes said. 'I should then have to find some excuse to peer inside his ears or nose. However, perhaps not everybody would be so quick to remark on the presence of a perfectly familiar facial feature.'

'I would,' I said. 'But an alopecia patient's baldness is a symptom, and I'm a doctor.'

'Then we should speak to Sir Newnham's friend Dr Kingsley,' Holmes decided. 'It is entirely possible that nobody else will even have noticed whether the man had lashes.'

I sighed. 'It's also possible it's not even Kellway's eyelash. He's been living there ten weeks, but Mrs Rust is not an enthusiastic cleaner. I'm not even convinced she heard him say he had alopecia, rather than jumping to her own conclusions. As evidence, it's useless.'

'Perhaps, but we can make one deduction from it. We may presume that Kellway did *not* tell his landlady that he was bald as a result of being subjected to accelerated evolution by intelligences from the planet Venus. I suspect that information at least would have stuck in her mind.'

I nodded slowly. 'So his claim to be an Evolved Man is one he only makes in company such as Speight's and Beech's, not to the world at large. That suggests a deliberate deception.'

'Perhaps,' Holmes said again. 'Or merely reticence about an account he knew she would be unlikely to accept. Then again, Kellway's assertion is that his hair has been lost because it lacks a useful function, yet eyelashes are helpful in protecting the eyes from dust and other foreign bodies. They might be considered essential, where other hair is a mere evolutionary vestige. Perhaps he is an Evolved Man after all. And who are we, Watson, to judge the honesty of a specimen of a superior race?'

He was still in a merry mood, evidently. As we passed through the grounds, I said, 'Speaking of medical matters, I've remembered something about epilepsy. Before a seizure, some patients report seeing patterns of light and colour, an illusion produced by the disorder in the brain. That sounds very like Skinner's auras, don't you think?'

We had come now to the little summerhouse, where the beetle-sized gardeners, now quite human in their bulk and solidity, were still laying down soil in the flowerbed. 'It is not locked,' Holmes observed as we reached the outbuilding. 'Well, there is no reason why it should be, during the daytime at least. We must ask Anderton whether it is secured at night.'

We went inside. The wooden cabin held two deck chairs and very little else. Where once it would have given a fine panorama across the lawns to the rear elevation of the house, its vista was now marred by the Experimental Annexe, the chemistry laboratories and the greenhouses. It did not look as if it was much used. Holmes ignored the view, however, and instead began inspecting the chairs, the floor and walls.

I said, 'Are you supposing that Anderton forgot to lock the door after the cat incident, and that Kellway escaped from the Annexe that way? Because Anderton was quite clear that he *did* lock up, and even if he's wrong I don't see how anyone could have predicted that.' Unless, I thought, Anderton was in on the conspiracy as well, but we had discounted that idea twice already.

'I have no such theory at present,' Holmes replied, peering into a dark corner. 'A-ha!' He pulled out his own tweezers, and after a moment's work held up between them a small length of dark thread. 'See, Watson,' he said, showing me the protruding nail it had been caught on. 'Someone has been here. Somebody wearing clothing of a dark material.'

'That could have been practically anybody, Holmes,' I pointed out reasonably. 'And at any time, too.'

'I fancy it has at least been in recent weeks. Over the summer the thread would have faded in the sun.' Sombrely he added, 'All data are valuable, Watson. We simply need to understand how they all fit together.'

As he led the way back to the house, I was left with the perturbing impression that my friend had at the moment no more lucid an understanding of the case than I had.

The Morning Chronicle

16th May 1887

Our correspondent has learned of a most discomfiting incident that has befallen a renowned scientist and innovator whose name (though the reader will not find it issuing from our Revolutionary-Spooling Finger-Powered Type-Writer) is familiar in households up and down the country as the originator of many a household boon.

It seems that the magnate in question, who the breath of rumour tells us may even now be under consideration for a knighthood, was last week accosted in the street by a distressed older gentleman who accused him of the most preposterous crimes. This gentleman contended, with many imprecations on the inventor's head and implorations to the passing public, that the man trucked with the Devil and that each of his machines was worked by tiny homunculi living within, all of whom were the ghosts of dead persons whom the gentleman had known personally, and moreover that he (the accosted) owed him (the accoster) a sizeable sum of money, which he would see repaid with menaces if necessary.

To this most lamentable and conspicuous scene the police eventually arrived, but they were beaten a little to the mark by the gentleman's friends, who helped him back to his residence, not altogether with his approval or acquiescence. One of these friends, recognised by some of those present at the scene as a peer of quite recent creation, from a family 'not exactly high-born', was heard to apologise to the inventor for the behaviour of his uncle, who had for some time been suffering from the most distressing delusions on the subject which he had so importunately raised.

His interlocutor, though

much embarrassed, accepted this account of the matter along with the apology, and the disquiet appears to have been laid to rest. We hear that the old gentleman is now visiting the countryside for his health, and is not expected to return to London this season.

Not one of Langdale Pike's best efforts, but suggestive nonetheless. — S.H.

CHAPTER SEVEN

After failing to make an appearance during the afternoon, Frederick Garforth continued to absent himself from supper at Parapluvium House. Rhyne informed us that, along with a message to Sir Newnham regretting his non-attendance, the artist had sent apologies to Holmes and myself, promising to call on us the next morning in Baker Street.

By way of making up for his guest's absence, Speight showed us one of Garforth's paintings which he had purchased and hung in one of the smaller guest bedrooms. It was, as Anderton had suggested, a frank study of a woman in a state of undress, executed in a sickly orangish hue. Although I do not pretend to any expertise in art I found it repellent.

Holmes, when we were out of earshot of Sir Newnham, confided his agreement. 'It is in the modern style,' he said, 'which will naturally antagonise a traditionalist such as yourself, Watson, but I regret that it is also a very shoddy example of the type. It is kind of Sir Newnham to buy a painting by an acquaintance who, I imagine, would otherwise have been unable to sell it. Garforth is evidently not a young man, but he must have come rather late to painting as a means of expression. I have not seen his name in the galleries or catalogues – although it is, I think, distantly familiar from somewhere.'

We gathered with Speight's other guests for drinks in the drawing room, which had resisted the inventor's modernising influence over the other rooms in the house, and retained its original Regency charm. Skinner was there, holding his glass awkwardly, his eyes flickering away whenever I looked at him, and so was Beech, drinking only water, and discoursing at length about teetotalism and other topics as they pertained to himself. Holmes and I were introduced to Major Bradbury, a florid, choleric man approaching his seventies, whose stiffness of bearing I thought owed more to rheumatism than to his military training.

'Can't imagine what Speight thinks he's doing, involving you fellows in this business,' he told us frankly. 'Skinner either, come to that. You're not going to find Kellway where he's gone.'

'You believe he's dead, then?' I asked.

Bradbury snorted his disagreement. 'If the fellow was dead, there'd be a body. He's gone exactly where he expected to – to Venus. Only way we'll see him again is if he finds his way back. Not sure I'd bother if I were him, eh?' He barked a short laugh.

'Did Kellway inform you of his likely departure, Major?' Holmes asked. His face was studiedly grave, and I could see that he was at pains not to be witty on the subject. 'We understood that the purpose of the experiment was to test his powers of telekinesis, not of translocation.'

'Quite right,' the Major confirmed shortly. 'Fellow couldn't transcend the earthly sphere on demand, could he? But he was expecting it to happen sooner or later, when he reached the necessary level of spiritual elevation. That last bit of meditation must've done the trick, I expect. I knew a guru in Calcutta who did exactly the same. Retired into a cave to meditate for sixty days and his followers walled him in. Huge pile of rubble they built. No way a man could have moved it on his own, and no other way out of the cave either – I looked over it myself. They came back two months later and took the walls down – not a trace of him. No body, no bones. He'd gone *somewhere*, and not in any usual way either. What do you make of that, Holmes, eh?'

'With no opportunity to examine the interior of the cave myself, nor to compare the composition of the wall at the beginning and end of the sixty days, very little,' said Holmes. 'That is the advantage of a controlled experiment.'

'Well, Kellway gave us a pretty clear demonstration of a psychic phenomenon on his way out,' Bradbury opined. 'Just wasn't the one we were expecting, that's all.' He had evidently recovered from his state of shock of the previous morning.

'Perhaps so,' said Holmes smoothly. 'This is what Sir Newnham has asked me to confirm.'

'I suppose you'll find a way to be sceptical about it,' Bradbury huffed. 'At least Skinner understands there's more to the world than what we Westerners call reason. They know all about that in the East, you know.'

'Major Bradbury has his little fads,' confided a high-pitched voice to my left, with a conspiratorial giggle. I turned to see the Reverend Vortigern Small, a man of a size to suit his name, dressed in dark clerical skirts and a white collar and bands.

While Bradbury continued to regale Holmes with his anecdote, the priest drew me aside. 'I would be hard pressed to call the Major a *student* of Eastern religion, because in all honesty I am not sure the poor man understands the difference between a Sufi and a swami, but he is terrifically keen *spectator* of it. If somebody told him that Methodism had originated on the banks of the Indus, I feel sure he would be knocking at the doors of the nearest chapel, begging for enlightenment. Not that I would condone any such practical joke, of course.'

I said, 'You treat these things lightly, for a man of the cloth.'

Small projected an air of self-effacing unworldliness which concealed a deeply irreverent sense of humour and, I was beginning to see, a very definite streak of malice.

He giggled again. 'I may appear to, but I am tremendously serious. This Society is a melting pot, my dear doctor, a positive melting pot of original and innovative faiths. Did you know we have a *genuine diabolist* among our ranks? Mr Aldous Horst is not here tonight, but his worship of Satan and his minions is touchingly earnest. Then there is Countess Brusilova, with the scriptures she has had dictated to her by the ghosts of pagan hierarchs from the vanished continent of Hy-Brasil.'

Small indicated a dumpy, veiled woman, of whom the hands were the only part visible; they were ropy and knotted with age. She stood nearby, leaning heavily on a stick, attended by her frighteningly stern young companion, who was in her early twenties, with delicate features and very pale blonde hair in a severe bun, and whose name I remembered was Miss Casimir.

The cleric continued, 'Those few who have read her books assure me that they too are *terribly* sincere, as far as they were able to understand them. As for Mr Beech, with his one-man religion based on evolution and the Will of Life – it is so *creative* of him to find a new way to scandalise convention, but of course he does it so well in his professional career that one must expect something of the same in his spiritual affairs.'

'And you, Mr Small?' I asked, tiring of this smirking litany of his fellows' defects. 'What is a Church of England pastor doing in such company?' The Reverend Small's character was so much at odds with the strait-laced, small-minded vicar whom Gideon Beech had described to us that I wondered whether the priest had been acting a part to discourage Beech's conversation, or whether Beech had merely disdained to listen to a word Small said.

The cleric affected an expression of indignant piety now, his face suffused with amusement nonetheless. 'Why, Doctor, I am searching for the truth, what else? Like everybody, I am here to observe the experiments. As the Lord tells us, "Ye shall know them by their fruits."'

'I see,' I said. 'And how should we judge Thomas Kellway?'

'I cannot say that, Dr Watson, until we know what exactly his fruits are. I will judge a tree that produces apples more favourably than one that grows mere wax imitations.'

'So you believe him to be a fraud?' I wondered. 'Yet as a man of the cloth, you must allow that miracles are possible.'

'I suppose I must, mustn't I?' Mr Small beamed. 'But I am not thereby obliged to believe that anything surprising that happens is a miracle. And believing such things *possible* is a rather different proposition from believing that they are *likely* to happen in a London suburb in our modern era, and to such ordinary people as ourselves.'

'Then why observe the experiments?' I asked. 'If you're not expecting anything out of the ordinary to happen...'

'Ah! But when I referred to my observations, I did not mean Sir Newnham's tests, but the whole panoply of religious experimentation which surrounds us all. I am a very *modern* sort of a clergyman, you see. In religion as in science, experiments must be essayed and results observed, failures as well as successes. How better to perfect my own faith than to observe the various and exciting failures of those around me here?'

I was sure there must be a clear answer to this, but being no theologian I was momentarily at a loss to put my finger on it. As I glanced around for inspiration, I saw Constantine Skinner, who was standing close by, barricaded from Holmes by a huge, enormously bearded man whose name I had not managed to remember and who, as far as I had been able to ascertain, spoke only Norwegian.

From the glare the occult investigator was giving Small, it was plain that he had heard his every word, including his comments about Beech. 'And I, Mr Small?' Skinner asked, with an attempt at hauteur. 'Am I another of your interesting failures?' He was, as I had already seen, the sort of man for whom dismissal rankled.

'Oh, Mr Skinner, I hardly know you. But an *interesting* failure?' Small beamed benignly, placing the lightest possible emphasis on the word. 'No, I can assure you, you could never be that.'

Skinner gaped abjectly before being rescued, whether by luck or design, by Dr Kingsley, who said, 'Oh, Dr Watson, I must ask you something.'

We had been introduced to the doctor earlier, a tall and dapper man with a saturnine beard. He was accompanied by the Honourable Gerald Floke, whose appearance, this evening at least, was quite extraordinary.

Kingsley continued, 'Mr Floke has been speaking to me about the irrelevance of hair and the appendix to human survival. He has been asking which other organs an Evolved Person might dispense with. Do you have any views on the matter?'

I considered for a moment. Distasteful though the topic was, it was an interesting medical question. I said, 'The tonsils and adenoids, I would think – the benefits to the system of both are minimal. There are a number of small muscles, like those which allow some people to waggle their ears, which are not generally used and have no practical application when they are. Fingernails and toenails are fairly dispensable, I suppose, and – ah, I can think of certain other structures.' Carried away with my train of thought I had been about to mention the mammary *papillae* of the male of the species, but given the nearby presence of the Countess and Miss Casimir, I demurred from so *risqué* an observation.

Kingsley's mouth turned up slightly, and he said, 'Quite so,' in a manner that reminded me irresistibly of Holmes. Like many of those present, the doctor exuded a strong personality, but he seemed to me a rational man, as if his medical background served to insulate him from some of the more outlandish excesses of his fellows. Or perhaps it merely seemed that way to me because the background was one I shared.

He said, 'Of course, one might take an even firmer line. Many organs in the human body are duplicated. This is useful in cases where one of them fails or is damaged, but there are individuals who live perfectly fulfilling lives with only one of the pair. Might not a truly efficient Evolved Man be organised on a monolithic basis, with a one-lunged, one-kidneyed torso atop a single leg, sprouting a single arm, and surmounted by a cyclopean head sporting a single ear and a single nostril?'

I smiled at his flight of fancy but he had, I suspect intentionally, provoked the Honourable Gerald Floke to earnest protest. 'But that would hardly be the peak of *human* perfection, would it, Doctor?' the young man expostulated.

At another time Floke might have been rather handsome, after the fashion of a thoroughbred racing-hound puppy. Tonight, however, his head was completely shaven, including his eyebrows (but not, I noticed, his eyelashes), and the skin was red and sore, suggesting that this state was both recent and uncustomary.

He continued, 'Why, such a grotesque creature wouldn't be a man at all. Perhaps the Venusians, or another of the races on our neighbouring worlds, might have developed in that way, but an Evolved *Man* must be the ultimate expression of earthly humanity. As Thomas Kellway is.' He said the name with some reverence.

'Young Gerald, I believe,' the insinuating parson said in my ear, 'is in the early stages of formulating yet another novel creed.'

'It's him we must imitate if we're to become Evolved ourselves,' Floke insisted, 'and elevate the rest of mankind. I'm rather hopeful that we have a channel of communication that will allow him to show us the way, but if not then the rest of us will just have to work it out between us.'

'The way?' I asked him, confused. 'The way to Venus?'

'The Way of Kellway,' Vortigern Small murmured. 'Or Kellwayism? Kellwianity, possibly?'

'The way to evolve!' insisted Floke, an evangelical light shining in his eyes. 'To attain that higher plane of enlightenment – *sphere* of enlightenment, I should say,' he added with a hasty glance across the room at Gideon Beech, who apparently had not heard. 'To ascend through the spheres towards the supreme effulgence of the Sun itself!'

'The shaving is a kind of *Imitatio Christi*, I think,' Small said quietly. 'But he is perhaps not *so* discriminating about which aspects of his new messiah he emulates.'

'So will you do it, Dr Kingsley?' the shaven young man cajoled. 'You've said I wouldn't miss it, and it would bring me closer to the ideal state.' When the Doctor snorted in amusement and shook his head, Floke appealed to me. 'What about you, Dr Watson? Will you remove my appendix?'

I was quite taken aback. 'That would hardly be a good idea, Mr Floke,' I replied. 'It's true that the body doesn't really need it, but the surgery bears risks of its own. It's quite inadvisable except in cases of medical emergency. No good doctor would carry out such an unnecessary procedure, and a bad one could hardly be trusted with it.' Floke looked crestfallen, so I added, 'You wouldn't want to die of septicaemia before you've transcended the earthly sphere, would you?'

'No. No, that would be dreadful.' Floke still looked distressed.

I took advantage of the moment to ask, 'What of the eyelashes, by the way, Dr Kingsley? They might be considered an example of hair with a function. Does Mr Kellway have those?'

Dr Kingsley looked surprised. 'I confess I hadn't noticed. Floke?'

Floke looked alarmed by the question, but said firmly, 'Of course he doesn't. He has no hair, he told us so.'

He blinked in realisation and touched his own eyelashes with a fingertip. I added hastily, 'Please don't pluck your eyelashes, Mr Floke. They can take a very long time to grow back, and there is again a risk of infection, though not normally a fatal one.'

I could tell that he was unconvinced. Feeling rather awkward, I elected to circulate.

Had Garforth attended as planned there would have been fourteen of us at the party, including our host, and I wondered how many of those present were sufficiently superstitious as to take alarm at our new number. Bradbury was holding forth to Skinner, while Beech similarly expounded at a rather peevish Sir Newnham. Being unable to join Holmes, who was annoyingly conversing with the Norwegian in his own tongue, I instead gravitated towards Talbot Rhyne, whom the forbidding Miss Casimir was addressing in somewhat Germanic English, apparently on behalf of Countess Brusilova.

'But Mr Rhyne, a person has not to be "dead", to use that distasteful term, to speak through a medium,' Miss Casimir told him. 'The Countess has held séances where the yet unborn souls have spoken through her, and the spirits of animals, as well as those of living men and women. Myself, I communicated with my grandmother on her deathbed through the Countess's mediumship, as clearly as on the telephone. And she was in Coblenz.'

Rhyne said, 'Well, Coblenz,' as if this were rather an everyday achievement. 'Venus is another matter, though, surely? The distance alone…'

'Not in the least,' began Miss Casimir, but she was interrupted by the Countess herself.

'Distance is an illusion,' the old lady declared, her voice quavering and accented far more thickly than her companion's.

'A desperate failing of human perception.' Rhyne and Miss Casimir waited respectfully for her to elaborate on this, but she stayed silent.

The younger woman resumed her discourse. 'For the Countess, the matter was merely of attuning her psychic resonance to the interplanetary etheric vibrations described to her by Thomas. Her earliest attempts did not succeed – she first channelled entities from the Moon and Mercury, before she was able to fully direct her attention on Venus – but Palú-Odranel, the Venusian with whom she established finally a sympathetic resonance, could reassure us that Thomas was alive and well, and benefiting greatly from the youthful atmosphere in that blessed sphere.'

'I... see,' said Rhyne. I sensed that his willingness to accommodate extraordinary possibilities might be nearing its limits.

I asked the old lady, 'So in your view, Countess Brusilova, we've nothing to worry about? Kellway is safe?'

'Safer than anyone in this sphere, certainly,' Miss Casimir replied for her employer, who remained as silent as if I had not been there. 'And the fact that we, through the Countess's mediumship, can communicate with him is invaluable to us. The Countess intends further séances where we can instruct ourselves from his wisdom. She hopes that they will attract large crowds.' Paying large fees too, I had no doubt.

Nearby Gideon Beech was affirming, 'But of course this news must be promulgated more widely! Surely all of us, however myopic, must wish a prodigy like this announced to the world at large, regardless of whether we take the proper view of the matter or assuage our fears of the unknown with some cowardly obfuscation of the obvious.'

'Don't be so reckless, Beech,' Sir Newnham said irritably. 'Such a precipitate announcement, before we have a definitive explanation of what happened, risks all our reputations.'

Beech scoffed. 'Oh really, Speight. If reputation is your lodestone, we can keep your name out of it altogether. I am due to be interviewed by a reporter from one of our less pusillanimous newspapers on Friday – an arrangement preceding this whole business, of course, but a fortuitous one nevertheless. The young man was good enough to approach me at my home on Monday morning, asking some fascinating questions about many overlooked aspects of my life, this Society included, and I arranged to meet him again later, to talk them through in the detail they warrant. I'll certainly bring this matter to the laddie's attention – he's a promising young fellow.'

Out of the corner of my eye I saw Skinner slipping from the room. I glanced around to see whether anyone else was absent, and realised that Bradbury was also missing. A moment later, however, the Major returned and started to regale Floke and Kingsley with his reminiscences of the accomplishments of a yogi in Bangalore.

Thinking to mention Skinner's departure to Holmes, I circled the room until I found him again. He was now listening to the Reverend Small as the cleric quizzed Miss Casimir in wondering innocence about the Countess's beliefs.

'I must say, Miss Casimir,' said Small, 'I understood that the Countess's devotion was to *ancient* wisdom, not to such up-to-date fads as the theory of evolution. I thought that her efforts were devoted to rebuilding the primordial religion of Hy-Brasil, in which the true names of all things in the universe were revealed, and are now available to those fortunate enough to be able to, ahem, *recover* that primeval knowledge. Such gnosis represents a full and accurate picture of the universe, as I recall. And yet as far as I can remember from our many chats in the past, neither she nor you have ever mentioned planetary spheres as entities that might have any effect on our lives, nor indeed as places that might be visited. Indeed, one of the Countess's many pamphlets opposes the astrologers' idea that celestial bodies might have any influence on our destinies.'

'I say, though, Miss Casimir,' said Floke, who had been listening in increasing concern, 'that can't be right, can it? Because you were telling me the Countess had been talking to Thomas Kellway. And he's on another planet, you know, and only got there because of the Venusians' influence.'

'What Mr Small says is true,' Miss Casimir agreed smoothly, 'but before now the public has been ready for the Countess to reveal only a small part of the wisdom of holy Hy-Brasil. There is much more yet to be disclosed.'

'Is that so? Goodness me.' Small smiled with needle-sharp gentleness. 'Because I had also understood that this ancient and changeless knowledge held that Man is perfectible in *his own* right, without the assistance of external influences, if only we can recapture that lost transcendence of the Hy-Brasilians. If that be the case, Miss Casimir, what need for influences from Venus?'

Unexpectedly the Countess croaked, 'Yet knowledge is itself an emanation, on the spectrum of the psychic aether.' Again she refused to be drawn further on the remark, whose significance to the discussion was questionable.

Miss Casimir sighed. 'Naturally, what holds on the Earth must hold equally in the other spheres. It may be that the Venusians like the Countess's guide have kept aspects of primordial knowledge that temporarily have been lost to our world – though the knowledge itself must always be the same. What is true in one sphere must be true in all.'

'Indeed.' Vortigern Small's smile became positively beatific. 'And yet it's almost as if – you must forgive the observation, my dear lady – this permanent, complete and *immutable* record to which the Countess has so miraculously been granted her unique access is being amended suddenly and rather hastily in response to the things the people around her want to hear. I know young Gerald here was *exceedingly* pleased to learn that he had found in the Countess – and her Venusian mentor, of course – the perfect conduit to learn more from Mr Kellway of the world to which he has travelled and the wisdom he has gained there. That *was* what you wanted to hear, wasn't it, Gerald?'

The red blotches on Floke's face had spread to cover most of it, and his eyes bulged froglike from his hairless face. 'My God!' he spluttered. 'My God! If you're deceiving us – if you're claiming falsely to speak for *Thomas Kellway*, just so you can make yourselves some money – well, I shall – I'll...' He seemed to remember belatedly that, regardless of his level of evolutionary development, he remained a gentleman, and finished rather tamely, 'Well, I shall have to ask Sir Newnham to remove you from his house at once, for a start. And then I might actually have to call the police.'

'The Countess has had the police called on to attend her before,' Miss Casimir said coolly, 'by better men than you. She is a guest in Sir Newnham's house, and while he extends to her his hospitality, we will stay. If you choose not to remain here while the Countess is in the house, that is your affair, Mr Floke – but you will then be cutting yourself off from further communication with Mr Kellway. You must do whatever you think is the best.'

She turned dismissively and took the Countess's arm in hers. As they crossed the room I heard the Countess observe rather gloomily, 'We think we choose, but we are deceived. Our minds are borne on the shoulders of animals.'

Floke stared silently after them, his nostrils flared with rage. The Reverend Small took a sip of his sherry and winked at me in sheer devilment.

Letter from Miss Charlotte Haborn to Miss Amelia North

King's Shelton
12th April 1893

My dear Amy,

It is so kind of you to write with your sympathy over the dreadful events of this past week. You cannot imagine how frightening it is to read in every newspaper stories about 'the mysterious disappearance of the Hon. Letitia Haborn, who was last seen', etcetera, and to know that they are referring to one's own dear sister.

If you have also seen these distressing stories, as I realise you must have, you will know that none of us have seen dear Letty since last Wednesday, 5th April, when she retired to bed a little early, having said goodnight just as usual to Mama, Papa and myself. The next morning when her maid Judith went to wake her, she found her gone, along with most of her jewellery and a suitcase of clothes.

After some frantic questioning of the servants we discovered that the gardener's boy had borrowed the trap to take her to the station for the early train to London, bringing it back before it was missed. It seems the foolish fellow was quite smitten with poor Letty and would have done anything she asked, even to the peril of his own job (from which he has of course been dismissed, with a further threat from Papa of criminal charges if it turns out that any harm has come to Letty!) He assures us that she met nobody there, and I believe that he is telling the truth.

Although there has been some terribly fervid talk of white slavers and opium dens and the like, the common conclusion to which the press are all so eagerly jumping is, I suppose, the obvious one for one who did not know her – that she has eloped with, or been abducted by, some unsuitable lover. I believe that that is also the assumption upon which the police are proceeding, though they have assured Papa that they are keeping an open mind.

As you will surely agree from your own acquaintance with Letty, this seems to us quite out of the question. Though at twenty-two she is three years my senior, she has never shown any interest in men, preferring the company of books and of her peculiar, and to all our minds quite unsuitable, 'researches'. You will, I am sure, recall her at the age of twelve finding that dead frog that Grimalkin brought in, and attempting to revivify it using electricity. And that is perhaps the least obscure and worrying of her experiments. A girl who is capable of that is unlikely to be considered quite the catch by any man, I fear.

Letty has, alas, always been an excellent liar, creative and always most persuasive – she once convinced me that the Queen had died, and earned *me* a beating from our governess for telling wicked stories! So we are less shocked that she was able to deceive us than that she would choose to do so. Our feeling of betrayal is, as I am sure you can realise, almost as horrible as our fears for her safety.

But as to where my dear sister has gone, or what her intentions there might be, I cannot for a moment fathom. London is no place for a young lady on her own, and yet as far as we can discover she seems to have done nothing to make herself conspicuous there. Papa and I are distracted with worry, and poor Mama is quite prostrated.

I will write more if we learn more. Though it seems disloyal to say so, my own life has not been uneventful since

I wrote to you last, but of Lieutenant Maurice Webster I will have to tell you on a future occasion. I will tantalise you with that for now!

In gratitude again for your concern, I remain,
Your loving friend,
Charlotte

CHAPTER EIGHT

After this prelude, supper itself was a relatively tame affair. Though there were tensions, with so many outlandish personalities clustered around one table and skirting with varying degrees of caution around the same subjects, we all survived it without major incident.

Skinner did not join us, which caused a detectable relief on the part of one or two participants – more because it brought our numbers down to an acceptable twelve, I hoped, than for any particular dislike of the pallid young detective, who I still feared could ill bear any further opprobrium. The atmosphere discouraged Holmes's attempts to ask questions relating to Kellway's disappearance, and we finished our meal little the wiser, although Holmes did succeed in establishing, through a whispered conference with Anderton during the port and cigars, that the only key to the summerhouse had been lost two summers previously, and that the outbuilding had stood unlocked ever since.

Before leaving Parapluvium House for Baker Street, Holmes and I returned to the Experimental Annexe. The room was darkened and unheated, so it was a surprise to find the shadowy shape of Skinner, sitting alone and thoughtfully gazing into

Room A. He leapt to his feet as I switched on the lights, and stared antagonistically at Holmes, who raised a placating hand.

'Forgive us, Skinner,' he said. 'We have no plans to hamper your investigation. We simply hoped to carry out a brief observation. If you are busy here, we can return later.'

'Oh,' said the young man, disarmed. 'Well, I suppose it's all right, actually. I wasn't really doing anything, you know, just thinking. This is a tricky case, you see. "A three-pipe problem", isn't that the term you use? Not that I'm a smoker, personally. I haven't the lungs for it,' he added with a shudder. 'I do find sitting in the dark helps my concentration, though.'

'But you do not need to be in this room particularly?'

He shook his head. 'No. No, I can leave you to it. I'm sorry I missed supper, I just... if you must know, I find the conflicting energies between the Society exhausting. Their auras are constantly sparking off one another. Not to mention the Countess and Floke fatuously claiming that Kellway is safe and happy on Venus, when I know full well he's nothing of the kind.' He added gloomily, 'Of course you won't agree, Holmes. I know you reject my claims, but –'

'And yet in some respects I do agree,' said Holmes. 'About the company, at least, and about the unlikelihood of both Miss Casimir and Mr Floke's views. I am not in a position to judge those of the Countess since her utterances, except when mediated by Miss Casimir, are so opaque.'

The Countess's one observation at supper had been to the effect that certain people had been born with their minds inside out, but that as the world inside the human mind so closely mirrored that outside it, this made very little difference. I had begun to suspect that the old woman was, while perhaps also an out-and-out fraud, nevertheless no longer in possession of her full complement of faculties.

Skinner said, 'I know you have little respect for me as a detective, Holmes, but I wasn't idle this afternoon. I've looked into the history of this house, and found something rather interesting.' I received the impression that despite his earlier hostility he was eager to find some kind of acceptance on Holmes's part, and I feared the rebuff he was likely to receive.

Holmes said, relatively politely, 'But surely the history of the house is unlikely to be of significance, since the Experimental Annexe is of such recent construction?'

'Perhaps,' said Skinner. 'But there's recent and there's recent, isn't there? For instance, there was a murder here, at Parapluvium House – Keelefort House, as it was then – just twelve years ago, a little before Sir Newnham bought the place.'

'Of course!' Holmes recalled the case immediately, I could see. 'Ralph Cordwainer, the MP murdered in his bed by the Honourable Percival Heybourne. I had not realised that the house was this one.'

Although nobody at the house had mentioned this dubious history, as the buyer Sir Newnham at least must be aware of it. I assumed that he had deliberately kept it quiet so as to avoid overstimulating his excitable guests.

'It was,' Skinner confirmed smugly. 'But there was another murder, nearly two hundred and fifty years before that, that became peculiarly important to the defence.'

'Heavens, yes. Heybourne's barrister tried for a verdict of insanity, because his client insisted he was driven to the act by a vengeful ghost.'

'Anne Heybourne,' Skinner agreed. 'The youngest daughter of the Royalist Sir Robert Heybourne, who was hacked to death at her home during the Civil War – on, as far as I can tell, this very spot. I did not detect the aura of her trauma earlier because it is so all-pervading – you know the way you fail to notice the background noise of the sea or the wind when you are listening to someone speak? Yet when all else is silent you can hear it loudly and clearly.'

'An interesting tale, Skinner,' said Holmes, 'though I am for the moment at a loss to divine its exact relevance to the matters in hand.'

Skinner looked smug. 'Has nobody mentioned? The spirit of Anne Heybourne has been seen again, and recently. Gregory the footman swears he saw a lady on the stairs near Sir Newnham's study just last week, when there were no ladies in the house, only the cook and a few maids. None of them would have had any reason to be outside the servants' quarters in the early hours of the morning.'

Holmes said, 'And what was Gregory the footman doing there in the early hours of the morning? If he was sampling the contents of Sir Newnham's drinks cabinet, for example, that would make him a most unreliable witness. Besides, where one servant can go, another might be found. Most probably it was one of the maids on a similar errand. Now, if you will forgive us…?'

'Oh, of course,' said Skinner, obviously disappointed, and made a few stumbling steps towards the door. He turned. 'Unless… could I stay and, um, observe your observations? As a professional courtesy?'

Holmes looked surprised and a little annoyed, but I welcomed the opportunity to ease the friction with our self-declared rival. 'Of course that will be perfectly all right,' I said. 'We won't be giving away any trade secrets, will we, Holmes?'

The readers of my reminiscences have more than once commented on the lack of tact which Holmes can display, but I have always maintained that this is more often due to simple distraction on his part than to any actual indifference to the feelings of others. When I drop a hint to the effect that he is exhibiting this failing, he is often willing to accept my guidance.

'No, I suppose not,' he said, perhaps a little shortly. 'We merely hope to ascertain as far as possible what exactly the observers mean when they say that they saw Kellway meditating in Room A throughout the night.'

For full verisimilitude, the electric lights in the antechamber being already alight, we turned on those in Experiment Room B, but left Rooms A and C in darkness. I then entered Room A at Holmes's urging, and subsided rather stiffly to the floor. He closed the door and I sat, staring at the dim light from the window, while Holmes and Skinner took it in turns to peer in through the window at me. I quickly began to feel most uncomfortable at their scrutiny.

After what seemed an excruciating interval, but can only have been a couple of minutes, Holmes opened the door again. 'I saw you quite clearly, Watson,' he said. 'At the centre of the window, the glass creates very little distortion. Your presence and position were perfectly clear, and even your face was tolerably visible. I could not have mistaken you for anyone else, at least.'

'You know me better than any of the observers knew Kellway, though,' I pointed out. 'Unless there's something they're not telling us.'

'True enough, though as yet none of our theories involve the person in the room being someone *other* than Kellway – except in that that identity may itself have been an assumed one. It is in any case remarkable how little detail the human brain needs to identify a face correctly. See for yourself,' he said, and ducked into the room, pulling the door shut after him.

I looked inside, but the room seemed dark. I pressed my nose to the glass and shaded my eyes, blinking to get rid of the after-dazzle of the electric lights. Holmes sat on the floor, framed by the odd curve that the glass gave the walls of the room, in the lotus position that Kellway had adopted, and which my troubled leg would never have allowed. It was unmistakeably Holmes; the light on his face was dim and shadowy, the room and its contents leached of all colour, but I could readily trace the lines of his intelligent eyes and proud mouth, not to mention the shadow of that prominent nose.

'Watson,' hissed Skinner next to me. 'How does he look to you? Are you satisfied that he's solid?'

'Whatever do you mean?' I asked, pulling away from the window.

'I'm hoping you're more open-minded than he is,' the young man told me. 'He's made it perfectly clear he hasn't the slightest interest in anything I have to say. But he looks solid to you? You couldn't be mistaken about that?'

I peered in again. Holmes waved playfully at me.

'Of course not,' I said. 'He's as solid as the Tower of London. How else could he be?'

Skinner gave a nervous grimace, midway between a scowl and a smirk. 'Kellway wasn't.'

I frowned at him. 'What can you mean?' I asked again.

'The later observers – McInnery and Lord Jermaine, who took the fourth shift – I visited them both this afternoon. They told Anderton that Kellway looked tired, but each told me independently that they thought it went beyond that. There was something insubstantial about Kellway towards the end of the night, they said. A *ghostly* look, as if he was already not quite there. Ghostly, Watson, as if he were fading away. Just as I told you all after reading the aura this morning.'

I said, 'Nonsense, Skinner,' but I said it rather uneasily. To tell the truth, the atmosphere in the chilly Annexe, not to mention the succession of strange beliefs I had been subjected to during the course of the day, had unsettled me.

'He was draining away,' Skinner told me obstinately. 'During the night, *somebody* did *something*. It may have been the spirit of Anne Heybourne, or of Percival Heybourne – he was hanged, you know, and spirits sometimes gravitate to the scene of their crimes – or just one of the observers. That person put a curse on him, if you like, though it would be more scientific to say that they altered his properties. It amounts to the same thing – from that moment he was doomed. They say he didn't move – well, probably he couldn't. He was becoming less and less a person, and more... Well, let me tell you this: if Countess Brusilova's Venusian spirit-guide is real, it has been lying to her. Thomas Kellway no longer exists in any sense that we would recognise.'

From Room A, Holmes rapped impatiently at the door and, Lord help me, I jumped.

'Remember, Dr Watson,' Skinner said. 'I told you because I thought your mind might not yet be entirely closed to such possibilities. You have to trust your instincts, not *his* prejudices.'

He scuttled away suddenly, leaving the room at speed like some startled nocturnal stick insect.

'What a peculiar young man,' I said, as I opened the door for an audibly tutting Holmes. But it did not seem quite fair to pass on what Skinner had told me. Instead I said, 'What did you make of his story about the footman?' I thought that he had been rather ready to dismiss what might turn out to be a clue to this intractable affair.

'Ah, yes. I did not wish to be indiscreet,' said Holmes. 'I suppose that for a man of Sir Newnham's wealth still to be unmarried at his age, he must have as little interest in the fairer sex as myself. But with a handsome younger gentleman like Talbot Rhyne living here, there might be other reasons for a young woman to visit unbeknownst to the servants. Unless it becomes clear that the matter is important, I suggest we keep our counsel.'

Returning to the main part of the house, we found that Skinner had already left, and that one of the footmen had been sent to secure a cab for Major Bradbury. We had learned during the meal that the Major was staying at his club in Mayfair, a short distance from Baker Street, so Holmes suggested that the three of us share the cab.

Bradbury protested about the value of a person's right to peace and quiet after a meal, but when the occasion called for it Holmes was as capable of blunt obstinacy as he was of tact. Despite the Major's bluster, in the end we all climbed into the rear of the cab and the driver set it on its way. As the gates and hedges of Parapluvium House receded into darkness behind us I remembered that we had left the door to Experiment Room A open, and wondered whether Anderton would think to lock it, or would assume it was to be left that way.

'A most stimulating evening, Major,' Holmes suggested. 'Your Society is to be congratulated on the diversity of its membership.'

The Major sniffed. 'They're tolerable, for the most part. Can't stand that little skulker Skinner, though.' I wondered whether he considered the epithet to apply to detectives in general.

'Since it happens we are spending this time together,' Holmes said, 'I wonder whether you might favour us with your own recollections of the night of Kellway's disappearance? All information is valuable, you know. I have already had Anderton's account, and hope to hear Garforth's on the morrow.'

Bradbury remonstrated, but, short of asking the cab driver to halt and climbing out, he was Holmes's captive, and he clearly understood this. Reluctantly, and with much complaint, he gave us his version of events.

He had been responsible for the second observation shift, from ten o'clock to midnight, alongside Rhyne, after they and others had dined with Sir Newnham, and had seen nothing out of the ordinary during those two hours. Kellway was certainly no slouch when it came to sitting perfectly still, Bradbury said, but he remembered knowing a fakir in Lucknow who once...

Holmes interrupted. 'Did Kellway remain still for the entire two hours?' he asked.

'Now you mention it I think he did change position once,' Bradbury said. 'He had his left leg crossed over his right at first, but by the end it was right over left. Can't have been comfortable keeping that position up for hours on end, although that fakir fellow I was telling you about in Lucknow—'

Holmes once again dismissed any likely relevance on the part of the fakir in Lucknow. 'Was anybody else with you during the two hours?'

Bradbury grumbled at being interrupted again, but answered the question. 'Anderton put his head round the door once or twice, to ask if we needed anything. Speight looked in to say goodnight at about half-past eleven. Nobody else.'

'Neither of them stayed for long?'

'Only a couple of minutes.'

'And you and Rhyne remained in the room the whole time?'

'Damn it, Holmes, I used to be a soldier,' the Major insisted angrily. 'I'm perfectly capable of standing two hours' watch without wandering off and getting lost.'

'I apologise, Major, no slight was intended,' Holmes said soothingly. 'During those two hours, did you notice anything unusual in the behaviours of Mr Kellway or Mr Rhyne, or any of your visitors?'

'Certainly not. Speight went over to look through at Kellway and the experimental materials, but Kellway didn't pay any more attention to him than he did to us. Anderton didn't go anywhere near the rooms. Rhyne and I alternated our observations, each of us looking in on one room every five minutes as per instructions.

In between we played cards, but he got tired of whist and I ended up playing patience on my own.'

Remembering the supposed purposes of the experiment, I said, 'Did you see any sign of any effect on the experimental materials, Major?'

Bradbury grunted. 'No, not a hint of movement there. Still, that isn't unusual, you know. Some of these fellows need a run-up, but when they get there the results can be quite spectacular. I was in Simla once and I saw this sadhu who—'

'Let us move on, then,' said Holmes hastily, 'to the later shift, Garforth and Anderton's, where you made an unscheduled appearance.'

Grudgingly, the Major gave his account of his early awakening on the Tuesday and his eagerness to find out what had been happening with the experiment. It conformed in all important particulars to what we had already been told by Anderton, and to the second-hand account originally given to us by Speight.

'I was going to sit with them a while,' Bradbury said, 'play a round or two of cards, but Garforth wanted to play chess. Then he looked into Room A and found Kellway gone, and the whole fuss and bother blew up. Anderton ran off to fetch Speight and Rhyne and I sat down and wished someone would offer me a drink, frankly. It was a tremendous shock.'

'You looked through the window to confirm what Garforth said, is that correct?'

'Absolutely. Fellow was gone. Five minutes earlier he was there, perfectly clear, then he'd vanished.'

'When he was there,' asked Holmes, 'which of his legs was uppermost?'

Bradbury looked irritated. 'Right over left still. Why on earth does that matter?'

'It may not in the least.'

'And did you notice any other change in Kellway?' I asked, remembering what Skinner had reported of Jermaine and McInnery's opinion.

Bradbury huffed. 'None at all, till he disappeared.'

'While Anderton was out of the room,' Holmes stated, 'did you move from one chair to another?'

'Did he say I did? Damn it all, I'm hardly likely to remember a thing like that, after the shock I'd had. Yes, now you mention it I think I did get up, to check the evidence of my eyes again. I probably sat down again in a different chair. Does that matter?'

'Do you remember where Mr Garforth had left his jacket?'

Bradbury shifted uncomfortably. 'No, I don't remember that either. For God's sake, Holmes, *you* may be able to spot a fleck of dust on somebody's cuff and guess that they've just been to Brighton to buy a new hat, but most of us don't notice the first thing about what another fellow's wearing or where he's put it down, unless there's something funny about it.'

'So I understand,' said Holmes. 'However, I am interested because you were present during both Rhyne and Anderton's shifts, and those two men, if any, are the ones most likely to have been in a position to copy a key to Room A.'

'A key? Is that what this is about? I tell you, sir, the man just disappeared from the room. Nobody opened the door and there was no key. If a man's going to transport himself ethereally to Venus, it hardly makes a difference whether the door's locked, does it?'

'In that case, very likely not. I feel there are other possibilities that we might explore.'

'I tell you nobody unlocked that room,' said Bradbury. 'I would have seen.' I noticed that his leg was twitching rapidly. 'When Garforth saw Kellway was missing, he tried to go inside at once, to find out what had happened. The door didn't budge. I tried it myself and it was definitely locked.'

'I see,' said Holmes. He asked the Major a few further questions, about the search of the rooms after Sir Newnham arrived, but again Bradbury merely confirmed what we had already been told.

As our cab left Notting Hill and began to trot along the north edge of Hyde Park, Holmes put a final question to the Major. 'There is one more thing I have been wondering, Major Bradbury. You were on watch till midnight, and you must have gone to bed some time later. You had no commitments prior to breakfast with the Society at eight. Why were you awake and seeking company at five o'clock?'

During this Bradbury had been looking more and more uncomfortable, and at this he exploded in anger. 'See here, Holmes, I will not be questioned like this! I am not accused of any crime – indeed, there has been no crime committed! You have no right to poke and pry into my personal affairs in this way, sir, and I will not stand for it!'

He rapped on the roof of the cab, and the driver opened the hatch to allow him to speak. 'Stop, please,' he said. 'I'll walk from here. These gentlemen are going the rest of the way alone.'

The driver called the horse to a halt. The Major fairly burst out of the cab, and walked at great speed into Hyde Park, where we lost sight of him among the trees and bushes. The cabby moved on, and so did we.

'I thought he was heading back to his club?' I pointed out. After a moment's thought, I added, 'He said he didn't notice where Garforth left his jacket or which chair he sat in. But he was pretty clear on which way round Kellway had arranged his legs.'

'I had made the same observation,' Holmes agreed calmly. 'Also, he has left us to pay the cab fare.'

The Daily Gazette

17th April 1885

The heavy hearts of the parliamentary constituents of Birlstone will be lightened somewhat today by the knowledge that the murderer of their popular Member of Parliament, Ralph Cordwainer, has been found guilty of his crimes.

The court heard how the Hon. Percival Heybourne, a cousin of the MP on his mother's side, invited him in November last year for supper at Keelefort House, his property in Richmond, and how once there, he so plied the other with drink that the normally sober Mr Cordwainer became incapacitated and had to be removed to the guest bedroom, and his manservant sent for from his home. In the morning the man went to awaken his master, only to find him dead, bludgeoned to death in his sleep. The unhappy servant broke down in tears in the witness box as he testified to his discovery of his master's grisly remains.

The police had never entertained any suspects in the investigation beyond those resident in the house, and the owner confessed after bloodstained clothing of his was found in the furnace, which the boy had that morning forgotten to stoke as usual in the unaccustomed excitement of the household.

Though Mr Cordwainer's solicitor gave evidence that Heybourne might have gained pecuniary advantage from the cold-blooded killing of his cousin, Heybourne's own account of his motives was a singular one. He maintained under oath that he had been tormented beyond endurance, and goaded into violence, by a ghost said to have haunted the house since the seventeenth century.

This spirit was named as that of Anne, the unfortunate daughter of the Royalist Heybourne family, said to have been murdered by Parliamentarian thugs in 1644; who, it was averred, retains such a grudge against all representatives of Parliament that she made her descendant the instrument of her vengeance upon the unfortunate Mr Cordwainer.

The judge, the Hon. Mr Justice Perchester, was unmoved by the defence counsel's plea for a verdict of insanity. Instead he was pleased to remind the jury that spirits of the dead cannot be found guilty in English law, and joked that the jury would have to make do with convicting Anne's accomplice, which they duly did.

Percival Heybourne is sentenced to hang at a future date.

CHAPTER NINE

Back in our rooms, Holmes paced, and sat, and stood, and paced some more, and smoked his pipe, while I wrote a few letters and attempted to exert a calming influence by example. Occasionally he would mutter incomprehensibly to himself, jabbing the air with his pipe as he reached some particularly emphatic point in his internal soliloquy.

Finally he threw himself with great force into his favourite armchair, which made a loud creak of protest, and exclaimed, 'I am baffled, Watson. I cannot express to you how frustrating the sensation is! And yet we can be sure that there is a real, definitive and absolute truth in this matter, if only we might capture it. It eludes us for the moment, and so we must persist.'

He stood once again, knocking a pile of magazines into the fireplace which he distractedly retrieved and placed, still smouldering, on Mrs Hudson's carpet. I eyed them uneasily as he continued. 'The only explanation – the one explanation that we could, under ordinary circumstances, possibly admit – is that Anderton obtained a key to the room, or copied it, and that he conspired with Garforth and Major Bradbury to release Kellway. That would be mundane and explicable: a trivial and sordid piece of fraud. And yet Sir Newnham is quite correct to ask how, in this case, his trusted butler, who could have turned to him in any difficulty, and who you and I, Watson, have judged to be a stolidly and unimaginatively loyal man, could have been suborned.'

I said, 'I've been thinking about that. The man has sisters, perhaps with families of their own – if someone threatened them, with dire consequences promised if he were to approach Sir Newnham about the matter, might he not be persuaded to go against his better nature for their sake?'

'There are times when our thoughts are in perfect accord, Watson. While you were out at Mrs Rust's I instructed some associates of mine to make discreet enquiries about Anderton's sisters and their families.' I knew that he was referring to his 'Irregulars', the street children who from time to time would help him in his investigations in return for small monetary considerations. 'There are two sisters, three nephews, two nieces and a great-nephew. All but the great-nephew, who is but four years old, are in service in respectable households around London, and all appear to be going about their business as normal. Even if there were some threat looming over them that they were unaware of, that knowledge would surely have created some signs of unease on Anderton's part, rather than the cheery optimism he showed this morning.'

'He would have to be a very good actor for it not to, certainly.'

'I do not consider that likely, and I am tolerably familiar with the acting profession. No – while such a threat might have the effect you describe on another man, I cannot believe that a man as guileless as Anderton would be capable of such deceit, of his employer or of us. He would break down in tears and confess, and throw himself on Sir Newnham's mercy.'

'But surely it is not impossible, Holmes. Your first thought was that Anderton, Bradbury and Garforth were in it together.'

'If this were a purely intellectual exercise, you might be

right. And yet I cannot believe it of Anderton. That may prove to be weakness on my part, but I will not recklessly implicate such a man. And there are attendant questions to consider, which may yet make a nonsense of the whole idea. Why have a third conspirator present when two would attract less attention? What was the true cause of Kellway's baldness? Why did he carry a broken sword-stick when thousands of ordinary, serviceable and intact walking sticks are available throughout London?

'Indeed, before we accuse Anderton of duplicity there is a more radical explanation we should consider. That is that the whole case, as presented to us, is a hoax on Sir Newnham's part. Several of the witnesses would still need to be involved, but most could be faithfully reporting what they saw, and Sir Newnham would have the means to reward the others well for their pains. And Anderton would still be loyal, to his employer if not to the truth.'

'That seems absurd, Holmes. Who on earth would benefit from such a deceit?'

'I offer it merely to illustrate the uncertainties of the case. But indeed, the reward money is Sir Newnham's own. If he wished to give Kellway ten thousand pounds, he need hardly justify it with such a charade.'

After a moment's thought I suggested, 'Unless perhaps Kellway was not part of the conspiracy. Perhaps Sir Newnham feared that his abilities were real, and connived with the others to do away with him.'

'Really, Watson?' Holmes said witheringly. 'That hardly seems likely given that Sir Newnham has devoted himself to researching the existence of psychic phenomena. Any true proof of such a thing would be a glorious vindication of his stance, and with his fortune he could hardly miss the ten thousand pounds. Even if he had some personal animus against Kellway, he would hardly remove him in such a showy fashion and then go out of his way to draw my attention to the affair.

'Indeed, the only motivation I can guess at for such a hoax would be to gull me, one of our era's most notorious defenders of reason, into endorsing the existence of psychic phenomena. Others have made attempts, as you will recall – showmen and charlatans every one. But such a coup would hardly benefit a reputable scientist, as to stand up to scrutiny any such phenomenon would have to be indefinitely replicable, under ever more rigorous experimental conditions. No, to risk his reputation on such a ludicrous gamble Sir Newnham would be a fool, and the man we have spoken to is no fool. Again, we founder upon an impossibility, not of science, but of human nature.

'Yet if we cannot accept one or other of these human impossibilities, the obvious solution – indeed, the only sensible and elegant solution – is that which scientifically speaking is quite impossible: that Thomas Kellway vanished from a locked room through some means presently unknown to science, and is now in some inaccessible place, Venusian or ethereal or otherwise, where the attractions of ten thousand pounds sterling hold no further appeal for him.

'And *that*, my dear fellow, is so unconscionable that I can only conclude that something I have thus far dismissed as an impossibility in fact conceals a reality. That Kellway did somehow contrive to hide himself in a completely bare room, or that the room has a secret exit that eludes detection even by me, or that he was never in the room at all. Taken on its own terms, *every* theory that could possibly explain the facts we have been given is unacceptable.

'Watson, my confidence that all things must have a rational explanation is unshakeable, but I am beginning to wonder whether my definition of the rational has not been too far limited hitherto.'

By now I had finished the last of my letters. I turned to smile at my oldest and dearest companion. 'I, too, have confidence, Holmes – confidence in you. You know it's not unusual for you to feel frustrated at this stage in a case. I have no doubt that with your own extraordinary powers you will find a way to shine a light into this murky space, and scramble out of this labyrinth of ifs and buts and maybes.'

He smiled thinly. 'I thank you for your faith in me, old friend, but I fear I cannot share it.' He lapsed into a melancholic silence which lasted for some time.

At last, struck by an inspiration, I said, 'Perhaps what you need is more data. Perhaps your Index has something about the histories of the people involved that will prove relevant.'

'Yes, that is possible.' Holmes cocked his head, more animated for the moment. 'Though I fear Sir Newnham's biography at least is thoroughly documented. Still, I thought I had heard Garforth's name before, for one. Bring me the relevant volumes, if you would be so kind, and we will look up the principals.'

It turned out that Holmes took a very broad view of who the 'principals' might be, and I had to fetch a number of files. They were heavy with paper, and I made several journeys between the shelves and the armchair where Holmes sat, distractedly filling his pipe. By the time I returned with R and S, he had it smoking, had already read the account of Anderton senior's death – 'A wholly inglorious suicide, Watson, notable only in that the father was of such a different character from his son' – and was working through the entries on Gideon Beech, Major Bradbury and Countess Brusilova.

We learned that Beech had been involved peripherally in an incident of burglary in 1891, when he had taken it upon himself to clear the name of a servant accused of stealing his mistress's ruby necklace. He had made a colossal nuisance of himself to the police in the process, and although in the end the footman was absolved of blame, his position in the household had become untenable, and the gems were never found. I had little doubt that Beech's own account of the affair would make it seem altogether more glorious.

Major Bradbury's sole entry in the files was a brief remark in a society column noting his return from India, kept by Holmes solely because the Major had served for some years under a person of far greater interest: Colonel Sebastian Moran. Bradbury had remained silent on this connection when introduced to Holmes, though as the latter's attempted assassination by Moran was a matter of public record, it was possible that he was embarrassed by the association. Holmes's information was normally drawn only from the British papers, however (primarily the London ones, in fact), and I had a growing suspicion that Bradbury's name had been familiar to me by reputation during my own time out East. I had already resolved to follow this up when I had an opportunity, but for now it was important for Holmes to continue approaching the problem in his own way.

'Countess Brusilova is undoubtedly a fraud,' said Holmes, moving on through the alphabet. 'Her imposture has been a successful one for many years, however, making her a tidy income. However, since her illness a few years ago it is Miss Casimir who has been at the helm of her endeavours, managing the Countess's displays of mediumship while the old woman acts as a passive, and perhaps even an oblivious, passenger.'

Miss Casimir had no entry of her own. Holmes guessed that there might be some record of her under some other name, but without some clue as to what that alias might be the Index was so sizeable as to make any search pointless.

'However,' Holmes went on, 'neither woman has attempted a deception of this kind before – their mediumistic tricks are all along the familiar lines of mysterious knockings and ectoplasmic apparitions, rather than anything more physical. And it seems that both were away from Parapluvium House at the time of Kellway's disappearance, though we might profitably confirm that point with the Star and Garter. Let us note that they are of suspicious character, and move on.'

It seemed that Gerald Floke's family was a venerable, dull and undistinguished one, of which nothing scandalous had been known since a non-fatal duel involving his great-great-grandfather's younger brother and the husband of one of the Prince Regent's mistresses. I imagined that young Gerald's fervour for the esoteric must be rather a worry to his elders, but beyond that, volume F of the Index was unilluminating.

Under G, it turned out that the Garforth whose name Holmes had remembered was not the artist nor even a person, but a village near Leeds: it had been the birthplace of two confidence tricksters who had been caught in a daring insurance fraud a few years previously. Holmes was amused by the audacity of the crime, which had traded on the strong family resemblance between one Simon Greendale and his uncle Theodore. Though Simon was eventually imprisoned, Theodore Greendale had escaped arrest.

Of Frederick Garforth there was no trace in the records; nor was there any entry for Thomas Kellway. As with Miss Casimir, this proved nothing in itself except that neither name had come to the attention of the criminal press.

For form's sake, we checked the record of the Hon. Percival Heybourne's murder of Ralph Cordwainer MP at what had been Keelefort House, but found nothing supporting his unusual defence. Indeed, Heybourne had a motive for killing Cordwainer that had nothing to do with seventeenth-century loyalties expressed via the spirit realm; he had been driven near to bankruptcy by a recent speculation, and Cordwainer had been refusing to sell a property in Staffordshire that they had jointly inherited. As it was, Keelefort House, which would otherwise have gone to a more distant cousin on the Heybourne side, had been sold to Sir Newnham to pay off the murderer's debts.

Dr Peter Kingsley had been an expert witness at a number of inquests and one or two criminal trials. I knew from our conversation at dinner that his medical specialism was pharmacology, but it appeared he was also a keen amateur practitioner of mesmerism. Like Sir Newnham, he was often called upon as an expert witness, and on one occasion he had apparently hypnotised a woman in the witness box, allowing her to recall without hysteria the details of her husband's ghastly murder, but the evidence had been ruled inadmissible. Again, Holmes noted all of this while also observing that the Doctor, having taken first watch in the experiment, had been away from the house during its later stages.

Talbot Rhyne was another participant who, it seemed from the Index, had thus far made no impact on Holmes's area of interest. Though not very much older, Constantine Skinner had appeared in the occasional news report, and had been instrumental in apprehending suspects in certain crimes judged by him to have had an occult dimension. Reassuringly from the point of view of public justice, these men had generally been convicted only when substantial non-supernatural evidence against them was also available.

Vortigern Small also lacked an entry, though establishing this enabled Holmes to spend a short while reminiscing about his namesake Jonathan Small, the one-legged ex-convict whom we had hunted up the Thames with his accomplice, the Andaman tribesman Tonga, in the case which first introduced me to my late wife Mary. At the time of Jonathan's crimes our Mr Small had, as I discovered from his entry in Crockford's, been publishing works with such innocuous titles as *On the Eschatology of the Gospels* and *A New Hermeneutics of the Revelation to St John the Divine*. His benefice was in Chiswick, a stone's throw from Mrs Rust's house, and I wondered whether it was the one her devout boarder Mr Brightlea attended, before remembering that she had said the man was a non-conformist.

Sir Newnham Speight's career was, as Holmes had said, a storied one, and there was no shortage of material even given my friend's idiosyncratic criteria for inclusion. In 1869, as a much younger man, Speight had been instrumental in foiling a robbery; in 1882 he had been a witness in the prosecution of one Ezekiel Whart, an accountant who had embezzled several thousand pounds from the Speight Company's head office; and in 1887, at the height of his fame and shortly before the awarding of his knighthood, he had been involved in an embarrassing street fracas with a madman who had levelled preposterous accusations against him. In 1890 it had been more credibly argued at an inquest that the deaths of two workers at his plant in Guildford were a result of negligence, but the coroner had fully vindicated the Speight Company.

Only one elderly clipping in the file gave us serious pause: an accusation that Speight, as an impoverished young man, had gained financial backing through a fraudulent demonstration of one of his earliest prototypes. A judge had dismissed the case in 1863, ruling it baseless – a decision that had relied strongly on the testimony of William Anderton.

'This proves no wrongdoing, Holmes,' I pointed out. 'Quite the reverse. The facts of the case were very likely as the court decided. The idea that there was somebody inside the machine's casing doing the work is rather far-fetched, don't you think?'

'Far-fetched but not impossible, Watson. You must remember

the case of the Mechanical Turk, the famous chess-playing automaton which proved to be a hoax. In that case the cabinet on which the mechanism was mounted concealed a skilled chess-player who operated the figure's arms. The folding of bed-linen is assuredly a less demanding task than the playing of chess.'

'Perhaps we should ask Mrs Hudson whether she would concur,' I suggested jocularly. 'But we have agreed that Sir Newnham is not the sort of man to perpetrate such a deception, nor Anderton to support it.'

'And so the judge ruled. But what if he was wrong, Watson, what then? Both men could be far better dissemblers than we have given them credit for.'

'Nonsense,' I scoffed. 'You'll be saying next that he killed those men at the factory.'

'I say nothing of the sort, Watson. I merely outline the possibilities as I see them. Well, I think I am done for the night. After all, we must be fresh for the morning, and our meeting with the evasive Mr Frederick Garforth.'

The Morning Chronicle

8th August 1863

A diverting Case was heard this week at the Magistrates' Court at Bow, as one Jeremiah Halborn, financier, contended that he had been the subject of a fraud perpetrated two years ago by a novice entrepreneur of business and his manservant.

Both Parties agreed that in January of 1861 the Defendant, a young man named Newham Spate, was seeking fiscal support for a remarkable new contrivance, a domestic linen-folding apparatus that would ease the work of maids, laundry-workers and humble housewives. He had arranged, for those whose interest he had succeeded in attracting, a series of private demonstrations of his prototype device.

The Plaintiff told how when the machine was shown at his house, he marvelled at the speed and dextrousness with which it had worked: unfolded linen was bundled into an opening on the top of the apparatus, to emerge minutes later, neatly laid out, from a slot in the side. On this basis he had agreed to finance the completion and manufacture of the machine, which the Defendant insists has since been much in hand.

The Plaintiff has, however, become impatient with the absence of pecuniary return on his investment. He is now convinced that the presentation he witnessed was fraudulent, and demands the return of his money in full.

The Defendant was able to produce in Court the latest model of the linen-folding contraption, which he demonstrated to operate exactly as the Plaintiff had described. He then dismantled it, to the amazement of those assembled, and showed how its components worked together to achieve the desired end of folded sheets.

The Plaintiff returned argument that, if it should

indeed prove that the funds have in the meanwhile enabled the defendant to create a machine that functions and may profitably be sold, he should be entitled to a full half-share in the patent and the profits therefrom.

Asked if he knew how a demonstration such as he described might have been counterfeited, the Plaintiff replied that, for all he knew, there had been a midget in the casing of the machine, folding the bed-clothes; and thus provoked much merriment in the Court-room.

The common sentiment of the attendant crowd was that, although Mr Halborn had made himself risible with this comment, nonetheless Mr Spate was 'too clever by half', and both Plaintiff and Defendant had factions of support among those present.

This opinion was amended when the defendant's man Wm. Anderson was called as a witness. This Anderson had already assisted with the demonstration of the device in Court, and it was he who had assembled the prototype machine *in situ* in the Plaintiff's house two years previously. He was therefore in a position to know with certainty of any such deception as the Plaintiff indicated.

Anderson attested that the earlier machine had functioned much as the one now in evidence, though less perfected and refined; that its parts had been exclusively mechanical and automatic, requiring no intervention by human hands; and, to further and greater hilarity in the Court-room, that he and his master were not acquainted with any midgets.

Such was the frankness with which the stout fellow presented his testimony that the crowd was soon in agreement that his was the truth of the matter, and sure enough the Magistrate judged in the Defendant's favour, considering the manservant's testimony to be 'unimpeachably honest, and such as to which I cannot take exception.'

CHAPTER TEN

I had drunk rather more port than is generally good for me, and so I spent a troubled night beset by dreams of shaven fakirs and of five-legged, five-eyed Venusians, who explained to me that the perfectly evolved state involved having one's organs quintupled, like the human fingers. At one point I beheld Vortigern Small, dressed in a loincloth and turban, giggling as he showed me how Sir Newnham had built the Experimental Annexe above an entrance to a network of subterranean tunnels, where Kellway had joined the other victims of his fiendish torture-machines.

All in all I felt little rested when Holmes shook me awake shortly after six-thirty the next morning, bringing with him a pot of coffee and an air of offensively vigorous enthusiasm.

'Rise and shine, Watson!' he insisted breezily. Needless to say he was already fully dressed. 'The sky is lightening, the sun strives to breast the horizon, and the cockerels are doubtless crowing somewhere, albeit not on Baker Street. We must be about our business. I have decided, given his reluctance so far, that we should no longer wait for the elusive Mr Garforth to attend our pleasure and will instead, like Mohammed, make our own pilgrimage to see the mountain.'

I struggled upright, and seized the coffee gratefully. 'Have we the mountain's address?'

'I heard what he said to the cabman,' Holmes reminded me, 'and it matches the address of the card in Kellway's pocket book. A brisk walk through the park to Camden should put us in an excellent state of mind for questioning him. If Anderton is right to say he is none too alert in the mornings, we may as well seize our advantage.'

Though I felt my own mental advantage over Garforth might be small, I could not fault my friend's logic, and a short while later I found myself enjoying the early-morning birdsong and fresh air in an almost deserted Regent's Park, while the sun climbed slowly above the stands of ash and elm, painting their autumnal shades with its own rosy hue. It was a fresh, bright morning, and by the time we left the park and turned onto Camden Road my lungs and my head were perfectly clear, and I was blessing once again the good fortune that had seen me settled in this leafy city, the metropolis of empire, at the side of the man who did so much to protect it from enemies within and without.

By a quarter past seven we were approaching Garforth's studio. It occupied the entire attic of a boarding house, but had its own entrance at the side of the building, reached by an iron staircase like the one we had used to ascend to the roof of Parapluvium House. At its foot FRED. GARFORTH, PAINTER was written on a wooden sign. Further evidence of Garforth's profession became obvious as we mounted the steep flight, in streaks of paint that stained the steps – boot-prints in paint, the left one blue, the right one green, becoming clearer as they approached the top. Alongside them, and overlaying them in places, was a pair of parallel streaks on each flat surface, one of white and a fainter one of green, that similarly became more pronounced as we climbed. Holmes touched the paint a few steps ahead of him, and clicked his tongue. I saw that his finger had left a slight imprint in the white streak.

He said, 'It is about time for some fresh development in this case, Watson, but this is not the form I would have wished it to take. Come quickly now, but try not to step on the paint.' He began to climb two steps at a time, treading only at the very edges, and I followed his lead.

At the top was a wooden door, its own paint faded and flaking. It hung not quite shut on its hinges. Holmes pulled it open and stepped gingerly into the studio.

The attic was large, light and airy, with two big east-facing windows letting in a generous amount of the early-morning sun, and their west-facing counterparts presumably offering a similar service in the evenings. It seemed to be a living-space as well as a workshop, with a cramped area under the sloping eaves holding a bed, a chest of drawers, a small gas-stove and a crudely plumbed washbasin. Whether Garforth lived here at all times, or whether he had another address he went to when he was not painting, I could not guess.

The rest of the room had apparently been given over to Garforth's work, with canvases, paint and what I assumed must be other artistic paraphernalia strewn everywhere.

I say 'strewn', because the room had been ransacked. The canvases, whether fresh or in use, had been slashed to ribbons, and everywhere tubes of paint lay trampled and burst. Wooden palettes were splintered in halves, two easels had been smashed to pieces, and so had some larger wooden structure whose planks – some splintered and broken, some still nailed together – lay in jagged heaps. There was much smashed glass, some of it crushed to powder underfoot, and a few intact bottles.

Huge strips of torn linen, looking like shredded bedsheets, festooned the scene of destruction. Among them were darker rags, and I peered at the nearest of these, which hung from the back of a flimsy wooden chair. It was a remnant of a jacket – not the Inverness cape which we had seen Garforth wearing the previous day, but something of a black material and a lighter weight.

A tin bath had been dragged from the living area under the eaves and apparently used to contain a fire. Its sides were blackened, as were the roof-beams above it, and the bottom was heaped with ash. Looped among the greyish powder, still intact, were several yards of wire to which a few black remnants clung, apparently also shreds of cloth. An oily film of soot clung to the nearest surfaces, and the stink of smoke suffused the room.

Holmes had gravitated towards a part of the floor where the glass shards and paint were particularly thickly smeared. Leaning forward, he grasped a roof-beam and used it to swing himself down without stepping nearer, the better to examine the traces without disturbing them.

He tutted. 'This is a bad business.' Hanging from one hand, he reached for his magnifying glass with the other. In the centre of the spillage, between distinct patches of green, white and blue, there was an area scabbed with blackish-red, which I knew from my medical experience had not come from any colourman – or not, at least, from his paintworks. Next to it lay an ebony walking stick, to which scraps of some residue – I did not need to look closely to imagine of what kind – still clung. Boot-prints of green and blue paint, together with twin trails of white and green, led from this area to the door.

Holmes said, 'Watson, pray speak to the occupants of the premises below us and find out whether there is a telephone to be found. We must send word to Scotland Yard at once.'

I found nobody at home downstairs, and the nearest neighbours stared at me in bafflement when I asked if anybody in the street owned a telephone. I returned ten minutes later, having dispatched a cabman with a message for Inspector Lestrade, and also bringing a constable whom I had happened to run into during the excursion.

We found Holmes at the bottom of the stairs, examining the stones of the pavement. I now saw that these, too, bore the faint traces of the variously coloured paints.

Without preamble, or greeting for the constable, he said, 'The body was dragged as far as the kerbside, then the same man loaded it aboard a vehicle. Whether it was unconscious or dead at the time I cannot presently tell, but the signs are ominous. We are dealing with assault and kidnapping at least, and most probably with murder. Whatever conveyance was used will be heavily stained inside with paint and blood, as will the criminal's clothes.'

'Crikey,' the constable declared, a little awed by Holmes's presence.

'There are some details I would show you, Watson, before Lestrade arrives,' Holmes said.

We ascended the stairs again, all three of us treading carefully. 'From the state of the paint,' Holmes told us, pointing, 'which is very nearly but not altogether dry, the violence took place rather less than a day ago.'

I said, 'We saw Garforth at Parapluvium House, Holmes, remember? It was about ten o'clock yesterday morning. He wasn't dead or kidnapped then. Although I suppose if he himself had just murdered or kidnapped someone, it would be understandable that he wouldn't want to run into us.'

'Yet he came to this address after leaving Richmond,' said Holmes. 'That is what he told the cabby, at least, and the cape we saw him wearing is here. Even if he had had the time to move the body and find clean clothing before visiting Rhyne, it hardly seems likely that he would have returned here after a crime yet still left it in its current state.'

Holmes left the constable on guard at the top of the stairs, then took me back inside the attic studio. He drew my attention to the sole surviving canvas, an unrecognisable daub of greys, blues and ochres. 'Does anything occur to you, Watson?' he asked.

'It seems to be just random brushstrokes in different colours,' I said. 'But I'm no art expert. Is it perhaps an early stage in a seascape, with more detail to be added later?'

'An inspired guess, Watson.' He smiled. 'But no, I think not. If it is an artistic composition, it is of a style more daring than the world is yet prepared for. And no care has been taken over the technique at all. It is not difficult to see why Garforth has made no name for himself in the art world. I think that this is not a real painting. It is not even a forgery. Its purpose is simply to mimic a half-finished canvas for the benefit of the uninterested observer. Presumably our friend has visitors – his landlord or landlady, if no-one else.'

'How peculiar,' I said.

'It is true of all of them, as far as I can tell,' Holmes reported. 'Some are too torn to be certain.'

'You think Garforth is a fraud? But he paints. We saw that example of his work at Sir Newnham's house.'

'If he does, then this room holds no evidence of it. But all we know for sure of his artistic career is that he sold Speight a canvas he claimed to have produced.'

'Then how does he make his living? Does he steal the paintings?'

'He may have an independent income. A studio such as this, with such large windows, would be the envy of many a true artistic practitioner. It would be a wild extravagance to indulge in if merely to keep up appearances.'

I looked around, trying to imagine the studio without its current devastation. The conditions were sparse, especially for a man who moved in society as a gentleman, but Holmes was surely right that such a room would not have come cheaply, and I knew many artists kept ordinary homes in addition to their studios.

He went on, 'No, plainly there is a deception of some kind going on here, but it could be as mundane as that of a wealthy man trying to prove himself as an artist and finding himself forced to cover up the fact that he has no talent at all.'

'Rhyne said Garforth knew his family,' I remembered.

'True,' said Holmes. 'We must ask Mr Rhyne what he knows of his family friend's affairs.'

He showed me the surviving bottles, which looked as if they had been used to store chemicals rather than paint; in any case, Garforth apparently favoured oils, which came in tubes. He said, 'As there are no pools of liquid other than paint, nor traces of corrosion or desiccation in the wooden floor which might suggest a chemical spillage, I suggest that the bottles were emptied down the sink and then smashed, to what end I cannot guess. Some residue may remain in the pipes. I shall ask Lestrade to have them swabbed so that I may analyse it.'

'One might expect a painter to own turpentine,' I ventured.

'True,' said he, 'but there are far more bottles here than that could account for. And turpentine has a distinctive smell, which would be noticeable even among those of paint and smoke, and which I do not detect here.'

We looked over the remainder of the room as we waited for Lestrade's arrival. The bed was unmade since it was last slept in. From the eaves hung two suits and half a dozen shirts, as well as some empty clothes hangers, while the chest of drawers held socks, underwear and shirt-collars. Though most of the clothing would pass muster at a society gathering, all was of the cheapest quality, and none would have had the durability of Kellway's ostensibly more modest belongings. It had not been interfered with during the altercation, beyond some spattering of paint and glass. Garforth's hat and, I now saw, the Inverness cape hung on a hook by the door.

The washstand held ordinary carbolic soap, a toothbrush, a shaving-brush, a packet containing a single remaining cigarette, and a tin of French throat lozenges. A mirror, mounted above it, had also escaped the devastation. A great many balls of cotton wool lay at its base, some of them still contained in a fragment of a jar. This piece had survived partly because it had had a lump of clay, about the size and colour of my fist, stuck to it, and this had evidently kept its shards together after it fell.

Beneath the bed were several empty cigarette packets and one full one, two more tins of the lozenges, a number of old newspapers, a discarded sock and a cardboard box containing a pair of shoes, which Holmes seized on with a cry of pleasure and compared at once with the coloured boot-prints.

'The size is a match,' he declared. 'Regrettably this is a new pair, so there is no pattern of wear for comparison. The boots that made the prints are older, but show no especial peculiarities. The wearer's stride is long and even, and he is a little heavy but not excessively so. It might be Garforth, but it might equally be five thousand men in London of a similar build and shoe size.'

In a chest by the window there were art supplies: tubes of paint, rolls of canvas, unused palettes, brushes and a palette-knife, a book-sized packet of clay identical to the lump we had already seen, wrapped carefully in wax paper, a drill-bit with its handle, and a writing-case, in which the only written material proved to be a few bills, mostly for art supplies and timber, and some papers pertaining to Speight's Society. 'Nothing from galleries or dealers,' Holmes noted. 'Nor any personal correspondence.'

'Perhaps he burns it all,' I suggested. Looking at the ashes in the bath, I added, 'Or perhaps someone else did.' We checked the room's fireplace, and found the chimney blocked with soot: no fire could have been kindled there for years. With its large windows, the room must get terribly cold during the winter.

Next to the chest was a stack of virgin timber, on which stood a hammer, well worn with use, a tin of nails and a pot of pitch with a stained brush stuck to its lid. 'What are all the other planks?' I wondered, looking back at the debris scattered around the room. I saw now that many of them had been daubed at the edges with pitch. 'Was he building something?'

'A crucial question, Watson, to which I have no immediate answer,' my friend replied. He added dubiously, 'Although I suppose an unsuccessful artist might resort to carpentry to make ends meet.'

Inspector Lestrade arrived shortly afterwards – a self-important, ferrety-looking man whose mind, I had found during our long association, was significantly sharper than his appearance and habitual conversation might have suggested. He was no match for Sherlock Holmes, but he was hardly alone in that.

'Well, this is a right to-do, gents,' he informed us sagely as he entered, accompanied by two Scotland Yard men. 'It certainly looks as if mischief was done here, doesn't it? What was your business here, Mr Holmes, if I may ask?'

Holmes said, 'The tenant goes by the name of Frederick Garforth. He is a witness in a matter I have been investigating for a private client – one which until today has presented no criminal ramifications.'

'Well, I'd say this was a ramification all right, wouldn't you?' said Lestrade. 'This Garforth's either dead or a murderer, I'd bet my best suit on it.'

'It looks highly likely,' Holmes agreed.

'And you just happened to be here to find the evidence,' Lestrade added, with a smirk.

'It was a great shock,' I objected. 'We had no reason to expect anything of the kind before we arrived.'

'Ah,' said the inspector. 'You may not have, Doctor, but in my experience few things come as a surprise to the great Sherlock Holmes.'

'In this instance I admit I was as surprised as Watson,' Holmes replied, with no trace of annoyance, 'though I perhaps should not have been. Mr Garforth has recently been most elusive.'

'Well, Mr Holmes, private client or no, you will have to let me in on the secret now. This has become a police matter, and anything you know that might be relevant, I need to be told.'

Holmes agreed readily enough, and between us we summarised for him the story Speight had told us, and what we had learned since.

When we finished, Lestrade whistled. 'Well,' he said, 'I stand by my first opinion. A right to-do is what this is, and no mistake. You don't believe all this nonsense, do you, about this Kellway fellow vanishing into thin air like that?'

'At present I believe very little,' Holmes replied. 'I am still gathering data, which was the purpose of our visit here this morning.'

'Well, it sounds like a clever confidence trick to me. And of course it gives someone an obvious motive to have done away with Garforth. If he was part of some scheme to defraud this Society and he threatened to expose it, then one of his fellow conspirators might just have decided to silence him, mightn't they?'

'It is, as you say, an obvious motive,' Holmes agreed.

'But you're not convinced,' Lestrade observed drily.

'Thus far there has been little about this case that conforms to the obvious. There may, indeed, be no connection between the disagreement here and whatever happened at Parapluvium House on Tuesday morning. We have some reason to suspect that Garforth was in the habit of passing others' work off as his own. That might have made him enemies.'

Lestrade sucked his teeth. 'In my experience – and we do deal with art theft at the Yard, Mr Holmes, and sometimes forgery as well – while artists may be disreputable, unreliable sorts, they're rarely the kind to do each other violence. A nasty review in the papers is more their line when revenge is on the cards.'

'You may be right,' admitted Holmes. 'But not everyone connected with the art world is an artist.'

'That I'll grant you. But why don't you show me what you've found here while you've been waiting? I'm sure you must have some theories by now.'

Holmes showed the inspector the patterns in the glass and paint, showing where the struggle had taken place, and the signs that a large body had fallen partly into the mess of green, yellow and white, and partly into a separate patch of cerulean blue.

'The man's clothes must have been smothered in paint,' said Holmes. 'After moving him, so will the attacker's have been, not to mention the upholstery of whatever carriage he was taken away in.'

'Couldn't he have undressed him first?' asked Lestrade. 'If he was dead, I mean.'

'And left on the shoes which made those trails down the stairs? Besides, there is no trace of the clothes here. The ash in the bath is not enough for them.'

'He might have come well-prepared and taken them away in a sack,' Lestrade suggested doubtfully. 'What are these bits of cloth and stuff?'

'A jacket, I believe,' said Holmes. 'I see no trace of blood on the remnants, nor of paint either, beyond the occasional light smear. I do not believe either party can have been wearing it during the struggle or afterwards.'

'We should ask Garforth's friends whether it was his,' I suggested.

'If so, he must have been cold afterwards,' said Holmes. 'His cape is still here.'

Lestrade smiled grimly. 'The cold won't have troubled him much if he was the corpse. But I'm sure you saw straight away what's troubling me now, about the scene of this crime, Mr Holmes.'

'I have observed several things that are perplexing,' said Holmes. 'The shaving-brush, for example. It is well worn and free of dust, suggesting Garforth uses it often, presumably when trimming the edges of his whiskers, but we have found no razor. Then there is the clay.'

Lestrade looked exasperated as I said, 'Surely that's an ordinary enough thing to find in an artist's studio?'

'You think so? Perhaps. But there is no other evidence that Garforth works in clay – no sculpting tools, for instance, and no completed work. There is the loop of wire in the bathtub – that might be used to cut clay, or perhaps as an armature, to give a model some internal structure. I am perplexed, though, as to why it was put in the fire at all. Wire does not burn at ordinary temperatures.

'However,' Holmes continued, 'I imagine that what has exercised you more, Inspector, is the clear evidence that this is not a case of an artist being attacked and his studio deliberately wrecked – at least, not in that order. For the signs of the struggle to overlay the spillage of paint and glass as they do, the destruction must have been carried out *before* the quarrel between our principals. The only footprints made afterwards appear to be those left while dragging the body.' By this time the inspector was nodding in agreement.

'Good Lord,' I said. 'You mean Garforth came back to his studio to find someone else already here, and smashing the place up? And then confronted him?'

'That seems the most likely story,' said Holmes. 'And yet it would have been surprising if he were to hang up his coat and hat first. For all we can tell, someone else might have arrived here to find Garforth smashing the place up. We should remain alive to all the possibilities.'

'Well, however the fight started,' said Lestrade, 'it ended in murderous violence.' We all looked at the walking stick, still lying on the floor next to the discoloured patch, and I was sure he was correct. The size of the bloodstain, and the fragments of blood, skin and hair adhering to the stick itself, did not look like evidence of the sort of attack someone would survive. 'And then the winner fled with the loser's body.'

'When we saw Garforth in Richmond,' I said, 'he was taking a cab – our cab, in fact. But no cabman would have accepted an unconscious passenger covered in paint. And it seems unlikely that Garforth owns a carriage. So the vehicle must have belonged to the other man, meaning that it was Garforth who was killed.'

I was rather pleased with this inference, so it irked me when Lestrade shook his head at once. 'No – if it was a private vehicle without a driver, either of them could have taken it.'

'Besides,' Holmes pointed out, 'we cannot know the exact time of the quarrel. Garforth might have had time to procure a second vehicle between Parapluvium House and here.'

We contemplated this for a moment. 'So,' Lestrade said, 'We don't know whether Garforth or this other person brought the carriage, or which of them went on the rampage smashing and burning things, or which one killed the other. Any of those could have been either of them, independent of the others. Is that right?'

'It seems an admirable summation. We might consider the further possibility that there were two vandals, one of whom turned on the other, and that Garforth was not directly involved at all, but given the presence of his coat and hat I think we can dismiss it as unlikely.'

I said, 'Surely we can rule it out entirely. There's only one set of boot-prints, after all. If Garforth wasn't involved, why has he not been back here since?'

Holmes said, 'Perhaps he became aware that violent men had been visiting his studio, and has hidden himself away somewhere. That would explain why he has not been seen anywhere else since. I admit, though, that this seems an unlikely contingency.

'In any case, one thing is clear. Whether Garforth is dead or merely keeping his distance, we should not expect him to return to the scene of this crime in the near future. Indeed, we may have seen the last of him in this case. In a city the size of London, it is very easy for a man – living or dead – to disappear and never be seen again.'

Letter from Mr Mark Admiral of the Admiral's Gallery, Camden, to Mr Robert Travis, 4th November 1896

Dear Travis

We have taken delivery of your latest canvas. I am afraid I can, in all conscience, only ask whether the degenerative illness from whose late stages you are evidently suffering has already affected your brain, or merely your eyes and fingers?

You spoke of a 'new direction' for your painting, and we all imagined some bold and imaginative use of colour, light and shadow, akin to the experiments we have seen from Mr Sickert or Mr Whistler. Instead you deliver us a pallid orange nude executed to look so sickly and emaciated that I can only suppose the reason for her unusual colouration is that she has been dead for some weeks. I can hardly bear to look at it, and I think you know that I do not object lightly to nudes.

Since I cannot exhibit this, and since nobody short of a magician could sell it, I return it to you with this letter. I can only suggest that you pass it off for a pittance to some neighbour wholly ignorant of art as the work of a genius too precocious for the hidebound prejudices of the galleries; that, or toss it on some nearby rubbish-heap and let it be scavenged for fire-lighters.

I beg to remain, your obedient servant,

Mark Admiral

P.S. Hettie is looking forward to seeing you and Roger for Thursday dinner. Don't forget to bring that bottle of whisky you owe me, you skinflint! Rgds, M.

I cannot of course be certain, but based on works from Mr Travis's hand that I have seen in less discriminating galleries, I believe this to be the one. —

S. H.

CHAPTER ELEVEN

One of the letters I had sent the previous night was to an old army colleague, asking if I might visit him during the day on a matter of some import.

Holmes had decided, doubtless for the best of reasons, that it was imperative that Garforth's monocle be found. As I could see that he and the Yard men would be engaged at the studio for some time, I excused myself as the morning drew on, and walked to the Anglo-Indian Club in St James's for luncheon with this friend, Captain Arnold Mayhew.

I came upon him in the club's lobby. 'How excellent to see you, Watson!' he cried. Some ten years my senior, Mayhew was a handsome grizzled fellow with a splendid handlebar moustache. Though these days he walked with a stick, I always found him as vivacious as he had ever been. 'Come and have a drink before lunch, old chap. Our chef here does an excellent curry, for these climes at least – though I miss my Madrassi cook, Naveen, I can tell you. Don't you remember his exquisite mulligatawny?'

He chattered affably away as I followed. While I had known Mayhew in Afghanistan, he had spent many years in service all over the Subcontinent, including a stint doing translation work for the Viceroy. He had been invalided home some two years previously, after catching a nasty injury in a skirmish with a particularly vicious gang of dacoits in Uttar Pradesh, and had been crafting his memoirs ever since; he had contacted me shortly after his return to seek advice on the practicalities of publishing. His recollection of the officers he had worked with was compendious, and while he was perfectly capable of keeping an official secret, in personal matters he was too talkative to be discreet. I suspected that his reminiscences, when finished, would prove unpublishable despite my best advice.

Over the meal, served with immense decorum by the club's Indian servants, we chatted about the exploits of our various mutual acquaintances. After a while, I steered the conversation to the reason for my presence. I said, 'I've run into an officer recently at Sir Newnham Speight's, a Major Bradbury. I believe he's been home for seven years or so. Did he cross your orbit out East at all?'

'Bradbury,' mused Mayhew. 'Yes, I think I might know the chap. Isn't his first name Cuthbert or Crispin or Chad or some such?'

'I understand it's Clement,' I said.

'Clement! I knew it was one of those saintly types. Yes, I recollect the fellow. Served under Moran, didn't he? By Jove,' he added excitably, 'is this one of Holmes's cases? Does he have Bradbury in his sights now?'

I said, 'The Major isn't under any criminal suspicion. But anything you can tell me about him would be helpful.'

'Ah,' said Mayhew. 'Playing your cards close to your chest, old man. I understand. Well, Bradbury was considered a good officer, for the most part – patriotic, tolerably brave, an able administrator and a moderately good tactician. Very popular with the natives, too, which isn't to be sneezed at. He used to lay it on thick to his men about treating the temples and the local holy men with the proper respect.'

'Frankly, I wish more of the officers I knew had done the same,' I said.

'Oh, I'm with you, old boy. But in his case there was more to it than just brotherly sentiment. Bradbury was fascinated by the local religions, although he didn't distinguish very well between them. He knew enough not to feed the Hindus beef or the Muslims pork, but the finer theological distinctions eluded him. He was in love with the idea of the mysterious orient and its teachings, and he didn't much care how they were mixed as long as he could drink them in.'

'There's virtue in an open mind, too,' I said, although after meeting Gerald Floke I suspected that a person's mind could be too open.

Mayhew grinned as he echoed my thoughts. 'Well, old boy, there's keeping an open mind and there's being played for a holy fool, isn't there? Did Bradbury tell you about that guru in Calcutta?'

'He seems to have a lot of colourful stories,' I said.

'Ha! Well, I'm not saying he didn't see some remarkable things, but my opinion is that most of them were stage-managed for his benefit. He once told me that the natives had their own name for him – "the White Gull" – which he took for a great compliment. Personally, I don't think they meant the bird. Once it became known that he took an interest in the miracles performed by the sadhus, yogis and the like, they were queuing up outside his door, and leaving very satisfied once he'd tipped them a paisa apiece. The man must have seen more rope tricks than I've had hot curries. His big mistake was giving the fellows cash, you see – we always advised against it. That's what identified him as a soft touch.

'From what I heard, that guru of his had a fine bag of tricks, but nothing much you couldn't see done at the Empire Theatre in Leicester Square on a Saturday night. To Bradbury, though, the fact that an Indian was doing the conjuring made the whole thing a mystical experience. The fellow took him in completely.

'What he was building up to, though, was asking Bradbury to give him the best part of his savings to build an *ashram*, where he'd teach all comers, native or European, the path to true enlightenment. Of course Bradbury handed over the goods, and that was when the fellow said he needed to pop into a cave for a couple of months to meditate. His famous vanishing act followed, and poor old Bradbury bought it completely. He was amazed to discover how holy the fellow must have been, and though he did make some enquiries among the man's acolytes about what might have happened to his rupees, he eventually accepted that the guru must have had them on him when he ascended, or whatever he was supposed to have done.

'That left Bradbury short, of course, and from what I hear he's still short to this day. He's always been one for the cards, and the guru had been giving him tips about making karma work in his favour, or some such nonsense. He was convinced he could win it back, but not surprisingly it didn't happen. Indeed, I have my suspicions that it wasn't just the guru who was fleecing the poor chap. And... well, it was a little while after the cave incident that the rumours started.'

'The rumours?' I asked, dutifully. It was obvious that Mayhew was relishing this, but the tale was so fascinating that I could not begrudge him his enjoyment. Nor did I resent supplying the punctuation in someone else's monologue, given that that was my usual role when Holmes was in full flow.

'Well, Bradbury had been appointed treasurer at one of the officers' clubs, you see. And some of the more eagle-eyed members began to find... gaps in the accounts. As I say, Bradbury was known as a skilful administrator, a man who kept his eye on the ball, but by this time he was rather distracted by his own problems. Some of his brother officers accused him of embezzlement, and it all became rather nasty. In the end it was put about that Bradbury had just been careless, and it was a native steward who'd actually been taking the money, but after that he was always under a cloud. Certainly he was never put in a position of trust again. A couple of years later he retired and came home.'

Mayhew sat back and gave me a self-satisfied smile while I thought about what his story might imply. At the very least, Bradbury had a history of placing his faith in profoundly unreliable people, with a certain wilful blindness to the outcome, which might explain his fierce insistence that Thomas Kellway had gone to Venus. On the other hand, given his need for money and the past suspicions against him, his involvement in a fraud was not out of the question either. He had, after all, had Sebastian Moran as an example to follow into criminal endeavour.

Remembering what Lestrade suspected had happened to Garforth, I asked, 'Were there any stories of disappearances surrounding the embezzlement case? Possible witnesses, perhaps?'

Mayhew whistled. 'Disappearances? Nothing that I recall, old chap. Why, what on earth do you suspect old Bradbury of doing?'

'Nothing, I hope,' I said. 'Certainly nothing we can be sure of at this stage. If something comes of it, I'll be sure to let you know.'

'Please do.' Mayhew smiled. 'I could always do with more material to alarm my publishers with. Don't worry, though, I'll keep it under my hat for now.'

As I stood to leave and shook his hand, he added, 'Incidentally, Watson... I wasn't sure whether to say, but if there's a disappearance involved I probably shouldn't keep it back. A little bird tells me Bradbury may have been running up more gambling debts – you know, recently, here in London. It's just a whisper of a rumour, but... still. You never know what might turn out to be important, do you?'

I took a cab back to Baker Street, feeling a little bloated after what had indeed been an excellent, though spicy, lunch. As I arrived at 221B, I had to stand aside to make way for two policemen carrying a pile of splintered planking into the house from a police van which had stopped outside.

'Whatever is going on, Mrs Hudson?' I asked our landlady, who was standing watching the proceedings with some distress.

'I'd be most obliged if you could ask Mr Holmes the same question, sir,' she told me with some emphasis.

I climbed the stairs, passing another pair of policemen on their way down, and entered our sitting room only by clambering over a large pile of broken board. More such stacks stood around the room, placed in positions seemingly calculated to be as inconvenient as possible. All the wood was heavily stained with pitch, and spattered with familiar shades of paint. Holmes and Lestrade stood by the fire, the former looking most pleased with himself while the latter seemed both puzzled and resigned. The pose was so characteristic of them both that I might have burst out laughing, had I not been so very indignant about the misuse of my living space.

I said, 'Is this the timber from Garforth's studio? What on earth is it doing here?'

'Ah, Watson!' exclaimed Holmes. 'Lestrade has kindly allowed me to take custody of some of the evidence from the scene of the crime. Whatever this wooden construction may have been, it was important enough for Garforth to have built it, and for somebody to have destroyed it. I intend to rebuild it and find out why.'

I looked at Lestrade, who shook his head gloomily. 'You know what he's like when he has a trail to follow, Doctor. I'd have left it all at Garforth's place if it were me, but Mr Holmes has got it into his head to find out all about it for us.'

The four policemen entered again, carrying between them two more piles of wood, which, at Holmes's direction, they set down directly in front of my favourite chair. They saluted Lestrade and tramped away again, not to return this time.

'For the Yard's part,' Lestrade continued as if he had not been interrupted, 'I think our most practical plan will be to find that vehicle, if we can. Either it's abandoned or someone's been busy cleaning it up, and either of those might get noticed. I don't think there's much more we can learn from all this stuff, anyway.'

My friend replied, 'Oh, but it has taught me so much already, Lestrade.'

'Nothing you care to share with Her Majesty's constabulary, I suppose.'

'When the time is right, my dear inspector. First I must test my theories, and assure myself that they match up against the facts.'

'I don't know why I asked,' Lestrade observed rudely. 'Well, I'll be going back to the Yard, then. We've always room for you there, Dr Watson, if he starts using your bedroom as a lumber-room.' And, smiling at his witticism, the inspector left.

'Really, Holmes,' I began indignantly, 'this is insupportable—'

'What did you learn from Captain Mayhew, Watson?' asked Holmes, disarming me at once. 'Did he tell you about Major Bradbury's gambling debts?'

'But Holmes...' I stared at him in astonishment, all thought of planking forgotten. 'I didn't tell you I was meeting Mayhew.'

He smiled. 'You did not. But there is a faint stain on your shirt-cuff, and the tint of turmeric is most distinctive. You mentioned that you were lunching at a club, and very few London clubs have chefs that routinely employ that spice in their cuisine. Those dishes which use it are a taste acquired largely by former officers in India. You dislike the company at the Oriental

Club and the ambience at the East India Club, though you are a member of both, but tolerate them at the Anglo-Indian, where you are not, for the sake of your occasional lunches with Captain Arnold Mayhew. And Mayhew has a nose for scandal second only in London to that of Langdale Pike, from whom I learned about Bradbury's gaming habit by letter on my return from Camden this morning.'

He showed me a sheet of paper bearing a brief note in the celebrated gossipmonger's effete hand. 'Indeed, in this case I have no doubt your source is the better one, as Pike's information is largely confined to London society and he rarely strays beyond it. Hence, I have no doubt, your pressing appointment with Captain Mayhew today, and hence my eagerness to learn what you now know of Bradbury's record in the service.'

I said, 'I'll tell you, Holmes, but not in here. It feels like my home's been invaded by an army of railway sleepers. Let's go to Harrington's.'

Though impatient to proceed with his self-appointed task, Holmes acquiesced, and shortly we were ensconced in a window-seat at our nearest tea-shop with a warm pot and some scones. Though Holmes and I rarely patronised it, preferring the restaurants of the Strand or the comforts of our own hearth, it was a cosy place, with many little booths and nooks for customers preferring privacy, and I had always found it congenial enough.

I told Holmes about the misfortune into which Bradbury's impressionable nature had led him in Calcutta, and the rumours of his embezzlement at the officers' club. Holmes seemed unsurprised. He said, 'There are worse afflictions than heathen religion that a man can acquire in India, Watson, and worse vices than gambling that can deprive him of money. I would that Colonel Moran had returned with no more deplorable habits than those. But – I say! Here comes the Reverend Small.'

And into the shop bustled the little cleric, looking rather tense and pale. Without preamble he said, 'Mr Holmes, Dr Watson – I *am* sorry to disturb you – your landlady said I might find you here. I *must* ask for your help, I am afraid.' His voice quavered and he sat down, unbidden, at our table. 'That poisonous young asp Skinner has been making the most unconscionable accusations – casting quite pernicious aspersions – *quite* unsupportable, of course, but some in the Society are so credulous – and if word were to reach my parishioners, or heaven forfend, the bishop—'

'Calm yourself, please, Mr Small,' said Holmes. 'Hi, waiter, more tea for my clerical friend! Pray compose yourself, sir, and tell your story from the beginning.'

With the help of the tea, and some medicinal brandy from the hip-flask which I happened to have with me, and from which his shaking hands added rather more to the cup than was perhaps strictly necessary, the Reverend Small achieved the required composure to continue.

'Mr Skinner has been... Well, the assertions he has been making are so ludicrous I hardly know how to describe them,' he began. 'He believes that I murdered Thomas Kellway. Young Mr Rhyne called at my vicarage this morning to tell me of it. He seemed quite distracted about the business, though I cannot imagine that it was wholly upon my account. Perhaps he fears that he will be the next to be falsely accused.'

'As an investigator, Skinner's methods are idiosyncratic,' Holmes noted, 'and his conclusions may border on the phantasmagorical. How does he believe you committed this crime?'

The cleric gave a short, rather desperate laugh. 'With a *curse*, if you can believe it, Mr Holmes. Mr Beech told him some libellous nonsense about my comportment during our watch together, and he – he seems to have concluded...'

'Ah.' Holmes nodded. 'Beech made a similar observation to

Watson and myself. He alleged that you were chanting outside the room, in a most unchristian fashion.'

Small coloured. 'Well, it would appear that that is also what he told Skinner.'

It had seemed to me at the time that Beech was attempting to steer Holmes and myself towards just such a conclusion, so it was natural that Skinner, Beech's own man, should have reached it. If anything it was surprising that it had taken him so long, but Skinner's mind evidently revolved in unusual ways.

'And why does Mr Skinner believe that you would... hex Mr Kellway?' Holmes asked, barely keeping his amusement hidden. 'What motive does he attribute to you?'

'He has concocted a most ludicrous fairy-tale to justify himself, Mr Holmes,' the cleric quavered. 'Are you familiar with the legend of Anne Heybourne, the ghost of Keelefort House?'

'Mr Skinner was kind enough to give us the pertinent details last night,' said Holmes. 'Not that I would trust his unsupported word, you understand, but it seems that such a tradition was at least attested as evidence in a murder trial twelve years ago. Supposedly Anne was killed by Parliamentary soldiers in the seventeenth century, and as a result her spirit is said to have goaded the last owner of Keelefort House under its original name into murdering a prominent Parliamentarian. She sounds oddly interested in politics, for one so surely beyond its reach.'

'I cannot attest to its *historical* veracity, but as a story it is much older than those twelve years.' Small sighed. 'I collect antique books of folklore, and I have seen the legend mentioned in them more than once. It seems that Skinner has unearthed evidence – of what kind and how he came by it, I do not know – that one of the soldiers who murdered Anne was a Yorkshireman, and he believes that her unquiet spirit now bears the same undiscriminating animus towards the denizens of that county as it does towards the representatives of Parliament. Mr Kellway, of course, also hails from Yorkshire.'

'And he believes you were induced to murder by the ghost, as Percival Heybourne claimed to be?' I asked in astonishment.

Small shuddered. 'I cannot say what he truly believes, Doctor, but that is without doubt what he told Sir Newnham and Mr Rhyne this morning. By his account the ghost has been tormenting me on my every visit to Parapluvium House, urging me to homicidal fury, and he will not accept *any* of my denials. At best, he says, I may have been attempting to exorcise the Annexe of her presence, and somehow – not that I have ever heard any account, in theology, folklore or the most lurid of popular fiction that would suggest such a thing is possible – botched the ritual such that it banished Kellway into another realm instead. But mostly he is inclined to believe that I acted malignantly.'

I tried to reassure him. 'But of course such a risible accusation would never convince a policeman, Mr Small, let alone a judge or jury. You are quite safe from any consequence more grave than social embarrassment, though I appreciate that that can be difficult enough...'

But Small was shaking his head. 'If I were a surgeon, Dr Watson, or a bricklayer for that matter, I am sure you would be correct, but as a priest the supernatural is my stock-in-trade. My membership of Sir Newnham's Society has already damaged my repute among a few of my more *backward* parishioners, and I regret to say they might seize upon such an allegation as an opportunity to discredit me altogether. Some of the old laws against witchcraft are still on the statute books, and sadly some in the Church still see this more as a wise precaution than an anachronism. Oh, criminal charges would be inconceivable – you are correct about that, of course – but as far as my position is concerned... of that, I fear, I would be much less confident.'

Holmes said, 'Much as Dr Watson and I sympathise, Mr Small, the prejudices of your parishioners are out of our purview, and I fear that I at least can spare you little of my time, for I have matters of some urgency to investigate. You may have heard that there has been some trouble at Mr Garforth's studio, and it will be a surprising coincidence if it is not related to the business at Parapluvium House. However, there is one point I fail to understand about your session on watch with Mr Beech, on which you can perhaps enlighten me. Since you were not, in fact, intoning an incantation to curse Mr Kellway into non-existence, what was the actual purpose of your chanting?'

Small looked abashed. He said, 'I fear the truth of that will be no more to my credit among my congregation than if it had been a prayer to Beelzebub himself. It is a chant which I understand to be used by monks of the Buddhist faith, and which I have found helpful at times of emotional strain. As I mentioned to Dr Watson, when it comes to religion I am somewhat of an experimentalist, and I am quite willing to accept the practices of other traditions when their utility is clear. I take an ancient Roman's view of this, I confess: I believe that the gods of other races, many of them the subjects of our empire, are merely our *own* under different names. I learned this *mantra*, as it is called, from a missionary, a friend of my father who returned from Tibet when I was a youngster. He was a remarkable man, and has been most influential in my own theological thinking.

'The mantra is helpful in calming the mind, and after an hour with Mr Beech I found myself sorely in need of it. The alternative would have been to have angry words with him, and as words are Beech's weapon of choice I would inevitably have come off the worse from such an exchange. I tried to make my chant inaudible to him, in the hope that he would think I was merely praying, but evidently his ears are sharper, and his knowledge of Christian liturgy more precise, than I expected.'

'I see,' said Holmes. He looked, I thought, somewhat more well disposed towards the little priest than before, and I remembered that he, like Mr Small's family friend, had visited Tibet and spoken with the monks there. 'Well, I think that clears up that matter satisfactorily. Now, if you will excuse me, I must attend to the urgent matters I mentioned. Will you join me, Watson?'

'I think not,' I said. I had little desire to return to the carpenter's workshop that Holmes had made of our rooms. 'I have some errands of my own to run.'

'As you wish, Watson, as you wish. You will find me at home. Good day to you, Mr Small. I hope you are able to resolve your difference of opinion with Mr Skinner.'

Small stared ruefully after Holmes as he left. 'I had hoped to find Mr Holmes more sympathetic.'

'He has a lot on his mind at present,' I assured him. 'I, on the other hand, have no pressing engagements. With your permission, I believe I will call around and have a quiet word with Mr Beech. I'm sure he can persuade Skinner to adopt some other avenue of enquiry.'

'Oh. If you would, Dr Watson, I should be *most* grateful,' Small said, with some relief. 'I find Mr Beech's conversation a great trial of my forbearance.'

'As do I,' I assured him, 'but I have less at stake if I lose my temper than you. Indeed, after the past day I admit that I might positively relish it.'

'I quite understand your sentiment, Dr Watson, even if as a man of the cloth I cannot condone it. But Mr Holmes said that something had happened at Mr Garforth's studio. Is he well?'

I supposed the story would be reported in the newspapers soon enough. 'It seems he has disappeared. I don't mean like Kellway,' I added, remembering that Small thought the Evolved

Man a fraud in any case, 'just in the sense that nobody can find him. There may have been some violence involved, but we're not sure who else was there at the time.'

'Ah,' said Small. 'Well, none of us know him well, of course.' A gleam of the old mischief came back into his eye as he added, 'Except for Mr Rhyne. He did seem *dreadfully* preoccupied this morning, you know. I wonder what they spoke about, he and Mr Garforth, that morning when Garforth came to Parapluvium House, and left so precipitately the instant you arrived? Well, it has been very *pleasant* seeing you again, Dr Watson. Do please give my regards to Mr Beech.'

Excerpt from *Apparitions and Hauntings of the British Isles, A Compendium, from the Scillies to the Shetlands, with Gazetteer and Map, and a Newly Formulated Theory to Explain the Persistence of Tales of Spectral Manifestation* (1879) by Samuel Marston, Gent

Accounts of the haunting of Keelefort House in Richmond (now belonging to Percival Heybourne, the last scion of the family by that name) must begin in 1644 with the slaying of the wife and daughters of Sir Robert Heybourne, an intimate of King Charles the First.

The current Keelefort House was built during the Regency, but it stands in the place of a Tudor dwelling erected by an earlier Sir Robert Heybourne, great-grandfather of the aforementioned, in 1568. It was here, in the Great Hall during dinner, that the latter-day Sir Robert's family and servants were ambushed and set upon by soldiers in the pay of the King's enemies in Parliament. Robert himself fled and hid in a garderobe, by which recourse he survived, while his wife and daughters were treated barbarously and ultimately killed along with many of the maidservants. Anne escaped from the house and into the grounds, where she was hacked to pieces by the pursuing soldiers.

Such indeed was Sir Robert's account after the event, but the matter was strenuously denied by those on the Parliamentary side, and indeed the scandal of the story did them poor service in the eye of the public. Others have averred that Robert himself ran mad and slew his family and servants, chasing his own daughter from the house to perform murder upon her outside, and once his wits were recovered placed the blame upon the King's enemies. Neither interpretation is altogether satisfying, but it may be agreed in either case that Anne's ending was a shocking, sad and painful one, of just the kind that I have suggested commonly result in a psychical *residuum*.

There was indeed no dearth of accounts of such over the following centuries: guests at Keelefort House under its later owners (beginning with Sir James, Robert's son, who being away at Oxford had escaped the massacre) noted such frightening phenomena as a wailing that might be heard at night in varying places among the buildings and grounds, the violent opening and closing of doors and windows in the house when no-one was present to touch them, and the inexplicable movement of furniture, some of it very heavy, likewise without human agency.

In addition a figure was occasionally seen, a young woman 'cutte and much bloodied but comelie of face and forme', as one guest put it in 1726. Family legend naturally named this apparition as the ghost of Anne, although no portrait of Anne survived for comparison, and her brother James, who had seen the spectre for himself in 1669, had noted no clear resemblance. Perhaps one of the unnamed servant girls who also perished on that night instead leant her *residuum* to the site, and was elevated in death to the position which in life she had merely served.

Regardless of the wraith's identity and origins, by the early eighteenth century her nuisances had become a trial to the house's owners, who were not only prevented thereby from receiving visitors but were themselves obliged to dwell for long periods away from the family home. In 1813 Sir Malcolm Heybourne had the original Tudor building torn down and replaced with the structure that stands there today, from which time to the present 'Anne' has remained both silent and unseen.

To kill so many with but one partial escapee would surely be beyond the capacity of even a madman, yet the tale of the Parliamentarian soldiers' atrocities is rather too convenient for the Royalist cause. Might we perhaps deduce that Sir Robert had decided to defect to Parliament's side, and was given a horrific warning to reconsider by the King's lieutenants? I must take this up with a historian when I have the leisure. — S. H.

CHAPTER TWELVE

Gideon Beech's home was in Belgravia, a tall white Georgian townhouse to one side of a leafy square. As I arrived there a young woman emerged from the house and hailed a cab, and I was surprised to recognise the pale blonde hair of Miss Casimir. As I paid my own cabman, she hurriedly bundled the frail figure of Countess Brusilova aboard the vehicle. As they departed I doffed my hat and called a greeting to them, but they were evidently in too great a hurry for conversation.

I rang the bell and was surprised when I was greeted by Beech himself, beaming with pleasure. His smile twitched as he saw me, then redrew itself with a dash of malice. He made a show of looking around for Holmes as he said, 'Why, it's Dr Watson – and alone! I had as soon expected to play host to Coster Joe in the absence of Fred Russell.' The reference would have been lost on me but for a recent evening spent at the Tivoli in the Strand, where I had seen this newly popular ventriloquist's act. (Coster Joe was, naturally, the doll.) Evidently Beech's tastes in entertainment stretched beyond even the popular theatre.

Gesturing expansively, the playwright told me, 'Come in, please. Ah – no, Jack, not the drawing room. Dr Watson and I will take tea in the conservatory.'

A pageboy, who had been about to open the drawing-room door, led us instead through to the rear of the house, where a veritable landscape of perennials, ornamental shrubs and small trees had been crammed into a huge glasshouse. Though my botanical knowledge is imprecise, I recognised a palm, an araucaria and some japonicas, and could guess from my visits to Kew Gardens that the others I could see were all foreign varieties. I thought I even recognised a shrub or two from my time in India.

'When the demands of my work, which are many and rigorous, become wearisome to me,' said Beech, 'I like to sit here in quiet, and contemplate the potent virility and illimitable variegation of Life. Though Man may be the more evolved type, plants such as these make for a powerful metaphor, don't you agree?'

I offered some non-committal comment, but Beech predictably required no encouragement.

He said, 'In their vegetal majesty, these humble organisms exhibit in its most honest form Life's purest goal: to propagate, grow and increase, to fit Herself for every place and every kind of landscape, drawing on the materials at hand to fulfil Her one sacred and eternal mission – to make more of Life. It is a calling which, in their respective, imperfect and partial ways, both the capitalist building his fortune and the pastor attempting to enlarge his flock are stumbling to answer. Though, as it happens, perhaps the highest human expression of this universal urge is found in the writer, who grows from the germ of his first insight, in the rich soil of his brain, a great organism of thought which may – publishers, theatrical impresarios and other mundane gatekeepers grudgingly permitting – disseminate itself into the wider world, planting its own seeds into the soil of other minds.

'I refer, of course, to those writers who create, and not to those mere stenographers who confine themselves to the dull business of transcribing reality; they resemble at best those collectors of butterflies who pin to the everlasting stasis of an index-card that which was once a vivid and irrepressible expression of Life.'

As I expected, having thus insulted me, he paused with a smile to see my reaction. I had been patiently awaiting such a moment, and so came immediately to my point.

I said, 'Speaking of pastors, Beech, your creature Skinner has been levelling the most outlandish accusations against the Reverend Small. Accusations which, though baseless, seem calculated to assist certain factions who would destroy his career. I am hoping you might prevail upon him to retract them.'

'I see.' For a moment I thought perhaps I could detect a trace of relief in Beech's superciliousness, but it passed. 'So poor wee Small's dogmatic mind is pothered by Skinner's untrammelled theorising, is it? And he has sent an intermediary to have me call off, as he sees it, my attack dog.'

I said, 'He didn't ask me to come, but he confided in Holmes and myself. Skinner is a loose cannon, but those who bear Mr Small ill will may doubtless say that there is no smoke without fire. I don't even believe you agree with his conclusions, Beech. Weren't you arguing that Kellway had been translocated to Venus? That would be difficult to reconcile with his being psychically murdered in the Experiment Room.'

'I try to keep an open mind, laddie. It's always imaginable that one day I might be wrong about something. But,' he continued magnanimously, 'as it happens I concur that, with his most recent aspersions, young Skinner is barking up the wrong tree. The boy's intellect has yet to develop the kind of rigour I am sure Holmes would wish to see in a person of his calling. And yet there is something to be said for understanding the virtue of humility in the face of others, caring about one's clients for their own sake rather than as logical conundrums, and preferring one's own imagination as a remedy for boredom rather than addictive narcotics.'

Again I ignored his jibes. 'And yet I believe you pointed him towards that tree yourself, Mr Beech, fully intending him to bark up it. Did you not tell Holmes and me, too, about Mr Small's use of a Buddhist mantra during your watch together?'

'Ah, is that what it was? I know little of such things, Doctor.' Beech smiled lazily. 'It's possible I *was* overly conscientious in giving Skinner all the information he might require, to the point of including some that was perhaps not strictly relevant. And certainly we wouldn't want to hobble Vortigern Small's illustrious career of promulgating sugar-coated lies to control the masses, would we? I suppose I could have a word with the lad, as a favour to Holmes and yourself, of course, and mention to him that I think he's labouring down the wrong garden path.'

'I would be grateful if you would,' I said, still biting back my anger. Infuriating though his condescension was, and despite what I had told Small about looking forward to losing my temper, I knew that feigning obsequiousness was the only way to stay on the right side of a man of Beech's temperament.

There seemed, however, little to be gained by staying to be lectured on the supreme grandeur of the Will of Life, or the role of interplanetary influences in evolution, or vegetarianism or nudism or eugenics or any other fad of Beech's, so I drank my tea quickly and made my excuses. Though he made some allusion to stray dogs running home to their masters, Beech seemed relieved by this.

As we passed out of the conservatory and along the hall to the front door, the page, Jack, said, 'The other gentleman's here, sir.'

I had already wondered whether Beech had expected to see someone else when he opened the door to me. 'I hadn't realised you were expecting company, Beech,' I said. 'It seems you're having quite a busy afternoon. I saw the Countess and her companion leaving earlier.'

Beech's annoyance was evident. 'It's just some business of the Society's, Doctor,' he said, 'and none of yours. It's nothing you should concern yourself with.'

'I see,' I said. 'And is your new visitor also a member of the Society Committee?' I hazarded a guess. 'Mr Floke, perhaps? If he's here I'd be interested to renew our acquaintance.'

A maid approached the drawing-room door carrying a tea tray, and Beech turned on her sharply. 'When I ring for it, Mary, not before,' he snapped, and she scuttled away – but not before I saw that the tea service was set for three. 'You must forgive me, Dr Watson,' Beech instructed me peremptorily. 'My visitor and I have a great deal of business to discuss, which I have no doubt you would find interminably dull.'

I turned to make a further comment, but by now Beech was standing in front of the closed door to the drawing room, his hand raised in farewell, while his page, abashed at his master's evident annoyance, held open the front door for me.

I could, I suppose, have pushed the illustrious playwright aside and forced my way into the drawing room, but that would have been as unforgivably rude as Beech was being himself. Had I suspected immediate wrongdoing I would have ignored such qualms and acted at once, but my only thought was that Beech was concealing a visitor, and however infuriating the man might be he was entitled to entertain whoever he wished in his own house without my interference. Indeed, if I were to barge in on his visitors against his will, he would be perfectly justified in calling the police. I bade him a stiff goodbye and returned in careful thought to Baker Street.

In the hallway I heard a loud hammering noise emanating

from upstairs, and met Mrs Hudson, dressed for the street and carrying a small valise. She shouted to me, as best she could over the din. 'I'm sorry, Dr Watson, but I can't stay in this house a moment longer.'

'You're leaving us, Mrs Hudson?' I cried back, flabbergasted. In all Holmes's and my adventures together, our landlady's self-effacing toil on our behalf had been a constant comforting presence. Even when Holmes's work had taken us on travels in England and abroad, we were both sustained by the knowledge that Number 221B Baker Street still had its loyal guardian to keep the pantry stocked and stoke the fire for our return. Though Holmes's behaviour had often been annoying, and occasionally outrageous – his habit of practising with his pistol from the comfort of his armchair making for a point of particular contention – she had never before been driven to such a recourse.

'I am, sir. I'm going to my sister's, and I'll come back once this latest craze of Mr Holmes's has finished, not before. I've left a cold collation in the kitchen, and the butcher's boy is due in the morning.'

She bustled off, leaving me aghast and bereft.

I ascended to our rooms, carrying with me a large tub of pitch that had been delivered for Holmes and had been sitting in the hallway, which I dumped without ceremony upon the carpet. I saw that in my absence the sitting room's other occupant had pushed most of its furniture up against one wall, and that the paint-spattered timber from Garforth's studio had been partially assembled in the centre of the space thus cleared.

I called out Holmes's name. The hammering stopped and my friend rose up from the ramshackle structure like a jack-in-the-box. 'Ah, Watson!' He beamed. 'I am making progress, as you see.'

'I can see you're making *something*,' I said. 'If only a nuisance of yourself, according to Mrs Hudson. For pity's sake, man, she's left us – for the time being, at least. I warned you the situation was intolerable. Whatever this contraption is, why do you have to build it here? Surely you know somebody with a convenient garden?'

'Garforth had set it up in an indoor location,' Holmes replied with infuriating calm. 'That factor might have been essential to its function, although it might just have meant that he wanted privacy. Until I reconstructed it I could not be sure. In hindsight I admit that that might have been done more conveniently in its original location, but it would hardly be practical to move it now.'

'And, pray, what is it supposed to be?' Though much of the planking still lay loose around it, the construction was beginning to look like a shed of the kind a gardener might use to store his tools and seedlings, vegetally majestic or otherwise.

'I have a theory on that point, my dear fellow, and a promising one, but I will not be able to confirm it until my present work is complete. If I am correct, though, it will allow for a very pretty demonstration at the appropriate time. The light is fading now, but I have hopes that tomorrow may be sunny.'

Baffled at his attempt to deflect the conversation, I said, 'The dimensions look similar to those of the Experiment Room. Is it possible that Garforth built a replica, for Kellway to practice escaping from?'

'Well, maybe so. But I fear that, as occasionally happens, Watson, your mind has found a promising thread and followed it in quite the wrong direction.'

With some annoyance I asked, 'So when do you expect that I may have my sitting room back?'

'Alas, I am not yet able to confirm that either. How was Mr Beech?'

I had not told him I would be visiting Beech, but I was

too vexed with him to rise to the bait for a second time that day. Probably, in leaving me with Small, he had intended that I should run such an errand all along, and had simply not thought it worth the trouble of mentioning.

'As self-important, stubborn and infuriating as ever,' I said, meaning Beech but perhaps putting some extra emphasis on the adjectives for the benefit of my audience. 'I do think he will ask Skinner to leave poor Mr Small alone, though.'

'A kind thought on your part, Watson. Although for all the sense Skinner makes, it is as likely to mean that you, I, or for that matter Her Majesty are instead accused of carrying out the psychical attack from afar.'

'I'm fairly certain that Beech set Skinner on Small deliberately, though,' I said. 'He called him his "attack dog", though he attributed the thought to Small. Do you think he's been trying to draw attention away from himself?'

Holmes gave a short laugh. 'That does not strike me as a habit of Mr Beech's.'

'Because he has something to hide, I mean.'

I went on to tell him everything about my conversation with Beech, of the arrival of another visitor shortly before I left, and of my suspicion that a third person had already been concealed in the house, and had already spoken to Miss Casimir and Countess Brusilova.

'I thought at first it was Kellway,' I said, 'and that Beech was soliciting the other Committee members to support his claim for the reward money. But on my way home I began to wonder whether perhaps it was Garforth. Beech could be harbouring him if he is guilty, or if innocent he might have gone to Beech for help.'

'Perhaps so,' said Holmes. 'But if he were innocent, your arrival would surely have occasioned him with a welcome opportunity to recount his side of the story. And if he is not, he would hardly have stayed there after learning of your arrival.'

'Unless Beech is keeping him prisoner,' I suggested.

'In his drawing room? That would be a most inconvenient arrangement. And if Beech considered himself to have apprehended a dangerous criminal, I cannot imagine him keeping the matter quiet. Speaking of Garforth, though, there is something that I must show you.'

From beneath an occasional table that he had stacked haphazardly on top of my favourite armchair, he pulled the ebony walking stick from Garforth's studio: the presumed murder weapon, if there had indeed been a murder.

'I'm surprised Lestrade has let you have that,' I said.

'The inspector has been most accommodating,' said Holmes. 'He recognises that my knowledge of the unusual background to this case gives me more than the normal advantage over him in solving it.'

Now cleaned of blood (though Holmes assured me that the marks had been meticulously documented), the cane's shaft showed clear abrasions where it had connected with the victim's skull. Its polished handle I took, in line with Garforth's general habit of gentility at the lowest possible price, to be pewter rather than silver. Similarly, when Holmes handed it to me it felt lighter than I would have expected of such a dense material, and I wondered whether it was really ebony or had been merely stained to give it the appearance of a darker wood.

'And what have you concluded from it?' I asked, handing it back to him.

Holmes gripped the handle in one hand, and the shaft in the other, and twisted.

'Oh, surely not,' I said, but it was true: this stick, like Kellway's, was a sword-stick. More specifically, it was a *former* sword-stick, now a hollow cylinder. As I saw when Holmes passed me the handle, the blade had been sawn off, this time with a deliberate, clean break, and its sharp edges filed down carefully.

'Well, this *is* remarkable,' I observed. 'Presumably it means that Garforth and Kellway were working together. And I suppose they must have been concealing something inside the shafts. I wonder what?'

'Wonder no more, Watson.' Holmes turned the shaft upside-down and tipped from it what seemed to be a long, narrow bundle of bamboo sticks. He passed it to me and I realised that it was actually a collapsed framework made of bamboo and wire, which unfolded into a much larger structure. After fumbling with it in the unwontedly confined space, I managed to set it upright, or in the orientation I assumed was upright. Expanded, it was around waist-high and cruciform in shape, with two hinged legs that formed a tripod with the base of the cross, keeping the whole assemblage roughly vertical.

'I've never seen anything like it,' I declared. However, there was something about it that seemed a little familiar. 'I wonder, though…' I poked at the hinges. 'Yes, I believe it uses the same sort of folding mechanism as a Speight's Super-Collapsible Pocket Umbrella.'

'Capital, Watson! Indeed it does. Of course, there are a great many such umbrellas in circulation, and it would not be so very difficult a challenge to copy their principles. But this device adapts them with some ingenuity.'

'Whatever is it *for*, though?' I wondered, and Holmes smiled secretly to himself. I sighed. 'Oh, I suppose you can't confirm that yet, either. Never mind. I'm going to take a bath.'

Bad-temperedly I stamped through to our bathroom, where I found my way impeded by several large rolls of linen cloth. The bathtub itself was full of labelled bottles of chemicals, arranged in neat rows.

'Holmes!' I yelled, marching back into the sitting room.

'Ah, yes – the bathtub,' he said, having the grace this time to look a little shame-faced. 'Forgive me, my dear fellow – I had to store the chemicals somewhere, and that seemed to be the safest place. You are quite at liberty to move them if you can think of a better one.'

But it was evident that our rooms would be uninhabitable for the duration. I reminded Holmes that Mrs Hudson had left out a cold collation, then after a rather terse farewell I walked the short distance to my club, where I took rooms for the night.

After a light supper, comfortable in a sitting room blissfully empty of carpentry, with a fire and a port-decanter, I directed myself to pondering further on the particulars of the case. Although my gifts of reasoning were in no degree a match for Holmes's, I flattered myself that I had contributed the occasional understanding to the investigations we had undertaken together. It was, I thought, possible that some such insight might occur to me given sufficient consideration, provided I kept awake.

I found, though, that I kept thinking of Miss Casimir, the Countess Brusilova's forbidding yet undeniably attractive young companion, who could have no part in the mystery of Kellway's disappearance at all. On the night of the experiment she had been at the Star and Garter Hotel with her employer from half-past nine in the evening until half-past seven in the morning, a fact which Holmes had been able to confirm. Not only did the Countess require constant attendance, meaning that her companion would have been unable to leave her side for any length of time during those ten hours, but the hotel concierge was prepared to swear that no female guests had left the hotel during that time.

Nevertheless, there was the incident of the young lady on the stairs near Sir Newnham's study, who had been mistaken for the unquiet spirit of Anne Heybourne. Holmes had spoken to Gregory the footman, who had been able to describe little beyond a figure of a woman wrapped in something like a toga, flitting in eerie silence down the stairs. He had also admitted, after very little pressure from Holmes, that he had indeed imbibed a quantity of his employer's whisky beforehand, a fact he had begged us to keep from Anderton.

Now I came to think of it, though, there was another unidentified young woman in the affair, the 'niece' who had visited Thomas Kellway. In our enquiries into the principals in the case, I thought we had perhaps rather neglected the distaff side – for in a business almost exclusively populated by men of strong personality, even a woman as forceful as Miss Casimir might be a little eclipsed.

I had no doubt that she would, if she wished, have some success in charming men of her own age, though I was a little too old to consider myself a likely object for such blandishments. Talbot Rhyne, though, would be a plausible potential conquest, although I baulked at the idea so casually espoused by Holmes that he might have let a young lady into Sir Newnham's house. This might, indeed, make her physical absence from Parapluvium House during the night less important than the influence she might have wielded upon those who remained. I wondered what it was that had been so distracting Rhyne this morning, according to Vortigern Small's account.

And then there was Constantine Skinner, a man whose raw and anguished sincerity might leave him peculiarly susceptible to such temptations. I had assumed that it was Beech pulling his strings, but perhaps he had some other puppet-master. He seemed like a man who might have need of money, and that, it seemed, was a primary concern of Miss Casimir's too. Was it possible that his accusations against Mr Small were intended merely to frighten the cleric, with the aim of extorting some remuneration from him for keeping them quiet in future?

And yet, Miss Casimir and the Countess were among those in Beech's confidence. Perhaps all of them were working together to the same end, though for the moment it was obscure to me.

I began to drift off into a dream in which I saw a set of strings lowering a body… I thought it was Sir Newnham's… into a bath of acid, watched over by Kellway… only instead of Kellway it was Constantine Skinner, wearing a bald stage wig and carrying his vermiform appendix in a jar, with Miss Casimir standing in the wings… but I was awakened a moment later by a rapping at the door.

A bath of acid. Could that be important? I wondered briefly, as the dream dissipated. Had Kellway's body somehow been dissolved without leaving the Experiment Room?

'Who is it?' I called out, very annoyed at being woken.

The steward called, 'There's an urgent message, sir, from Mr Sherlock Holmes. He says to tell you they've found Mr Garforth's body.'

The Morning Chronicle

6th March 1894

In *Jack Commonsmith's Crime*, Mr Gideon Beech's new play at the Architrave Theatre, the eponymous servant (played ably enough by Mr Bernard Carhill) stands accused of a theft. The audience understand from the start that this stout man is innocent of the crime, indeed of all possible crimes, but he is in all respects the natural suspect, as those others who had the opportunity are all respectable ladies and gentlemen.

Such is the dilemma which Mr Beech outlines, and the reprehensible actions of many of its principals enable his players (including Mr Pryce and Miss Mittern as Lord Highgrace and the young Lady Highgrace) to educate his audience most imperiously on the iniquities of wealth and the evils of social class, subjects to which he has not infrequently turned his pen in the newspapers and journals as well as for the stage. In this aspect of the play it is difficult not to detect a reflection of Mr Beech's own experiences, and in the plodding Inspector Knassock in particular (a study of stolid ignorance well observed by a newcomer to the stage, Mr Myles Briggs), a condemnation of some of the individuals involved in the affair of the Clitheroe Rubies, in which a servant was likewise accused, it eventually seemed unjustly, and Mr Beech was personally involved in clearing his name in the face of opposition from the police and the household.

This imitation of life becomes inescapable in the final act when the Highgraces' most thoughtful guest and Commonsmith's truest friend among them, the poet Gordon Bastion (Mr Carew) demonstrates almost incidentally the stalwart servant's innocence, before taking this as his cue to deliver a supercilious and exceptionally lengthy monologue on how the ills of society at large have been reflected in microcosm in Highgrace Manor. Those who have had the pleasure of Mr Beech's acquaintance may feel that certain aspects of life need not be quite so closely imitated as others.

CHAPTER THIRTEEN

'I was sent a note,' Talbot Rhyne told us. His face was pale and his voice, always somewhat adolescent in pitch, was squeaky with nerves. 'It *said* it was from Freddie Garforth. I didn't recognise the handwriting, but... Well, after what you found at his studio I thought he might have been in a bad way. I thought perhaps he'd dictated it or something.'

He sat, a tumbler of brandy untouched in front of him, in one of the interview rooms at Scotland Yard. It was completely dark outside, and the single dim electric bulb made his face a mask of shock. I had rushed there at Holmes's instruction and found him delaying Rhyne's interview for my arrival, much to Lestrade's irritation – a peace offering of sorts, I supposed, after his inconsiderate behaviour at home.

'Did you keep the note, sir?' Lestrade asked Rhyne, who shook his head.

'It said I was to burn it,' he said, 'so I did. It came around one o'clock this afternoon – well, it's yesterday afternoon now, I suppose – by messenger. I know I should have contacted the police then – your people had already asked us about Freddie's studio, Inspector – but the note was very clear that I shouldn't. It asked me to meet Freddie at ten o'clock tonight, at a particular address in Limehouse, and not to tell anyone – not Sir Newnham, not Mr Holmes or Dr Watson, and *definitely* not the police. The only person I did tell was Anderton, just as I was leaving, but I swore him to secrecy unless I failed to return by the morning. It had occurred to me by then that it might be a trap, you see, although why they might want to trap me I couldn't imagine.

'Oh Lord, I've just realised he's probably sitting up worrying about me. Poor old Anderton.' Rhyne picked up the brandy, lifted it to his lips, sniffed, stared at it, and asked Lestrade, 'I'm sorry, Inspector, could I possibly have a glass of water?'

Lestrade summoned a constable to bring the water, sequestered the brandy for himself, and gestured for Rhyne to continue.

'I took a cab, but then it struck me that if it *was* a trap they might send a cabman to wait near the house for me, so I had him put me out when we got to Hammersmith. I walked to Kensington and took another cab from Olympia, then switched cabs again in St James's. I suppose I thought I was being rather clever, though of course I was still going exactly where whoever wrote the note had told me to.

'Anyway, by the time we reached the address in Limehouse after all that dithering I was half an hour late, and the building turned out to be a big warehouse, dark and completely shut up for the night. I asked the cabman to wait and walked around the building to see if I could find a way in. And there *was* a door ajar, around the back. I was very nervous, of course, but the only thing I'd been able to find to bring with me for a weapon was a kitchen-knife. I hadn't thought to bring a lantern, either, so all I had to light my way was matches.

'The door led into a small back room – I suppose it must once have been a post room, as it had a row of pigeonholes on the wall – with a door into the main warehouse. I stepped through as quietly as I could and listened, but there was no sound of movement or breathing. I struck another match and that's when I – saw him.'

He took a deep breath and rubbed his forehead. 'I'm sorry. It was a terrific shock. He was… hanging, you see. Not *hanged*, you understand, but hanging – someone had tied a rope round both his ankles and suspended him from a beam. Not that I saw that straight away. He was just… dangling there in the air, upside-down, with that great gash in his head. I didn't recognise him at first, but I could see at once he was dead.

'I'm not ashamed to say I cried out and dropped the match,' he added ruefully. 'In fact I would have run away and never looked back, but I couldn't immediately find the door to the office. My hands were shaking so much it took me three tries to light another match, and by then I was half-hoping that it would turn out to have been some horrible figment of my imagination. But no such luck.

'I looked more closely then, and eventually I realised that it was Freddie Garforth. It… took me a couple of matches, actually.'

'We can talk about the state of the body in a moment, sir,' Lestrade said, with that stolid brand of comfort and menace that is the policeman's stock-in-trade. 'What did you do after you'd satisfied yourself of its identity?'

'Well, I ran back outside and round to the street of course, but my cabman had taken off. I can't say I altogether blame him – it was a pretty rough-looking neighbourhood. He must have decided to give up the fare rather than chance it. Then I wandered round for a while looking for a policeman. I don't know how long it took me to find one. I was in a terrible state. When I did, he blew his whistle for help, and three of us went back to the warehouse together. I… couldn't bear to go inside properly that time; I just waited in the office. Then the second policeman stayed with the body, while the first one flagged down another cab and brought me here. I asked for you, Inspector, and for you, Mr Holmes, so they called you in and… Well, I'm terribly sorry to have woken you all, but here we are.'

Lestrade said, 'Please don't trouble yourself, sir; it's all part of the job. Well, mine at least,' he added, with a twinkle in his eye, and I remembered that he was often at his most sprightly at this time of night. 'Between ourselves, I believe Mr Holmes and Dr Watson enjoy it.'

Holmes said, 'You say this letter came by messenger, Rhyne?'

'That's right. I didn't see the man, though. He gave an envelope to Gregory, the footman. I asked him what the man looked like – as casually as I could, as I didn't want to cause anybody in the household any alarm – but he didn't remember anything notable about him.'

'He'll have been an innocent party anyway,' Lestrade said sagely.

The constable came in with Rhyne's glass of water, and spoke briefly to the inspector, whose eyes gleamed with anticipation. 'Well, well, gentlemen,' he said, 'it seems the body's arrived. Shall we?'

Rhyne drained the water quickly and we all went down to the mortuary. The whole building was deserted, aside from the duty sergeant and a handful of constables passing through. The law never sleeps, but in my experience police detectives often value their night's rest. One of the constables who had assisted Rhyne was awaiting us, along with the dead man on his slab. The constable respectfully unveiled the corpse, and I came face to face for the second time with Frederick Garforth. The wound which had killed him was plain to see: a great fissure in his skull, scabbed with blood, just above the left temple.

I recoiled in surprise, and even Holmes raised an eyebrow.

'*Is* this Frederick Garforth, Mr Rhyne?' Lestrade asked with some doubt, and I could see the source of his confusion.

'Oh, it's him all right,' Rhyne replied grimly. 'I know him now.'

When Holmes and I had glimpsed Garforth, he had sported a fine pair of muttonchop whiskers and a mane of silver hair. Though I had only seen him for a moment, I had also had an impression of bushy grey eyebrows above the monocle.

The corpse in front of us had been shaven, face and brow and scalp alike, until it was as bald as Thomas Kellway – or Gerald Floke.

'Good heavens,' I exclaimed. Shorn of its hair, and with some signs that it had suffered from its time suspended in the warehouse, Garforth's visage was still distinguished by a noble brow and an equally prominent chin.

Lestrade asked, 'Was the body dressed like this when you found it? No hat, no coat?' Garforth's body was still wearing his trousers, a waistcoat and shoes similar to the new pair we had found beneath his bed. All were torn and abraded from the dragging the corpse had been subjected to, and liberally smeared with green, white and blue paint, as well as spatterings of other colours, over which was a layer of dirt and grime.

'Of course,' said Rhyne. 'I'd hardly have removed them.'

'And you saw nobody else at the warehouse?'

'Only rats,' said Rhyne with a shudder. 'I must have surprised a dozen of them.'

Holmes's interest was piqued. 'That is perhaps suggestive.'

It would not do to discuss the details of the case in front of Rhyne, though, and Lestrade stepped in smoothly. 'Well, sir, I don't think we've any further need for you down here. The constable here will take you to the duty sergeant, and he'll take down your statement. Then you can go home and rest – we'll send for you if we need you again.'

'Thank you,' Rhyne said, his voice exhausted. 'It has been a very trying night, as I'm sure you can imagine.'

'Just one moment, please,' said Holmes as the young man was about to leave with the constable. He had been inspecting the small pile of objects placed beside the corpse, which the constables had found beneath it, their assumption being that they had fallen from its pockets. There was a cheap pocket-watch without a chain, a matchbox, a crushed packet of cigarettes, a cigarette holder, a paintbrush and a handkerchief. 'Mr Garforth's monocle is not here.' I remembered that Holmes and Lestrade had not managed to locate it at the studio either. 'Did either of you see it at the warehouse?'

Rhyne shook his head mutely, and the constable said, 'No, sir. Might have rolled away, though. The men will have a look in the morning when it's light.'

'Thank you, Constable,' said Holmes, adding once they were gone, 'I think we can do better than that, Lestrade. There's no time like the present, after all. Once Watson has examined the body, we shall all go to the warehouse and inspect the scene. Can you muster a dozen men and some powerful lanterns?'

'I'll try,' Lestrade said with a grin, 'though they won't thank me for not letting it wait till the morning.' He called in another constable and sent him to round up the men and equipment.

I said, 'You are aware that some of the younger members of the Society for the Scientific Investigation of Psychical Phenomena are shaving themselves in tribute to Thomas Kellway, Lestrade?'

'Holmes did mention it,' Lestrade agreed sceptically.

'I doubt, however, that the Cult of Kellway has progressed so far in a few days as to have inspired a religious purge,' Holmes observed drily. 'This may be a crude attempt to throw us off the scent.'

'It looks more like a warning to me,' Lestrade said. 'Displaying a corpse like that for a friend to find? That's the sort of thing we'd expect from a criminal syndicate. Perhaps this fellow Floke's in deeper than we know – Kellway, too. There could be a whole gang of shaven men out there.' He sounded a little doubtful.

'Yet the presentation may not have been a matter of pure theatre,' Holmes said.

I said, 'You're thinking of the rats, aren't you?'

'Indeed. The murderer – or, if we avoid making any unwarranted assumptions, the person who placed the body there – knew that a cadaver left on the floor would attract the rats' attention. They hoped that by suspending it they would deter the vermin, at least for a while. We may infer that it was essential to their purposes that the corpse be recognisable.'

'In that case, why the dickens did they shave him?' asked Lestrade incredulously.

'All in good time, my dear Lestrade. Let us first satisfy ourselves as to the condition of the body. Watson, if you would be so kind…?'

I began by removing the shoes and socks, to inspect the damage left by the rope, and was quickly able to verify that it had been done post mortem. The corpse's feet were rather hairy, and further inspection confirmed that only those portions of the artist that were visible when clothed had been shaven, simplifying the job considerably. I presumed that the same was not true of Floke, though naturally I had not enquired. Nonetheless, the impression given when the corpse was clothed was of a man wholly without hair.

Looking more closely at the shaven hands, I saw that in the fingers, and particularly under the nails, were splinters of wood, and that two of the nails themselves were torn. I said, 'You were right to reject the idea that Garforth surprised a vandal in his studio, Holmes. By the looks of it, he tore apart that wooden thing himself in something of a frenzy, I'd say. It must have taken some force.'

'Well, he looks to have been a burly fellow,' Lestrade observed.

I moved on to Garforth's head. It was a grisly sight, but I must spare the reader no details. The facial features were distended from where the clotted blood had sunk into Garforth's face during his suspension, and, despite the murderer's best intentions, it was evident that at least one determined rat had gone to the effort of climbing down the rope. 'I'm not surprised it took Rhyne a moment to recognise him,' I said, 'what with the shaving as well. It's a marvel he did, in the dark and with only a match to go by.'

'I think you may be on to something there, Doctor,' Lestrade said meaningfully. 'I think young Mr Rhyne may know more than he's telling us.'

I inspected the wound on Garforth's skull, which I confirmed was the size and shape of the ebony cane's shaft. I calculated that unconsciousness would have followed immediately from such a blow, and death not long afterwards. Then I leaned in to peer more closely, and said, 'Oh – that's peculiar.'

'What do you see, Watson?' Holmes asked.

'There are fragments of hair among the blood, adhering to the scalp,' I said. 'As you would expect from a wound of this type. But… it's all short, Holmes. Practically stubble.'

Lestrade said, 'But I thought this Garforth cove had long hair and whiskers.'

'He did,' I said. 'We saw them. He must have shaved soon afterwards, for heaven alone knows what reason. This is a day or so's growth of hair. But that conflicts with the time of death.'

'When *did* he die, Doctor?' Lestrade asked.

'Well, medically speaking I can say only that it was probably between one and two full days ago. Rigor mortis has taken a complete hold of the joints, but decomposition is minimal. But that's not what I mean. Holmes and I saw Garforth on Wednesday morning, and he certainly had his hair then. It's equally clear from the paint on his clothes, and the scene at the studio, that he died in the struggle there, which happened sometime soon afterwards. Yet somehow during that time he was able to shave and regrow his hair – at least a little. The rates of growth vary, but I would say this had been left unshaven for a day or so.'

Lestrade frowned. 'I don't see any stubble on his chin, though.'

'Ah,' said Holmes, pointing, 'but here are a few hairs on the neck, also very short, which have been missed.'

I said, 'There is also a small cut on his cheek consistent with the bite of a razor, that has not bled. The body was shaved for a second time post mortem.'

Lestrade groaned. 'So you're telling me that this man saw you both at Speight's house, went home and shaved off his hair and whiskers, grew a day's worth of stubble, smashed up his own work, then got into a fight with someone else, who killed him and then shaved him again for good measure, all in the space of a couple of hours?'

'It certainly seems that way,' I said. 'And no man could grow his hair to this length in that time. It looks as if we have a second impossible problem, Holmes.'

Holmes said, 'Not in the least. This matter is a perfectly simple one. Unlike Kellway's disappearance, which requires a very ingenious solution.'

I said, 'Well, I wish you'd tell me what either of them are.'

He smiled. 'All in good time, Watson.'

'I thought you said there was no time like the present?'

'And so I did. Lestrade, to the warehouse if you please.' And with that, it seemed, I would for the moment have to be satisfied.

We rode to the warehouse in a police-van, pulled by a team

of police horses who were fretful and skittish at being so hastily roused. The building itself was a tall brick construction, one of a line of such, hulking like beached leviathans along the banks of the Thames.

A team of constables had taken over to secure the place, and the one stationed at the front sent us around to the rear, which was guarded by another policeman. This turned out to be the man who had stayed with the corpse while he and Rhyne went to the Yard.

He told us, 'This place gives me the creeps, sirs, I don't mind admitting. When I think of that poor bloke strung up upside-down like that, like something out of a penny dreadful, and shaved all over like a newborn baby... well, it gives me heart palpitations something horrible.'

I sympathised, but Holmes was impatient to get inside and begin his work. Lestrade's men had brought powerful kerosene lanterns whose reflective shutters could be arranged to supply a strong directional beam, and while the policemen searched the remainder of the warehouse space Holmes appropriated one of these to make his own inspection of the place where the body had been found.

Looking around us, I could imagine only too well the state of mind in which Rhyne must have been when he made his horrific discovery. The warehouse was musty and smothered in dust, the scrabbling of rats an ever-present horror, and in the beams of the policemen's lanterns the monstrous shapes of mechanisms loomed.

'As I thought,' Holmes concluded after some consideration. 'Garforth was suspended, not from a beam, but from a winch. The mechanism is still functional, and was used to raise the body off the ground. To suspend it directly from a beam would have taken two: one strong man to hold it aloft, and one more nimble to climb and tie the knots. This way one man could work alone instead. See, he laid the body here, and tied the pulley rope around its ankles, then stood here to winch it upright and into the air. The shoe prints in the dust are of Garforth's own size, yet cannot be Garforth's own, confirming that the victim and assailant had similar feet. It is not so great a coincidence.'

'What I don't understand,' Lestrade said, coming back from speaking with one of his men, 'is why remove the body from the studio at all? Why go to all that effort to have it found somewhere else, when the bloodstain and the murder weapon were at the crime scene, plain for anyone to see?'

Holmes said, 'Because the shaving was important. One would not do that at the scene of the crime, if only because of the delay it would introduce. We know the man had a vehicle waiting outside, and that might attract attention.'

I said, 'Not every murderer is as rational as you, Holmes. Perhaps the man just panicked and took the corpse with him, intending to come back and clear up later, but realised that that would be too great a risk. He tried to disguise it by shaving it, but then he feared that if the body were not recognised the hunt for Garforth would never let up. So, rather than have the police continuing the search, he arranged to have it found and hoped that would be an end to the matter. Of course it must have been someone who knew of Garforth's friendship with Rhyne, not a passing housebreaker.'

Lestrade said, 'Or else it *was* Rhyne, and he hoped to prove his innocence with this charade.'

'My dear inspector!' Holmes expostulated. 'Have you seen the man's feet? They are positively dainty.'

'A man can wear boots that are too big for him, Mr Holmes,' Lestrade said stubbornly. 'He just needs to put on enough socks.'

'That would mean the murder was premeditated,' I

objected. 'That wasn't how it seemed at the studio.'

'I'll grant you that,' the inspector said, 'but maybe that's all part of the same plan, to make it look like a different kind of crime than what it was.'

I said, 'I have difficulty imagining Talbot Rhyne even dragging the body. *He's* not a burly man, Lestrade.'

'Well, I'm not insisting it was so, just saying it might have been. We've let Mr Rhyne go for now, but I'll be keeping my eye on him all right.'

'What of the murderer's vehicle, Inspector?' Holmes asked. 'It must have been outside Garforth's studio for some minutes at the very least, and outside this warehouse for rather longer than that. Somewhere in London there is a coach or a cab or a tradesman's cart that is either smeared with three distinctive colours of paint, or has been very recently and thoroughly cleaned with turpentine.'

'Oh, we've been looking, you can be sure of that. There *was* a carriage found on fire in Leytonstone last night, but we're fairly sure the owner's just a careless smoker who fled to avoid being held responsible. We've impounded it just in case, but we haven't found any traces of paint yet, and I don't need to tell you how much more quickly turpentine would have made it burn. We've been making enquiries in Camden, of course, and tomorrow we'll start asking around here, too.'

The constables had begun by now to return to Lestrade to make their several reports. It seemed that nothing else in the warehouse had been disturbed, except by the rats, and no items found that might not be explained by the building's former occupancy. To Holmes's annoyance there was still no sign of Garforth's monocle.

It was but a few hours from sunrise when Holmes and I finally shared a cab home – or rather, to the temporarily inhospitable number 221B, from where I would walk to my club. As we alighted, Holmes remarked, 'I have now entirely recreated the structure from Garforth's studio, Watson. Would you care to come in and inspect it?'

'In the morning, gladly,' I told him. 'For now, I am afraid sleep calls.'

And with that I left him to his own devices, and returned to my fireplace and my bed.

Report of Dr Damocles Strye on Patient J.H., 1887

J.H. was committed to my care following a public outburst against an individual with whom he has developed an unfortunate preoccupation. His family report that, while he has mentioned this person, N.S., unfavourably over the years, the strength of his animosity against him and his delusions surrounding him have grown exceptionally strong over the past two, and they fear that if not contained they may express themselves in grievous and perhaps murderous violence against N.S. or others associated with him.

This opinion is one which, regrettably, I must endorse. J.H. converses lucidly on most topics, and with relative coherence even upon those which are touched by his delusion, but left to his own devices he returns repeatedly (in a manner typical of obsessive patients) to discourse at length on his erroneous beliefs, and the resentment he bears against N.S. is implacable and asserted in bellicose terms.

J.H.'s contention that N.S., with whom his relatives confirm he was at one time acquainted, has taken possession of his house and is now living in it is, they assure me, false. His conviction that N.S. cheated him out of a sum of money years ago is one which I would (speaking as a doctor and not as any authority on criminal matters) more readily assign to the realm of the possible, were it not for J.H.'s coexistent belief that N.S. achieved this through the operation of witchcraft, and that the same black arts underlie N.S.'s business practices wholesale. There is (as once again is common among obsessives) considerable elaboration as to the system by which these dark powers operate, the details of which hold a certain grotesque fascination but are irrelevant for diagnostic purposes.

If his infatuation had taken another object I might venture to suggest that J.H. should be protected from any chance sight or mention of that person, to test whether he is capable under such insulated circumstances of sustaining a normal life of no danger to others. Unfortunately, mention of N.S. is ubiquitous (in that his name routinely appears on a number of common household items), and it would be impossible to be confident of isolating J.H. from such stimuli outside the bounds of an institution such as this one.

I cannot therefore justify his release at this time, nor in the foreseeable future.

CHAPTER FOURTEEN

For a second time I was awoken by an insistent banging at the door, but a bleary glance at the clock admonished me that it was no longer night-time and that I should be abroad. Nor was the voice calling my name that of the club's steward; it belonged to Sherlock Holmes.

'Watson!' he cried. 'Lestrade has found the hansom cab!'

I dressed and joined him in the club's breakfast room. Holmes was far too excited to partake of the kippers, though, or the excellent kedgeree, preferring a pot of coffee and a cigarette.

'So it was a cab, then?' I asked.

'Indeed, my dear fellow. A brace of constables found it in a back-alley half a mile from the warehouse, without any sign of a horse. By now I would imagine the poor beast has been sold to a crooked dealer or a slaughterhouse. The vehicle has been impounded and is now at the Yard. As I predicted, the interior is positively smeared with paint and blood.'

'Well, that was hardly one of your more astounding predictions,' I told him with ill grace. 'But I'm glad Lestrade's found it. So our villain is a cabman, then?' I was reminded of the first case on which Holmes and I had worked together, the murder of Mr Enoch Drebber of Utah, with its strange and bloody aftermath.

'I would regard that as far from settled, Watson, though I gather the driver has been traced and constables sent to bring him in for questioning. The name he uses is Jonas Flatley, and unless that turns out to be a pseudonym he is not among the principals in our case. But this is one of the points you will need to verify.'

'I?' In my befuddled state I was unsure that I had heard him correctly.

'I have a certain matter to attend to, Watson,' he told me airily. 'The morning is a fine, clear one, and if it holds I should be able to spare my attention for other business by around luncheon. Can you summon me an errand-boy? I have an urgent telegram to send to one Inspector Utterthwaite of the West Riding Constabulary.'

Grumpily, I did as he asked, then retired to my room to shave before joining Lestrade at the Yard. As I applied my Speight's Accurate and Dependable Safety Razor – a present from my late wife Mary – to my chin, it occurred to me to wonder whether a skilled inventor might design a kind of razor that could remove most but not all of a man's hair, leaving behind a remnant so short as to give the impression of stubble, and if so whether it would be possible to discern the difference. I stepped out again, thinking to put the point to Holmes, but he had already left. Since Baker Street was so close I determined to call around after I finished my ablutions and ask his view on the matter before continuing to Scotland Yard.

I blinked my way through the dazzling streets; I had slept well past sunrise and it was, as Holmes had predicted, an unusually bright day.

I had forgotten that Mrs Hudson was away. To my surprise I was greeted in the hall at Baker Street by a small, grubby and untidy child who I eventually recognised as one of Holmes's Irregulars. Evidently, in our landlady's absence, he had turned to others for his household arrangements. Loud crashing noises from the kitchen suggested that this child's comrades might be attempting further feats of domestic service. I desperately hoped that Mrs Hudson was content at her sister's, and would not return unexpectedly.

Ransacking my memory eventually yielded the urchin's name. 'Hullo, Daphne,' I said to her. 'Is Mr Holmes in?'

'You're not to disturb him,' she told me solemnly. 'He said as you might want to, and as you wasn't to anyways, not on no account.'

'But what on earth is he doing?' I exclaimed. I felt that this really was the limit, that Holmes should not only bar me from my own rooms but detail a street child to give me the message.

'He says you can look, only don't go in and don't talk to him,' Daphne elaborated. 'He's got to constentrate, he says.'

'Well, I... I never did,' I retorted weakly.

I made my way up the stairs and found the sitting-room door ajar, with a cardboard sign tacked to it reading emphatically 'DO NOT DISTURB'. Silently I pushed it open a little and peered in.

Holmes was sitting on the floor in front of a huge wooden box, a cube around six feet to a side. It had been constructed neatly and with great care, evincing a facility with carpentry that I would not have imagined my friend to possess. Though the planks were still variously splashed with paint, they had been stained over again with pitch where the timbers met. The whole construction loomed like some heathen shrine, an impression reinforced by the way Holmes faced it, his legs arranged in the lotus shape, his hands spread palms upward upon his knees. Arranged thus in such an attitude of prayer or meditation or who-knew-what, with his hawkish nose and high brow outlined by the light from the windows, he looked the very image of an Indian fakir of the kind that featured in Major Bradbury's inexhaustible fund of stories, got up in Western garb.

'What in heaven's name are you doing, Holmes?' I hissed at him, but he ignored me austerely. Despite my irritation and my curiosity, his prohibition against interrupting him, as relayed by Daphne and the sign, were so very definite that I did not dare interfere further. Shaking my head and hoping that I would not need to arrange a trip to an asylum at any point in the near future, I descended the stairs again and set out for Scotland Yard.

There I found Lestrade awaiting the cabman Flatley. The inspector seemed surprised and a little put out to see me rather than Holmes. 'It's always a pleasure, Dr Watson,' he said, 'but I'd thought Mr Holmes was taking a personal interest in this case.'

'He's still busy with that object from the studio. He has rebuilt it, but evidently he has… further investigations to make. I'm sure it will prove to be crucial one way or another to the solution of the mystery,' I optimistically asserted.

'Well, Mr Holmes's methods are his own,' Lestrade said grudgingly, 'and I won't deny they get results. If only he wasn't so infernally secretive about them, and so dashed pleased with himself afterwards.'

Old and trusted colleague though Lestrade was, it felt disloyal to be discussing Holmes in this way, so I changed the subject. 'What do we know of this Flatley fellow, then?'

Lestrade puffed out his lips and blew. 'The cove lives in Whitechapel, I understand. He's been a cabby for thirteen years and has never been in trouble with the law. If he's suddenly decided to turn murderer now, he must have had pretty good reason.'

Flatley, when he was brought in, proved to be a fellow of about thirty, with a quick tongue but a rather surly look, especially when addressed by Lestrade or any other policeman. He was insistent that the police had no right to keep his cab from him, and was also demanding compensation for the loss of his horse.

'Now see here, my man,' said Lestrade, 'you're lucky we've found your cab at all. If you go along with our enquiries and we're satisfied with what you have to say, well, maybe you can have it back when you're done with it. As for your horse, I doubt any of us will be seeing him again, except perhaps in a rissole.'

'Her name's Joanna,' Flatley said truculently. 'It was my auntie's name.'

'Well, sonny, it would've been a miracle if she hadn't vanished seeing as how she was left unattended in Limehouse. Perhaps you can tell me how that came to happen.'

Flatley stared dubiously at me, and Lestrade said, 'This gentleman is Dr Watson. He's helping us out with our enquiries, see? Now you'd better start talking, my lad, and make no bones of it.'

I could see that my name meant as little to Flatley as his to me. He was a small, dark cockney with the muscular arms of his profession. Though of course I must have encountered many hundreds of London cabbies, and taken little note of their appearance, I did not think that I had ever seen him before.

Flatley said sullenly, 'It was stolen, wasn't it? Yesterday morning it was, Wednesday. I left Joey on her own with the hansom for a few minutes while I stepped into the Joker's Arms on Bellinger Street to pick up a pot of ale – for later, you see, 'cause I wouldn't never drink on duty and that's God's honest truth – and when I come out again she was gone. Nothing to do with me where the cab ended up after that. Did it get used to do crimes, then?'

I thought he was rather quick to jump to that conclusion, and I could see that Lestrade was also suspicious. He asked, 'Did you see the man that took it?'

Flatley considered carefully. 'I reckon maybe I did. There was this bloke leaning up against the wall of the Joker's when I arrived. Big fellow he was, built like a docker, but he had glasses on and a little beard, like a gent. I reckon it was him.'

'How old? How was he dressed?' Lestrade asked.

'A bit younger than me, I reckon. He had on ordinary working clothes, tweed jacket and trousers like you'd wear for any rough job.'

'Hair colour?' Lestrade demanded. 'Eyes?'

Flatley looked nervous suddenly. 'Well, I didn't get close enough to see his eyes, 'specially with those specs on. Dark hair, though, like his beard.'

'What sort of accent did he have?'

'It was – Look, I don't know, I didn't talk to him, did I? I told you, he was just leaning up against the wall of the pub, waiting to waltz off with someone's horse and hansom cab. What did he do with it, anyway? Why are you talking to me about this?'

Lestrade leaned back and folded his arms. 'Ah, but you've told us a lot about him, Flatley. A lot more than you'd have noticed if you'd just walked past him in the street like that. You talked to him, didn't you? So what was his accent like?'

'Well, I s'pose I might have passed the time of day, like. He didn't sound like he was from around here. Not foreign, though. Scottish, maybe? I didn't ask.'

'But you had a proper conversation with him, didn't you?' Lestrade insisted. 'More than just passing the time of day. You had long enough to hear what he sounded like and take note of his hair and clothes. Long enough to get some ideas about what he might be planning to do with your cab, too. Isn't that right, my man?'

Flatley sighed. 'All right, peeler,' he said. 'All right. Cards on the table, then. Yes, I spoke to the bloke and yes, we talked about the cab. He might have mentioned that he had a use for it, like, and I might have said something like, "It's more than I can afford to lend it to you, I could lose my licence that way." And he might've said something like, "How about if I borrowed it while you was looking the other way, and brought it back here later? I'd only need it an hour, and there's fifteen shillings in it for you."'

'Fifteen shillings?' Lestrade whistled appreciatively. 'You could buy a new nag for that.'

'Not a decent one, I can't. Not like my Joanna. Besides, I drank half of it last night when I realised the bloke wasn't going to bring my cab back. What did he do with it, mister? I'll kill him when I see him, running off with my Joey and treating her like that.'

'We'll have no threats of violence, my lad,' Lestrade said. 'Remember you're in a police station. It would be no trouble at all to book you in and throw you in a cell. Especially since it looks like your cab was used in a murder.'

'Coo!' Flatley seemed excited to learn this. 'That'll be one to tell the lads. Who was it what got offed, then?'

'Excuse me,' I said, and left them to continue without me. It was perfectly apparent that Flatley was guilty of nothing more nefarious than a willingness to bend the rules to make some ready cash. It was also quite clear that Lestrade had always been capable of conducting this interview on his own. It was, after all, his profession, and the man was quite in his element.

I wondered whether Holmes had been expecting some more significant revelation to emerge, but for the life of me I could not think of what it might be. Flatley's description of the 'thief' did not match anybody else in the case – not Rhyne nor Skinner, who were young but not burly; not Kellway nor Garforth, who were burly but not young; not Beech nor Kingsley, who were bearded but matched none of the other points; not Anderton nor Small, who were fat and not tall; and not Sir Newnham, who was far too elderly. Evidently whoever it was had employed an intermediary, as they had when they delivered Garforth's purported message to Rhyne.

I wondered whether the reason for my presence was simpler still – Holmes was, he had insisted, frantically busy on whatever work he was still doing with Garforth's peculiar indoor shed, so perhaps he simply wanted me out of his way for the morning. For the sake of my own feelings I hoped that this was not the case, but it would not have been entirely uncharacteristic of my friend at the times when he was most preoccupied with a mystery.

Determined that I should prove my worth regardless, I asked the desk sergeant whether I might inspect Flatley's cab. It was the same man who had been on duty in the small hours, and he remembered me. He cheerfully assigned a constable to show me the way through to the stables.

In the yard, next to the burned-out wreck of the carriage found in Leytonstone, was an ordinary black hansom cab, considerably the worse for its sojourn in the slums of Limehouse. A window had been smashed, the paint was scratched, and not only the horse but all her harness and tack were missing. The interior presented an altogether more grisly picture.

We had all expected the paint – the same blue, green and white as I had already seen on Garforth's studio floor, his steps and his trousers – but even I had not realised that there would be quite so much blood. Evidently the painter had still been bleeding profusely when he had been loaded into the hansom. Whether his assailant knew it or not, his victim had not been dead, though I had no hopes that he would have regained consciousness. Certainly there had been no blood at the warehouse, meaning that Garforth had been dead by the time he arrived there.

Further inspection quickly established that this was where Garforth's body had been shaved for the second time. A myriad of small flecks of grey stubble adhered to all the paint stains, and were scattered liberally over the seats as well, particularly in one corner. The razor was nowhere in evidence, but the murderer could easily have cast it into a soil-heap, or the Thames, after abandoning the cab.

Having satisfied myself as to the condition of the visible surfaces, I lay down gingerly on the floor, doing my best to avoid the smeared paint and congealed blood, and peered beneath the seats, where I had already noticed something faintly glinting. I reached beneath the corner where the largest quantity of hair had been heaped, and with a cry of triumph retrieved – not the razor, but Garforth's monocle.

The frame was of cheap metal, plated with silver, and attached to a smart black ribbon. I examined it carefully for any inscription. There was none, nor could I gather anything from the occasional scratches to the lens and housing. Holmes might be able to deduce a man's vices from the marks on his pocket-watch, but I was not Holmes. Emerging from the cab, I held the glass up to my right eye, and frowned.

My view of the stable-yard around me was completely undistorted. There was none of the bending and thickening of the image that characterised, for instance, the windows in Sir Newnham's Experiment Rooms, or any ordinary pair of spectacles. The glass in this monocle had no optical properties at all. It would be useless as a corrective for anybody's eyesight.

I remembered Holmes's observation that the canvases in Garforth's studio were not real paintings, nor even forgeries, but objects intended to give the impression of paintings. It seemed that Garforth's monocle was likewise a mere facsimile of a monocle. It was the kind of accoutrement I might have expected to be worn on stage by an actor.

Did Garforth wear it purely as an affectation, I wondered? An artist might do such a thing, I supposed, if he wished to cultivate a particular impression. In any case, Holmes had thought the monocle would be significant, and that meant that this information was important to him. It was time for me to return and make my report.

I stopped by Lestrade's desk, and he related cheerfully that he had let Flatley go for now, with a threat of misconduct proceedings hanging over his licence. 'To keep him to heel,' the inspector explained. 'Unless we turn up something new, though, I think we'll leave him be. He made a stupid mistake and he's suffering for it. He's proper cut up about that nag of his.'

I gave him an account of what I had discovered, and left the monocle in his keeping, with a suggestion to search for the razor in the area near where the cab had been found. I then returned again to Baker Street, determined this time that Holmes would pay attention to the important questions in hand.

'Two gents was here,' Daphne revealed as I arrived. 'Sir Newting Something and Mr Turbot Something Else. They wanted to talk to Mr Holmes. When I said as he wasn't to be disturbed on no account – what he still isn't, in case you was wondering – they wanted to talk to you.'

'Sir Newnham Speight and Mr Talbot Rhyne?' I asked in alarm. I could only imagine the impression Holmes's unconventional new pageboy must have given those two worthy gentlemen. 'Did they tell you where they were going?'

'I said they couldn't wait in the sitting room 'cause that was where Mr Holmes was, and he wasn't to be disturbed on no account, and besides it was full of his old tat. And Mrs Hudson's rooms are just a little bit sooty just now, 'cause of how Pete reckoned as he could remember how to sweep a chimbley. So I said as they could wait in that tea-shop what's just round the corner.'

'Thank you, Daphne,' I said, passing her a penny. I should have realised that Holmes would have left a relatively sensible child in charge, though I shuddered at her description of Mrs Hudson's sitting room. 'I'll go and see them now. Did they say what it was they wanted?'

'They said,' Daphne informed me importantly, 'as how Mr Kettley's turned up, and he's round Mr Bleach's house right now.'

Excerpt from *Discoverer of the Esoteric Wisdoms: A Life of Her Illustrious Highness the Countess Irina Grigoriyevna Brusilova* (1920) by Callum Carpenter

Irina's acceptance into London society had not been free from obstacles. Her manner, though not as tantalisingly enigmatic as it would become in later years, was found by her contemporaries to be oblique, a quality that in conjunction with her faltering English was sometimes uncharitably taken for rudeness. Though assured by her nobility of entry into the highest levels of society, she was also at the mercy of the English prejudice that saw Russians as uncivilised, a view that would mellow only somewhat with the Tsar's visit to England in 1874. Her wholly innovative explorations of the arcane were thus often mistaken by the ignorant for the backward superstitions of her mother country.

Of greater personal import, however, were the malicious rumours begun in early 1873 by one Captain Ivan Viktorovich Kotovsky, newly arrived in London. After being introduced to Irina at one of Arkady Garbuzov's receptions, Kotovsky impudently announced to all who would listen that Irina was, if not a fraud as a medium, then certainly no true Countess. He impertinently insisted that he had known her and her family in Smolensk in the Sixties, that they were mere servants working in his uncle's household, and that her account of her noble descent, her education in Moscow and St Petersburg and her tragic widowhood were pernicious fabrications.

A gallant protector but always a cautious one, Garbuzov tried gently and discreetly to discover whether there might be any truth underlying these rumours, but his contacts in

Smolensk failed to make contact with the family Kotovsky had described. They reported that the family had moved away some time before, leaving only a senile uncle behind, and they could never be traced.

Captain Kotovsky's perfidy sowed grave distrust of Irina among the city's expatriate Russian community, which had always been excessively conscious of class politics. At the same time, though, thanks to a succession of revelations in her private séances, which would culminate in her defining vision of Hy-Brasil in March 1874, Irina's reputation among the metropolis's home-grown occultists and esotericists had grown sufficiently that she no longer needed to call so often upon the dubious support of her unreliable countrymen.

CHAPTER FIFTEEN

At Harrington's I found Sir Newnham and Rhyne waiting for me in a booth, with a nearly empty pot of tea and a plate mostly denuded of scones. I saw that the younger man's face was still drawn, exhibiting traces of the shock and dismay it had displayed in Lestrade's office in the early hours. I remembered that Holmes and I had a number of questions to ask Mr Rhyne, not least about his acquaintance with Frederick Garforth, but for the moment it seemed there were more pressing matters.

Sir Newnham's visage mostly betrayed his irritation. 'Thank you for coming, Dr Watson,' he told me, politely enough. 'I admit, though, that it was Mr Holmes who I was most hoping to see. Indeed I must confess that I've been increasingly disappointed in his conduct of this case. As a reader of your reminiscences I understand that he has certain eccentricities, and that is perfectly understandable – the same is true of other associates of mine, as you have had ample opportunity to observe – but when I engage a person's services I do expect them to be available for consultation during reasonable business hours. I do not expect to be fobbed off by a small girl with an instruction to await his associate's pleasure at my own expense.'

'I can only apologise, Sir Newnham,' I told him.

'I do not blame you for his peccadilloes, of course – Mr Holmes is his own man if he is anything. Nevertheless, I trust you understand the reasons for my displeasure. The matter at hand has become most urgent, and I have at present no indication of when Mr Holmes is liable to spare it his attention.'

'When Holmes is preoccupied by an idea he becomes quite single-minded, and he can occasionally forget social niceties.' I was aware that this was the second time today I had been called upon to justify my friend's absence, and I wished I knew enough to be more reassuring. 'I can promise you, however, that whatever has his attention at the moment will be germane to the case, and may even prove decisive in solving it,' I concluded, fervently hoping that this would prove true. 'I gather there have been developments since we last spoke.'

'There certainly have been; grave developments. It seems highly likely that I will be forced to give ten thousand pounds of the Society's money to an obvious fraud, and become the laughing stock of the scientific world. That the whole affair is a fabrication is more transparent than ever, yet the majority of the Society Committee appear to support it. Beech, Floke and the Countess present a united front, and just as I feared they have induced Mr Small to go along with them.'

'Small? But he believes Kellway is a fraud, and he and Beech loathe each other. Oh… now I see. Beech told me he would ask Skinner to leave Small alone, but he must have placed a condition on the favour. That odious man!' I exclaimed. 'I should have realised he capitulated too easily.' I supposed this had been Beech's intent all along in suggesting Small's guilt to Skinner, and for that matter to Holmes.

'The Society's promise must be honoured, of course,' Speight lamented. 'After that I shall have no choice but to resign my Chairmanship and my entire interest, in protest. To distance myself from the entire debacle will be the only way to salvage my reputation. I fear this is a play for power on Beech's part; he covets the Society for himself, it seems, and if he must embarrass me to achieve it, then so be it.'

I said, 'Perhaps you should tell me from the beginning what has happened, Sir Newnham. I was only told that Mr Kellway has returned.'

Speight and Rhyne exchanged a dubious look. 'That's the contention, Dr Watson,' Rhyne said. 'As Sir Newnham says, it appears on the face of it ridiculous. And yet...'

Sir Newnham gave a cry of despair, to the consternation of the other customers. 'If that man is Thomas Kellway, then I am the late Prince Albert, returned from the grave.'

I was shocked at this disrespect for royal persons from a man who had been appointed a knight of the realm by the Queen herself. 'Nevertheless,' I said, 'it would be helpful to have an account of the events in order...'

'Oh, very well,' Sir Newnham groaned. 'We received a message from Gideon Beech, early this morning. He said nothing about Kellway's return, but intimated that he had solved the mystery of his disappearance, and would reveal the truth to the Society Committee at ten o'clock.

'We hurried over there, naturally, and found Gerald Floke, the Countess Brusilova and Miss Casimir already in attendance along with Beech. Professor Scaverson has gone up to Camford to deliver a lecture, but Mr Small and Dr Kingsley joined us very shortly afterwards.'

'Can the Professor vote in absentia?' I asked.

'Alas, no, the rules preclude it. Though I fear his vote would avail little in any case.'

'This wasn't a formal committee meeting, you understand,' Rhyne explained. 'Only the Chairman can call those. Instead

Beech said that he'd assembled us to tell us his solution to the mystery. Constantine Skinner was there, too, but from the way he was sulking I don't think he had much to do with it. Beech claimed all the glory, of course.'

'He assembled us in the drawing room, with all his usual pomposity,' Speight went on. 'Then he delivered a lengthy monologue to us, like those interminable prefaces he appends to his published plays. After a long preamble about the Will of Life and how it pertained to Evolved Men, he rehearsed what we all already knew of the events occurring on the night of the experiment, and then got to the meat of his pronouncement.

'He explained that Kellway had recently been in touch with him, and had requested his assistance in collecting the reward money for the very clear demonstration of phenomena beyond the ordinary, namely his disappearance. "At first," Beech told us, "and for reasons which I feel sure will not elude you over the coming hour, I betrayed my good judgement by entertaining certain intellectual doubts that my correspondent was indeed Thomas Kellway, but he has answered all my questions very satisfactorily and you may all take it as a settled fact that he is indeed the same man."' Sir Newnham's impression of Beech's voice was rather good, and I smiled a little.

'By now, I'm sure you can imagine, we were getting rather impatient for him to come to the point,' Rhyne put in. 'At least, Sir Newnham and I were. I had the impression that Floke and Miss Casimir, at least, knew what was coming.'

'I have reason to believe that they did,' I said. 'Please continue, though.'

'Well, I asked him to come to the point. I said something like, "Whatever do you mean? Surely this person's either Kellway or he isn't?" And Beech gave that infuriating grin of his, and one of his servants ushered in the fellow he was talking about.

'He looks a lot like Thomas Kellway, I'll give him that – the resemblance is quite uncanny, in fact. I've no idea how or where Beech found him. He was quite bald, and just as big and muscular as the real Kellway. But – well, as I've told you, Kellway looks to be in his early fifties. This fellow isn't even half that age.'

'Good heavens!' I exclaimed. 'But however did Beech think that he could pass a young man off as Kellway?'

'When Sir Newnham says the resemblance is uncanny, Dr Watson,' said Rhyne, 'if anything he understates the case. Set the difference in age aside, and the pair could be twins.'

'But why on earth would you set it aside?' I expostulated. 'That alone makes the contention insupportable.'

'You say "on earth", Doctor, but...' began Talbot Rhyne, but such was Sir Newnham's agitation that he spoke quite rudely over his subordinate.

'This was perfectly obvious to me as well, Dr Watson, but it seems that Gideon Beech would indict us both for having insufficiently open minds. To his credit, the young fellow puts on quite the performance – he has Kellway's voice, accent and mannerisms down just as well as his appearance. He greeted us by name as he arrived, as perfectly naturally as if he had seen us but a few days previously. He spoke knowledgeably about the Society, and the details of the experiment. I could see that young Floke was entranced, and I might even have said that Beech was taken in as well, were his interests in the matter not so evident.'

'Beech must have coached him to say the right things.' I nodded. 'When did Beech say he had arrived?'

'Yesterday, at around lunchtime,' Rhyne said. 'Beech told us he wanted to be sure of his identity before showing him to the rest of the Society.'

'Well, he was showing him to some of them yesterday, I'm sure of it.' And I told them what I had seen and heard at Beech's townhouse. 'You must be right that this is a plot to take control of the Society from you, Sir Newnham. Without your level-headed presence at the wheel, Beech could allow the wilder excesses of the members' beliefs their full rein. It would become a vehicle for his bizarre personal religion, and all your scientific work could be wasted.' Sir Newnham groaned, and I carried on more tactfully. 'It's plain that the man is both ambitious and amoral. What isn't clear is whether he planned it all along, perhaps with Kellway's connivance, or whether he's merely taking advantage of an unexpected circumstance.'

'With Beech it could be either,' Speight admitted ruefully. 'The way his conceit exaggerates his genius works leads many to underestimate him, but he is a genuinely clever man. Indeed, I wonder whether he contrives his public personality to provoke just that response.'

'I still can't see why he thought you would accept a different man as Kellway,' I said. 'Did the fellow have any explanation for such a remarkable rejuvenation?'

'Indeed, though it was a lengthy one. Rhyne, may I have my notes?'

Rhyne fished out some hastily scrawled papers from his briefcase and handed them to Speight. (I was able later to take possession of these, and I have since supplemented them with notes found in the Yorkshireman's own hand, detailing his story. I can thus be fairly sure that what follows reproduces with a reasonable degree of accuracy what he told the assembled group at Beech's house.)

'"My friends," he began,' said Sir Newnham, doing a creditable imitation of a Yorkshire accent, '"since last you saw me I have made an astonishing journey, to the place that is the source of all my enlightenment, past and future. You shake your heads at the change you perceive in me, and believe me I understand your bewilderment, for it is a transformation I myself can scarce credit. And yet it is the truth.

"'For as you have suspected I have been on Venus, the sphere that first created me, an Evolved Man, whose intelligences have cultivated me from afar in the service of evolution and of the Will of Life. The meditations which I carried out towards the culmination of your little experiment brought me, instead, to the very culmination of my time on earth. There was no more that I could achieve here, without first having unmediated communion with my Venusian principals, and so they removed me to their own sphere.

"'There I have embarked upon the second phase of my enlightenment: one which has entailed intense physical and mental training, and which has lasted for many years.'"

'Years?' I said, interrupting Sir Newnham's flow. 'But this story becomes ever more absurd. If this man were indeed Kellway, then he would have only been away for a few days.'

Talbot Rhyne grinned rather mischievously. 'Sir Newnham interrupted him to make that very point, quite forcefully. You waxed quite lyrical about it, Sir Newnham.'

Speight looked a little embarrassed. 'Well, I was furious at how gullible he must believe us to be – though of course the confounded fellow hasn't been proven wrong on that score. And of course he had an answer ready to my question. I suppose it was so obvious that I should hardly have expected otherwise.

'He said, "One of the things I learned on Venus was that time moves differently on different worlds. Like Life, of which it is merely an aspect, Time pours in a torrent from the great sun of our local universe, and trickles out across the worlds, from fleeting Mercury to slow old Neptune. Because Venus is closer to the sun than our Earth, time flows more quickly there. Had I instead visited Mars, I might have returned here believing that it was just a day or so later, to find instead that years had passed. As I have been on Venus, while from your point of view I may have been absent for a mere three days, I have experienced a span closer to the measure of three decades.

"'However,'" he said, "'thanks to my Venusian principals and the exceptional spiritual techniques they have cultivated – techniques which affect the body also, because spirit and body are one – for every day I spent there by my own reckoning, instead of ageing I grew a day younger. By the count of the days I have lived, I am now eighty years old, my friends, and yet I have the youth and vigour of a stripling in his twenties. That is the reason you find me so changed, but I know that from my manner and my voice – why, from my very face, free of its wrinkles and the work of earthly time and care upon my features – you will know me nonetheless as your friend – by your reckoning, your very recently vanished friend – Thomas Kellway.'"

'Then, if you'll believe the gall of the man, he explained that the return journey had so exhausted his reserves of psychical energy that he had none left to demonstrate the many thoroughly miraculous new abilities he had acquired while among the Venusians, though he could describe them at length. When we left, the others were all clamouring to ask him further questions about his experiences. A more unconscionable and blatant fabrication I have never heard, and yet Beech has them all believing it.

'Floke is delighted to have his idol back – and so much closer to his own age, making the imitation of him all the easier. The Countess is pleased – or at least, Miss Casimir assured us she was – because the impostor confirmed the name of Palú-Odranel, her mediumistic contact on the planet, as one of his Venusian tutors… thanks, no doubt, to Beech's coaching. Now that this has been corroborated, Miss Casimir has high hopes of the Countess channelling further Venusian wisdom in future séances, with hefty attendance fees of course. Mr Small gave his support rather wanly, but spoke of biblical sanction for the idea of life on other worlds and speculated that Venus might be an unfallen world, untainted by the sin of Adam.

'And Beech, of course, takes the whole business as the most magnificent vindication of his evolutionary philosophies – though I am quite convinced that he, at least, is acting in the worst possible faith.'

I said, 'Will not your further investigations, with the repeated experiments and the testing of hypotheses, prove that this false Kellway has none of the psychical capacities he claims? That he is in fact a baseless fraud?'

Rhyne said, 'Oh, undoubtedly, if he sticks around. That doesn't seem likely, though. He's perfectly within his rights to take the money and go.'

'He'll go back to his own name, grow his hair back and never be identified,' Sir Newnham predicted gloomily. 'Beech will get the Society to reshape as he wishes, Skinner can claim a successfully concluded case, the Countess and Miss Casimir get a whole new story for gulling the public, and Floke and his clique... well, they'll probably believe Kellway's ascended to Venus again. They'll have built a church to him by the end of the century.'

'I have to say this is one of the most outlandish cases that Holmes and I have been embroiled in,' I mused, 'not excepting those involving gigantic rats, hounds and cormorants. Aside from explaining Kellway's original vanishing, I'm completely baffled as to why, if this whole situation is a hoax – whether it started out as an attempt to take control of the Society, or merely to claim the reward money – he has not appeared himself to deliver the *coup de grace*, rather than sending this young proxy in his stead. It appears that it will be effective, but it could have fatally weakened the conspirators' case.'

Speight shuddered. 'My only thought on that score, Dr Watson, and it is a sordid one, is that the trick was one that could only be carried off by killing Kellway and somehow smuggling out his body. Holmes joked about his having left in small pieces through the window, and perhaps that is what happened. Perhaps the original Kellway was a harmless madman, despicably taken advantage of and done away with by a ruthless group of conspirators. And yet, despite my low opinion of the man, I find it hard to imagine Gideon Beech resorting to cold-blooded murder. He thinks too highly of himself for that.'

Privately I agreed with Sir Newnham on that point, but I felt that I should prepare him for disappointment. 'I have learned,' I said, 'that men who might present the most harmless fronts to the world are capable of hatching devilish plots against their own children, whilst those whom one might believe utterly without compunction can display the most unexpected scruples. But this is Holmes's area of expertise, and I'll see he's told of these latest developments. I shall ask him to discuss the matter with you as soon as can be managed.'

Sir Newnham said, 'I have arranged for the Society to convene at four o'clock at Parapluvium House, with this purported Kellway present, so that the matter can be decided; though I fear the Committee's minds are made up and that any discussion of the matter will be a travesty. Four o'clock, Dr Watson. I would very much appreciate it if Mr Holmes could join us there. Come, Rhyne, we should go home and prepare.'

'You go on ahead, Sir Newnham,' Rhyne suggested. 'I have to place an order with Cavendish's, for those electrical components you were wanting. The specifications are complicated, and it's a short walk to Oxford Street. I'll join you by four.'

The three of us parted our ways, and I returned thoughtfully to 221B Baker Street, where a small boy was energetically beating the hall-carpet on the front steps.

'Is Mr Holmes in... Danny?' I hazarded.

'I'm Ronnie, sir,' the boy told me cheerily. 'Yes, sir. He's upstairs, sir, and he said as you was to come right up.'

I thanked him, tipped him a halfpenny, and left him to his task. Though his zeal was commendable, he was using a broom rather than a beater, and one which by the looks of it had recently been used to sweep up the excess soot released into Mrs Hudson's room, so that the overall effect was not one of improved cleanliness.

Upstairs I found Holmes pacing back and forth as best he could in the constrained space, and chuckling to himself as he smoked his pipe. 'My dear fellow!' he cried when he saw me, with an air of extreme good humour. 'I am delighted to see you home at last. I have cracked it, Watson – I know how the thing was done, and what's more I have done it myself. The crucial thing in science is that the results of an experiment should be reproducible, as Sir Newnham would tell us if he were here.'

'He *was* here,' I said, a little sourly. 'As was I. I can't say I approve of your new staffing arrangements, Holmes. I can only hope they're short-lived.'

'Ah! Well, that too is an experiment, of a different kind,' he said jovially. 'Though perhaps it is one which we might venture not to repeat, once Mrs Hudson has returned home.'

'If she can be persuaded to return home, after the chaos those wretched imps have wreaked here,' I replied gloomily. I told him of what Lestrade and I had learned from Jonas Flatley, and of my discoveries in the hansom cab, and gave him the best summary I could of all I had learned from Speight about Kellway's miraculous return, its ramifications for the Society and its implications for Sir Newnham himself. Recounting all the details required some elaboration, and by the time I had finished our four o'clock appointment at Parapluvium House was fast approaching.

'Capital, Watson!' exclaimed Holmes after I had told him everything. 'A most satisfactory account, my dear fellow. It seems that we may expect a persuasive resolution to this matter shortly. I must say I am delighted by this new appearance of Kellway's, though I confess I have been expecting something of the kind.'

'Kellway's emerging to claim the money is what this case has been lacking from the beginning,' I agreed, 'but I can't say I expected an impostor to arrive in his place.'

'That is because you have not been paying sufficient attention, my dear Watson. Some representation by proxy was inevitable, although it has taken a most stimulating form.'

'I am glad that you find it so,' I told him. 'I'm afraid Sir Newnham is less sanguine, particularly about your approach to the case. He's also most exercised about this imminent Committee vote.'

'I hardly think it will come to that, Watson. Still, we must away to Parapluvium House at once, naturally. Pray be so kind as to have one of the Irregulars hail a cab for us. You may also ask them to dismantle this,' he said, waving a dismissive hand at the structure which had so dominated his attention over the past day. 'That is perhaps a task better suited to their talents than those they have been attempting of late. They should bundle the whole lot up for dispatch to Inspector Lestrade, care of Scotland Yard. It may be required as evidence at the trial.'

'There'll be a trial, then?' I asked, but Holmes merely waved me away.

I went downstairs and found a small clutch of children surrounding a raw fowl that must have been delivered by the butcher's boy. One of them was saying, 'My mum always boils ours in beer, with the greens. D'you think we should stuff it first, or after?'

Mrs Hudson's larder-door stood open, and when they realised I was present the children all gazed at me with guilty faces and tried to hide marzipan-sticky hands. I told them supper would not be required that evening, and sent Ronnie to summon a cab.

By the time I had explained their other task, Holmes had joined me, wearing a jacket which it took me a moment to place as the one that Kellway had left behind in the Experiment Room.

'Well, Watson,' he said, brandishing a cane that I recognised as Frederick Garforth's. 'Our carriage awaits, and so does the Evolved Man. It seems we are all set for the end of our first interplanetary adventure.'

Second Excerpt from *Discoverer of the Esoteric Wisdoms* by Carpenter

Kristina Casimir, the young German woman who would become Irina's constant companion during this late phase of her earthly existence, first appeared in her life in June 1893. She attended a séance given by Irina at Francesco Ribisi's London townhouse, as a guest of Ribisi's friend Mariella van Houten. Ribisi had been pioneering a use of an early form of the Ouija board, and asserted that through it he had been receiving a series of spectral dictations, which would later form the basis of his book *The Seven Worlds Within Our Own*.

Since her stroke, Irina had become physically frail and more than usually elliptical in her speech, and she probably hoped that this new technique might allow her to automate some elements of her mediumistic practice. Despite her normal reluctance to embrace novel approaches, she sat as a full participant in the séance and, much to the surprise of all present, received what appeared to be a number of unusually clear communications from a spirit calling itself 'Hanuman', the name that had earlier been revealed to her as that of the last High Hierarch of Hy-Brasil. She would later publish these in a pamphlet entitled 'New (Old) Revelations from the Hindmost Keeper of the Inner Lantern', with the help of Kristina Casimir, whom the messages had explicitly instructed her to choose for the task.

According to her own statements, Casimir came from Coblenz, from an academic family who had encouraged her intelligence and desire for learning as long as they followed a conventional course, but had been scandalised at her burgeoning interest in esotericism. She had, she always stated, made use of an independent income left to her by an aunt to emigrate to England, hoping to join the circles of occultists surrounding the famous Countess Brusilova.

The reader should know that Casimir is a divisive influence among the followers of Brusilovan Wisdom, and there have been many who disbelieve this account of her origins, suggesting that she was a fraudulent occultist, perhaps of British birth, who used this false background to insinuate herself into Irina's confidence. Certainly much interest has been taken in the mechanics of the séance at which her services were recommended to Irina, and the question of how far one of the participants might have been able to direct the planchette's movement on the board.

CHAPTER SIXTEEN

We were ushered into the drawing room at Parapluvium House to find that most of those involved with the case were already present. While Holmes had a quiet word with Anderton, who stood in attendance, I greeted Sir Newnham, who stood uncomfortably by the window, looking quite isolated in his own domain.

'I am glad to see Mr Holmes here at last,' he told me, sincerely. 'I can only pray that his presence is not too late.'

I scanned the room. Dr Kingsley stood at a discreet distance from his host, with an air of clinical detachment whose underlying sentiments I could not read. The gigantic Norwegian, whose name I supposed I now had little chance of discovering, was moodily staring out of the window. Countess Brusilova sat on a wicker chair next to him, temporarily abandoned by Miss Casimir. The latter had joined a group being held court to by Gideon Beech, including Constantine Skinner, Gerald Floke and two others, equally shaven. For a moment I supposed that one of them might be the false Kellway, but both were slight, weak-chinned specimens like Floke himself, one of whom wore eyeglasses, giving the lie to any suggestion of superior evolutionary development. Vortigern Small, who sidled up to me immediately, pointed them out to me as Felix Herrisham and Lord St Andrews.

The clergyman had a fretful look on his face. 'Dr Watson, might I beseech a word? The vote – that is to say, Mr Beech – intolerable, of course – I very much regret...'

'It isn't likely to come to that, Mr Small,' I told him, hoping that Holmes had been right to say so. 'Holmes expects a conclusion to this affair quite soon.'

'I see. Well... that is excellent, of course.' Small sounded rather doubtful. 'But if I may ask... a conclusion of what nature?'

'That,' I said wearily, 'is for Sherlock Holmes alone to know, for now. The rest of us can only wait to be instructed.'

Major Bradbury, who I had seen briefly in the hallway as we arrived, now rejoined the group in the drawing room. Unlike Skinner, Miss Casimir and the bald young men – and, I supposed, Holmes and myself – he appeared to be the guest of no particular Committee member, but I supposed he had as much right as anybody else here to learn the outcome of the experiment.

Holmes finished talking to Anderton, who left the room quietly, and strode over to speak to Sir Newnham. Before he could reach him, however, Gideon Beech clapped his hands and called for silence. 'Ladies,' he declared, beaming at Miss Casimir, 'and also, regrettably, gentlemen. You all know for what momentous reason we are here, and how it is that I have become the humble stimulus for such a happening. By the grace of all the divinities that shape our evolutionary ends, for the first time in this Society's otherwise insipid history we have in our midst the living proof of a miracle defying all the pusillanimous strictures and shibboleths of our conventional science.'

I will not weary you, my patient reader, with all that issued from the playwright's mouth along these lines. Suffice to say that Kellway's reappearance was, in his view, an unprecedented prodigy certain to rewrite all the annals of science, metaphysics and theology in favour of the religion of the Will of Life, and that among the myriad outcomes of this revision, one of the most profound and satisfying would be the increased prominence, in all these histories, of Gideon Beech, Esquire.

Eventually he said, 'But all of this depends on acquiring through the stagnant channels of authority sufficient authentication of this miracle to convey its validity to the honest British public, with their servile deference to any self-appointed expert. And so we must, in the plodding habit of the English – honouring your exceptional presence by tactful omission, ladies – vote on the matter in Committee, so that the respectable formalities can be observed. To which end—'

'Oh, for God's sake get on with it, Beech!' cried Major Bradbury, who had been listening with increasing restlessness and who now at last lost all semblance of restraint. 'Damn it man, call in Kellway and let's all have a look at him!'

Beech gave an aggrieved smile. 'Very well, Major. I have been attempting to prepare you for the historic nature of what you are about to see, but if you have not the patience for that, then so be it. Miss Casimir, if you would…?'

Demurely, the Countess's companion left the room for a moment, then returned, leading a young man in an awkwardly fitting suit. Though bald, he was built to a far more formidable frame than Floke and his cronies. I had heard Thomas Kellway described so many times by now that this younger individual, with his remarkable resemblance to somebody I had never even seen, looked hauntingly familiar. Certainly Speight's account of Kellway's magnetic personality applied equally to this man, to whom every eye was drawn as he entered the room. Despite his pleasant demeanour, something about his appearance made me shudder.

The man whom Beech had introduced as Kellway smiled and spread his hands, and said, 'My friends. Mr Beech has asked me to tell you my story today.' His voice was light and held an echo of laughter, and though his words held little hint of dialect, his accent was the purest Yorkshire. 'During the three earthly days since I was last in this house I have, as you know, spent many years on the second planet of our star, bathed in the life-giving light of the sun, and hence have regained the appearance I had as a young man, though I believe I have grown in wisdom beyond the years of any here present.'

I heard Major Bradbury whistle. 'Upon my soul,' he muttered. 'I wonder whether the creatures would have me.'

The Yorkshireman went on. 'You knew already that I have, since ere my birth, been guided by benevolent intelligences from the world that we call Venus, whose influence has been to me every kind of care, from a gardener cultivating a seedling to a tutor instructing a beloved pupil. Thanks to their patronage I have been allowed to develop such mental disciplines as are required to evolve beyond the mundane bounds that constrict the remainder of Mankind, so that I may, in turn, teach all our people to become Evolved Men... and Women,' he added, with a smile at Miss Casimir, and I wondered whether their newfound alliance was wholly confined to enlisting his endorsement for the Countess.

'It is as an effect of this development – and quite an accidental one, I assure you, since my patrons have little interest in what we would call parlour tricks – that I have also developed certain abilities, of the kind that Man's limited scientific understanding in our age calls psychical.

'When I informed Sir Newnham that these peripheral gifts of mine included the ability to move objects placed in a room next-door to me, I was being discreet, and I admit a little mischievous. Such action at a distance I have discovered to be a challenging exercise, and difficult to achieve with any precision, especially without a view of those objects. I could have asked to be shut in your Room C, whence I would have been able to see the box, but I knew of an easier and more surprising way.

'My plan was not to reach out with my mind beyond the wall to move the objects there, but simply to step *through* the wall into Room B, and there remove the ball from the box, then knock upon the door to be set free. I thought that such would be a powerful enough demonstration, if any there were, to earn Sir Newnham's ten thousand pounds. From your nodding I can see that many of you agree.

'I was telling all the truth when I said that to effect this feat I would need some hours of meditation, to elevate my psychical state to the appropriate point. When I spoke to Sir Newnham, he compared the process to the charging of an electrical battery, and those of you of a scientific inclination may appreciate the analogy. Once I had reached a certain level of what one might call "psychical charge", I would be able to vanish from Room A and reappear in Room B in the twinkling of an eye.

'Such a plan, I thought, would be simplicity itself. I had performed similar acts in private for my own amusement, watched with tolerant resignation by my Venusian tutors as a teacher might indulge the tricks of a child. Yet this time their response was different.

'For, at the moment when I made myself incorporeal, I found myself seized as by a giant hand and dragged bodily up into the heavens. I saw the Experiment Room recede beneath me, and the Annexe, and then the whole of Parapluvium House, laid out like a living plan upon a table. In the space of a few breaths – had I the need for breath in my insubstantial state – I saw the whole of England's coastline as I have seen it in maps, obscured here and there by cloud but quite clear, as the sun came into view beyond a horizon that I now saw quite clearly was curved, like the edge of a billiard ball…'

As the man continued with his fanciful and absurd account, I became conscious of a sensation of crawling horror that was as surprising as it was disagreeable. The disturbing familiarity of this man whom I had never seen before began to feel, not merely curious, but frightening, as if he was no man at all, but something wholly different that had taken the shape of one. Though two hours earlier I had been ready to dismiss the idea of visiting another world as the wildest fantasy, I now wondered whether there might not be some truth in it – and yet, if one were to believe such a thing, why one would stop at that. Who was to say that this man, who was so clearly not Kellway, was not indeed some substitute, some unnatural creature sent back by his extra-terrestrial abductors, to impersonate him?

Such fancies are, as my regular readers will be well aware, quite outside my usual habits of mind, and I ordered myself firmly to keep them in check. Nevertheless, there was something about this false Kellway – for I remained certain that he was false – that made me feel he was something quite unlike a living man. Something like a living corpse…

While I had been brooding in this morbid fashion, the impostor's story had taken him to Venus, where he had already encountered some of the local wildlife. He was saying, 'You see, the life of that planet has evolved far beyond the sophistication of our own world's forms, and many of the animals and indeed some of the plants have reached a level of sapience not un-akin to some of the less developed of our human races. The intelligence of the Venusians themselves, of course—'

'Was it warm there, or chill?' asked Sherlock Holmes's voice suddenly, in ringing tones which immediately held the attention of the room.

The man paused and smiled. 'I don't understand your drift, my friend.'

'Please allow Mr Kellway to continue, Mr Holmes,' said Miss Casimir severely. The Countess sat forlornly alone across the room from me, and I began to wonder whether she had been entirely abandoned.

'I merely wondered,' Holmes was musing, 'whether this mist you mention chills the flesh, like the pea-soupers we get here in London, or whether it warms it, like the sunlight you say it conducts. Venus is nearer to the sun, to be sure, but the fog you describe is unlike the meteorological phenomena of our own world.'

'It was warm, my friend,' the impostor said, 'like a summer's day or a mild bath of water.'

'And the gravity?' asked Holmes, his voice calm and curious still. 'I wondered about the gravity. I believe that Venus is a smaller world than our own, which might mean that objects – and persons – feel lighter there.'

'Now that you mention it, there was an unaccustomed spring in my step when I arrived, even before I began to regain my youth,' the other replied. 'But as to the nature of the human Venusians, their intelligence is far beyond anything anyone would encounter here, except in the most—'

But Holmes had been making his way from the back of the room to stand in front of him. 'So in a warmer world, and one where your body was lighter, you would I suppose have had little need of the jacket and cane you left behind. Here, allow me to give them back to you.' He handed the man the cane he carried, and made to remove the jacket.

I saw the false Kellway's eyes widen in horror, and Holmes nodded in satisfaction. 'Ah, of course,' he said, shrugging the jacket back on, 'how foolish of me. That cane is not the one that

Thomas Kellway left behind him. I fear I have confused it with the one found in Frederick Garforth's studio. The one you used to beat him to death with.'

Miss Casimir recoiled violently, and Gideon Beech blanched as white as bone; and with the mention of Garforth I finally recognised the man, and knew why seeing him walk and talk had been the cause of such creeping unease in me.

His age aside – for the other had undoubtedly been some thirty years older – he was the very image not of Thomas Kellway, whom I had never seen, but of Frederick Garforth, whom I had observed lying on a slab in the Scotland Yard mortuary.

My shock prevented me from immediately reacting as, aghast, the young doppelganger turned in panic and ran for the door. Almost any of us in the room could have stopped him, but the rest were as paralysed as I by Holmes's revelation. The man thrust aside Gregory the footman, who stood beside the door, and the servant staggered into the Reverend Small, knocking the cleric over. Whatever else this impersonator might be counterfeiting, his muscular bulk was no deception.

'After him!' Holmes cried. 'That man is the murderer of Garforth *and* of Kellway!'

The pretender tore open the door and passed through it, slamming it as those of us with sufficient presence of mind began finally to scramble after him. It was Major Bradbury who reached the doorway first, showing a surprising turn of speed. He wrested it open to reveal a laden coat-stand tipped across the doorway, and a second footman lying in the hallway beyond it, laid out by a heavy blow.

By the time we had unblocked the door and struggled through it, there was no sign of the Yorkshireman. Anderton, who had just entered the hall from the servants' wing, now hurried up to us and said, 'It's all done, Mr Holmes. I've sent for Inspector

Lestrade, just as you asked. All the gates out to the street are locked, and I've stood servants everywhere he might climb over any walls. The beggar can't escape from the grounds now.'

'Excellent work, Anderton,' Holmes replied, and turned to address the men and women of the Society who had followed us out. 'Now listen to me, all of you. Your differences are unimportant now – a murderer is loose, and must be caught. Fortunately he is trapped within the grounds of Parapluvium House. He will be hiding, but we must flush him out. Sir Newnham will organise the search with Anderton – they know the grounds best.' It suddenly occurred to me to wonder where Rhyne was – I had not seen him since Harrington's.

Holmes continued, 'Watson – and Gregory, if you are quite recovered – come with me.' He set off at a run towards one of the side-doors, and the winded footman and I followed him.

Outside, however, rather than racing off into the grounds like a hound after a hare as I had expected, Holmes made for the iron staircase which led up to the roof.

'Why, Holmes, whatever are you doing?' I asked as he began to climb, though of course I followed him without hesitation. 'Would not our efforts be better devoted to the search? Or do you suppose the fellow has made for the roof?'

Was Garforth's double mad enough to believe his own story? I had visions of him calling on the Venusians to snatch him once again from the house's gables. Then, of course, I remembered what Speight had built between those gables, and Holmes's intentions became clear.

Once we had reached the rooftop, Holmes asked Gregory to wait outside as the two of us bundled into the camera obscura, and waited for our eyes to become accustomed to the total blackness within.

Just as before, the outline of the house's grounds came slowly into view, emerging from the dark like a dream. This time the image was a picture of activity, the grassy hinterlands between the house's outbuildings thronging with uniformed servants and members of the Society in quest for our absconding fugitive. We stood and watched in silence for a few moments, and I began to pick out individuals: Beech, in his tweed suit; Sir Newnham, with his white hair left uncovered in his haste; the great bear-like bulk of the Norwegian. I even caught a glimpse of Miss Casimir's dress as she joined in the search, doubtless hungry for retribution against the man who had so disappointed her.

Again I experienced the vertiginous feeling that I was a god or a giant, looking down upon the antics of tiny people... or perhaps, just as disquietingly, a schoolboy watching a nest of ants busily at work.

'What I would not give, Watson,' murmured Holmes, 'for a device such as this that could encapsulate the whole of London! Had I such a contraption I doubt that I would stir from it. I would solve crimes from my armchair and become the corpulent image of my brother.'

For a few moments more, we watched. Though I strained my eyes trying to comprehend all of the display at once, I saw nobody running, or trying to hide, or acting differently from those around them. Then Holmes's finger shot out. 'There!' he said.

I saw a figure wearing a footman's livery, walking across the lawn from the summerhouse. 'It is one of the footmen, I presume,' I said. I thought I had seen him enter the outbuilding a minute or so previously, but I had neither Holmes's needle-sharp eye for detail nor his comprehensive memory.

'No, Watson. The footman who went into the summerhouse was slighter, and walked with a different gait. That is our man.'

But by then the fellow had already passed between the workshops and the generator-house, and I could not tell which of the liveried figures milling about on the other side of them was him.

Holmes rapped on the door. 'Gregory!' he said. 'Have Anderton assemble all the footmen in the kitchen at once. And tell Dr Kingsley that there is a man in the summerhouse who requires his attention.'

I said, 'In the uniform he might pass at a distance, or in a crowd. But the servants will know he is not one of them.'

'Exactly so. He will not join them in the kitchen, therefore, which means that anyone outside in footman's livery will be our man. Watson, stay here and continue our watch. I fear I must rejoin the fray.'

I had the sense to close my eyes against the blinding light of the door, then continued to watch the projection as Holmes's instructions were relayed across the grounds. One by one I saw the uniformed figures of the footmen hurry towards the house, while the others – the Society men, the gardeners, even some of the maids – continued with the search. I saw the rotund figure of Anderton hurry towards the summerhouse along with a long-legged shape I recognised as that of Dr Kingsley; a couple of minutes later they emerged, carrying between them a recumbent figure wrapped in a blanket.

A minute later I saw Holmes himself, his energetic stride unmistakeable even from this strange perspective, hurrying about directing the others, and it occurred to me how strange it was that at that moment I was the one who could see further than he. Remembering my experiences in Afghanistan, I thought I could perhaps imagine how it might feel to be a general, watching as battalions were moved around a map and forgetting that each represented men whose lives he might be sacrificing. It was a strange fancy, on a day which had been serving up an exceptional number of them.

And then I saw our man – a bulky shape in footman's livery making his way stealthily along the side of the flotation tanks. I glanced about for Holmes but he was several buildings away, directing a search of the greenhouses. The only figure in the fugitive's vicinity was a lanky, clumsy figure who I recognised immediately as Constantine Skinner.

I ran out onto the roof, reeling for a moment at the onslaught of late-afternoon daylight after that stygian darkness. It took a moment to orient myself, and then I located the occult detective on the lawn below. He had paused in a gap between two of the tanks to blow his nose.

'Skinner!' I cried, and he dropped his handkerchief with a start, before gaping around foolishly to see who was shouting. 'Skinner, he's just the other side of the tanks!'

To his credit, the man stopped trying to guess whence I was directing him, and ran around the tanks instead. For all I knew, he often found himself following orders from unseen voices. Unfortunately the fugitive had heard me too, and had started running for shelter elsewhere.

By now, though, Anderton had joined me on the roof, and I bade him stay put while I plunged back into the inky blackness of the camera obscura. I blinked desperately, willing my eyes to work, and once again the image swam into focus.

I saw the man at once, running towards the Experimental Annexe and the greenhouses beyond – and now I saw where he was heading, for there was a coal-bunker on the very edge of the grounds, positioned so that the coalmen could fill it up from the street, and Sir Newnham's people could then carry the coal across to the forge or the glassblowers' kiln. It looked like an easy climb onto its roof, and from there onto the wall surrounding the property. Presumably it had been one of the places where Anderton had stationed a footman to keep watch, but all the footmen had been summoned to the kitchen.

I rapped on the door. 'Anderton!' I cried. 'Tell Holmes and the others that he's coming their way!'

I heard the butler relay the information, and the small knot of figures surrounding Holmes began to mill towards where the escapee would emerge. He saw them at once, and turned back, disappearing through the door into the Experimental Annexe. I remembered that it had been left unlocked after Holmes had completed his first inspection of the building.

'The Annexe!' I yelled, bursting out once more into the dazzling light. 'Tell them he's in the Experimental Annexe!'

I hurtled down the stairs and into the house, through the hall and along the passageway into the chemistry laboratory before bursting into the Annexe, where I found the bald man struggling with Holmes and the Reverend Small. He was immensely strong, and bulky where Holmes was slim, and they were having difficulty containing him. I barrelled into the fray, and with my extra momentum the man was catapulted into Experiment Room A, whose door we had left open after the dinner at Sir Newnham's two days before. He struggled to escape, but with the aid of a pair of gardeners who came to help us, we fought the door closed and jammed one of the chairs beneath the handle.

And, as quickly as that, it was over. The man who had been impersonating Thomas Kellway had been imprisoned just as Kellway had – if indeed there ever had been a real Kellway – in Experiment Room A, while Holmes, Small, the gardeners and I stood by, all grinning with satisfaction at a job well done.

While Sir Newnham was sent for, and various others trickled in from outside or the house to join us, I looked in through the distorting glass at the young man who had led us all such a merry chase. He looked far from serene or meditative; indeed, his face was contorted with fury as he banged against the glass.

Remembering that it was supposedly unbreakable, I gave him a cheerful wave before turning away.

'Well, he isn't Kellway, obviously,' I said over the thumping as the young man raged. 'Who on earth is he?'

Holmes smiled broadly. 'A very apt question, Watson. Here on earth, it seems he is Simon Greendale, the nephew of the late Theodore Greendale.'

I blinked at him, aware that I had heard those names in the past few days, but quite unable to remember where.

Statement by Inspector Utterthwaite of the West Riding Constabulary

The first I knew of it all was in the early afternoon of Friday the 5th of June in 1891. I was summoned to the Ridings Hotel in King Street to find the establishment's concierge and manager in a right state of distress, with an elderly guest complaining fit to burst about some lost valuables, and other guests milling around them all in great alarm.

It took me and my constables some time to quiet them all enough to take their statements, but we got there eventually. It turned out that this complaining guest, one Mr Elmet, had taken rooms at the hotel the previous day, and at this time he had deposited a case containing a quantity of jewellery, which he described as family heirlooms, in the hotel safe. Because it was the hotel's usual practice in such cases, the manager, Mr Ridley, had itemised the gemstones individually, and had from Mr Elmet an estimation of their value, before putting them in the safe and locking it with his own hands.

Mr Elmet had then spent the afternoon in the hotel lounge writing letters, eaten a very hearty supper and retired to bed.

At eleven o'clock the next morning, a person who Harold Shawcross the concierge identified at the time as this same Mr Elmet came up to the desk and asked to check his items out of the safe deposit. The reason he gave was that he was taking them to an assayer in town to have them formally valued. Shawcross summoned Mr Ridley, who handed them over willingly enough, and the fellow took the case and left.

An hour later, Mr Elmet came back to the desk and

asked again if he could retrieve his valuables, this time because he intended to deposit them at the local branch of his bank, for more permanent safekeeping. Well, Harold Shawcross was right bewildered, and reminded Elmet that he had not returned them since checking them out earlier. Elmet insisted that he had not checked them out, and Harold begged to assure him that he had.

Ridley was called for once again, and he confirmed his employee's story. Elmet then flew into a towering rage, accusing the both of them of robbing him blind. That was when we were called in, and I arrived shortly afterward with my men. Elmet insisted he had been sitting right there in the morning room since breakfast, reading the papers, and that he had been nowhere near the desk, the safe or the jewellery; he also said a dozen other guests and waiters could attest to this; which, being called upon by us, every one of them proceeded to do.

Meanwhile, however, Harold, Ridley and two guests who had passed through the lobby at the time confirmed the story that the valuables had been handed over to a man who appeared the spitting image of Mr Elmet.

We came round to the view, then, that a robbery had indeed taken place; but that it was one where an impostor had disguised himself as Elmet so he could avail himself of the latter's jewellery. Of course Ridley apologised to Elmet, and told him that the hotel would cover the loss as well as his hotel bill, though he told me afterwards that the value Elmet had assigned to the jewellery would be a shockingly heavy price to bear. He seemed very relieved when I reminded him he should be able to file a claim with the hotel's insurance company.

My men got nowhere with finding the thief. He had

been seen in the street, hurrying away from the hotel clutching the case, and soon after that in the railway station, but it looked as if by the time his imposture was discovered he had already left town by train, and none of our enquiries could locate him after that. My view was that he had taken off his disguise and got rid of it the moment he was in private.

From the start, though, there were a number of things about the case that didn't sit right for me. This Elmet was a man of striking appearance, and although some of that was because of his white hair and whiskers, Harold Shawcross was adamant that he had recognised the thief's facial features as being his. Both he and Ridley were quite clear that if they had had any doubt about the fellow's identity, they never would have handed the jewellery to him. There was also the strange coincidence of the real Elmet, as we were supposed to call him, deciding to withdraw his valuables so soon after the impostor had already done so, after so clearly establishing his alibi for the morning.

I wish the police could take credit for the discovery that the jewels were all forgeries, but this was established by the investigator for the insurers, a very smart lad, who had had the idea of talking to all makers of costume jewellery in the area. He found out that a set exactly matching the description of those which Elmet deposited had recently been made to commission, as cheap as dirt relatively speaking, by a theatrical costumier in York.

This meant that the case was not one of robbery but of fraud, and that our supposed 'Mr Elmet' was now not the victim but the perpetrator, with an accomplice who resembled him closely enough that the two of them could be twins. Between them they had got a long way towards extorting a princely sum of money from the hotel and its insurers. In fact the first, very substantial, instalment had already been paid, though there was a lot more waiting for the outcome of the insurers' investigation.

Fortunately the costumier's clerk could describe the young man who had placed the order for the counterfeit stones, and from that description and our knowledge of the local criminal element we were able to identify the perpetrators of the fraud. One of them, Simon Greendale, was a lad from a small village nearby who had only been involved with the police on occasions of petty affray, but his uncle, Theodore Greendale, was a seasoned confidence trickster who had evidently started training him up in the family business. A few of my colleagues had had serious dealings with Theodore in the past, though never over a crime this ambitious.

I had never met Theodore myself, but allowing for some alterations to his hairstyle and other easily achieved cosmetic changes, I could see he was a good match for the description of 'Mr Elmet'. More significantly, Simon, although he was so much younger, bore such a close resemblance to his uncle at the same age that we were told it had been much remarked upon in their home village of Garforth.

CHAPTER SEVENTEEN

'Greendale?' I repeated, recalling the name at last. 'Isn't that the family who were involved in that fraud case in Leeds?'

'Indeed, Watson,' said my friend. 'They hailed from the village of Garforth in Yorkshire, hence Theodore Greendale's choice of pseudonym here in London.'

'So Frederick Garforth was *Theodore* Greendale?'

'Quite so. And our friend here is his nephew, Simon. They have traded on their close family resemblance before.'

For the benefit of Sir Newnham and the others who had joined us by now, Holmes explained the nature of the Greendales' fraud. 'I have been in correspondence about the case with Inspector Utterthwaite of Yorkshire's West Riding Constabulary,' Holmes revealed. 'It seems that when he realised they were discovered, Theodore Greendale absconded with the first payment of insurance money, leaving Simon with nothing to show for his pains but the paste jewellery. Once the Leeds police knew who they were looking for he, being so much less experienced than his uncle, was more easily found. He was arrested and convicted, and only recently completed his prison sentence.'

Sir Newnham looked little the wiser. 'But how came they to be here, Holmes? And why was Theodore Greendale impersonating Frederick Garforth? *Was* there ever a Frederick Garforth, or was he only an alias?'

'I shall explain all, Sir Newnham,' Holmes replied. 'According to Utterthwaite, though Simon Greendale has been understandably aggrieved against his uncle, he has rebuffed several overtures from the police soliciting his help in entrapping him. It would seem he had plans of his own for revenge.

'From what we have learned, it now seems certain that following his release he followed his uncle's trail to London, with the express intention of recovering what was owed to him. He located Theodore and observed his activities, which included impersonating Frederick Garforth and attending the meetings of your Society. I cannot confirm this for certain, but I believe that the journalist who visited Mr Beech seeking more details of the Society's activities was Simon himself.'

'Drivel, Holmes,' Beech asserted hastily, 'quite quintessential drivel. The young man who visited me looked nothing like that thug. He was from one of the quality papers. Indeed, he is probably at my house for our interview now.'

'Yet Inspector Lestrade has spoken to the editors of all the major newspapers by telephone, and each disavows any knowledge of such an interview. I would surmise that young Greendale has learned a number of useful skills from his uncle, including some aptitude at disguise.'

Before the gaping Beech could reassert his own infallibility, Holmes pressed on. 'With his hair and whiskers grown far beyond his usual custom, and affecting a monocle, Theodore Greendale would have provided his new artist character, Frederick Garforth, with a most distinctive countenance. I found evidence at his studio that he also adopted certain theatrical techniques, involving flesh-coloured clay and cotton wool, to change the shape of his nose, ears and cheeks.

'To be precise, though, whilst I believe that Theodore did originally sport his own hair and whiskers as Garforth for long enough to avoid any suspicion that they might be false, by the time Simon caught up with him he would have shaved them off. Indeed, he must have removed all his hair, with the exception of his eyelashes. For with this new and distinctive appearance, and lacking the amendments to his facial appearance he had adopted as Garforth, he reintroduced himself to the Society in the new person of Thomas Kellway.'

'Good Lord!' exclaimed the Reverend Small, with no little relish. 'So when you told us that Greendale was the killer of both Garforth and Kellway...'

'I was alluding to but one murder, though that is distasteful enough. For a year or so, Garforth established himself fully as a member of the Society in good standing, and if his status as an artist was nonexistent, that impinged little on the interests of those here. I would imagine Greendale chose Garforth's profession to precisely that end. His selling on to Sir Newnham of a second-hand canvas acquired elsewhere – a very inferior one, I am afraid, Sir Newnham, of lesser value even as a curiosity than if it had been truly painted by a murder victim – sufficed to establish his credentials in your respective eyes.

'For the past month, Greendale has been using a wig and false eyebrows and whiskers when appearing as Garforth, but as you were all so used to his striking appearance they have escaped the suspicious scrutiny they might have inspired earlier on. Greendale has shaved regularly – at Garforth's studio, not at Kellway's rooms – to maintain Kellway's baldness. He has smoked only with a cigarette holder to avoid staining his fingers, and has freshened his breath with lozenges so that Kellway might pass as a non-smoker, despite Garforth's excessive smoking. Thus he has appeared to the Society in both personas at different times. Anderton told us that the two of them met once, in the street outside this house, but his only witness to that meeting was Garforth himself.

'In this way, Greendale maintained a dual identity for the weeks required to establish the deception. Indeed, he may have had further identities during this time. Given the poverty of both Frederick Garforth's and Thomas Kellway's accommodations, and the substantial value of the payment from the hotel fraud, it is possible that Greendale maintained yet another establishment at which he resided between times. Although the payment for the hotel fraud was partial, the full sum claimed was large, and he would have been able to bear such an expense for the necessary time.

'Such, in any case, was Theodore Greendale's routine when his nephew Simon caught up with him. From observing his uncle's movements, and with the information you gave him, Mr Beech, Simon was able to deduce what Theodore's current money-making scheme must be – as I am sure you must all have done by now. He intended, of course, to stage Kellway's disappearance with the help of the Garforth disguise, and to reappear in person as Kellway to claim the ten thousand pounds before disappearing more permanently. Whether he intended to carry on living as Garforth and develop further schemes in that person, or simply to abscond and allow both identities to lapse, I cannot tell. I doubt he intended to continue attending Society meetings, though – the risk of recognition would have been considerable.'

Several of the Society had clearly been straining to interrupt during this speech, and as Holmes paused for breath their voices sounded forth.

'But *how* did he disappear, Holmes? You haven't covered that!' Sir Newnham expostulated, and the others made similar protests with differing degrees of rudeness.

'All in good time – gentlemen, Miss Casimir,' Sherlock Holmes replied with insufferable calm. The Countess Brusilova had been put to bed and was being attended and chaperoned by one of the older maids, freeing her companion to listen with the rest of us to Holmes's account. 'I have a little demonstration planned which will, I hope, set all your minds wholly at rest on that score. If I may continue in the meantime, however:

'I imagine that Greendale's plan for his reappearance involved arriving at Parapluvium House as Garforth on Wednesday morning and changing *in situ* into his Kellway guise, before emerging unannounced from the Experimental Annexe, to the awe and admiration of Sir Newnham and any others who chanced to be present. In the commotion Garforth would not have been missed, at least not at first. Greendale would then return to Kellway's rooms and create some less spectacular evidence to suggest that Kellway had once again been taken up into interplanetary space, more permanently this time.

'Instead of which, he had a nasty shock. On arrival he learned not only that Sir Newnham had engaged my services to investigate Kellway's disappearance, but that I was expected at the house at any moment.

'I flatter myself that the reputation I have earned during my modest career –' I distinctly heard Gideon Beech snort, but Holmes continued implacably '– would cause all but the most confident criminal mind to experience some trepidation at such news. In any case, Greendale panicked. He left at once, taking the cab in which Watson and I arrived, and fled back to his studio to destroy the evidence he had been keeping there. He had nearly completed this process when, to what I would imagine was his extreme surprise and dismay, his nephew arrived at the studio.

'Simon was unaware that matters had reached such a head.

He knew from speaking to Kellway's landlady that the experiment had taken place on Monday night. He knew that the first half of the deception, Kellway's disappearance, had come off without a hitch, and that Theodore needed only to reappear to claim the reward, which Simon had every intention of taking for his own. He had, in fact, arrived in a cab that he had commandeered for the purpose of abducting Theodore, taking him to a vacant warehouse of whose existence he had learned, and there insisting with menaces that Theodore complete the job and hand over all the proceeds to Simon, cutting out his accomplice.'

'Accomplice?' Miss Casimir frowned.

'With Simon harbouring such an intention, and with Theodore already in an agitated state of mind, we can well imagine the conflict that might have developed between the two men. How Simon ended up killing Theodore with a blow of the latter's walking stick is less clear. Possibly Theodore, who though older was no feeble specimen, offered such a fight that Simon was forced to defend himself by any means that came to hand, or possibly the news that Theodore was abandoning his carefully laid scheme to defraud the Society enraged Simon beyond reason. Whatever the reason, he gained nothing by killing a goose which might yet have been persuaded to lay him a golden egg.

'Whether in anger or by accident, however, he did so, and thus was he faced with a problem. He still intended, as we have seen today, to claim the money Theodore had earned through his meticulous planning. To do so, however, he would have had to disguise himself as Theodore – and not in his Garforth appearance, which would have been relatively easy to mimic, but in the person of Thomas Kellway.

'The family resemblance between the two men is quite remarkable, but it is not perfect – the most striking difference, of course, being in their ages. When disguising himself as Theodore during their Yorkshire escapade, Simon had needed to pass muster only for a few minutes. Methods such as growing his hair and whiskers to resemble his uncle's, whitening them with talcum powder or some similar agent, and creating wrinkles on the visible parts of his face with spirit gum, would have sufficed. But "Kellway"'s lack of facial hair, or even hair on his scalp, to draw attention away from his unadorned skin made such a deception all but impossible.

'Nevertheless, Simon had a notion of how he might, given this Society's unusual openness to unconventional ideas, pass himself off for long enough to claim the reward and make his getaway. First, however, Garforth's absence needed to be accounted for. If the artist had merely disappeared – if, say, Simon had filled his uncle's pockets with bricks and dumped him in the Thames – the coincidental timing would have raised associations that would have been all too pertinent. The police and others would have been looking out especially for Frederick Garforth, and would have been more likely to recognise the echo of his features in Simon's.

'However, were Theodore to be found in his state at the time of death – his wig and whiskers held on with spirit gum, clay clinging to his nose and ears and cotton wool stuffed into his cheeks – the imposture would have been discovered, and all would have been lost. Dead hoaxers claim no rewards. Theodore's body must be lacking all evidence of disguise, which of course meant it must be hairless. For a man to be shaven after death is grotesque, but for him to sport a day's stubble when he was seen earlier that day with a full head of hair is unnatural. As for the facial discrepancies caused by the removal of the disguise, Simon was fortunate indeed that I had caught only the most fleeting glimpse of Garforth, or I would certainly have detected them when Watson and I viewed the body.'

I could see several of the Society itching to interject once again; Sir Newnham, in particular, looked thunderstruck and furious, and I was beginning to understand why. Once again, however, Holmes pressed on.

'Simon Greendale was faced with the grisly business of ferrying his uncle's corpse to the warehouse where it was found, and shaving it so that it appeared Garforth's hair and whiskers had been removed post mortem. He also required the services of someone who could identify the body definitively *as Garforth*, with no ambiguity suggesting that it might belong to Thomas Kellway.

'This forced Simon to enlist Theodore's accomplice, the same person he had hoped to induce Theodore to cut out of the deal. With the knowledge he had gained from observing meetings between the two, however, he was able to blackmail this person into assisting him, by threatening to reveal their complicity in the attempted fraud. They seem to have dug their heels in rather, creating a delay to finding the body which was to nobody's advantage, but evidently they capitulated in the end.'

At this point Major Bradbury, a little slower on the uptake than his fellows, succeeded in interjecting, 'But who—?'

'This was the man who introduced Garforth as a member of the Society,' Holmes announced, 'and one of very few who had the opportunity to duplicate Sir Newnham's key to Experiment Room A. He planned the observation rotas which were crucial to the deception, and warned Theodore of my imminent arrival on the Wednesday morning. You do not need me to tell you who this person was. It was the man who ultimately identified Frederick Garforth's body – the body, he claimed, of a dear family friend – without noticing that its appearance had changed, giving it a marked resemblance to that of Thomas Kellway.'

From the ensuing animated discussion, it emerged that nobody had seen Talbot Rhyne since he had excused himself following my conversation with him and Sir Newnham at Harrington's.

A search of his bedroom revealed that a number of his personal effects were missing, and the luckless Gregory revealed that he had, at Mr Rhyne's request, sent a valise by cab that morning to be held for collection at Victoria Station. By now Inspector Lestrade had arrived to take Greendale into custody, and he at once dispatched two men to Victoria, but Holmes agreed with him that they would almost certainly be too late.

'I fear,' he said, 'that Talbot Rhyne has joined the legions of the capital's vanished men.'

Simon Greendale was hauled away, still swearing blood-curdling oaths against us all, by four strong policemen, and bundled into a wagon bound for the Yard. We all relocated to the drawing room, and the men lit their pipes and cigarettes. Lestrade remained, out of curiosity to hear the rest of Holmes's explanation.

'It was Rhyne who betrayed me, then?' Sir Newnham asked bitterly. 'I would have trusted that man with my life. If you had asked me, I would have said that he was no less loyal than Anderton, though I admit that having known him but a few years I would have had less firm grounds for saying so. Was he treacherous from the start?'

'I do not know for sure,' said Holmes. 'It seems just as likely, however, that he had no such intention before he was suborned by Greendale. He may have been as unwilling an accomplice of Theodore's as he later was of Simon's.

'What I am sure of is that Rhyne borrowed the keys you keep in your office safe for long enough to copy those that open Experiment Room A and the exterior door of the Experimental

Annexe, and that he arranged the watch rotas to allow for the cunning scheme that Theodore had planned.'

'But this is nonsense, Holmes,' the Major insisted. 'You must see that it is. Why, I stood outside that room with Garforth and looked in at Kellway. If what you say is true, the man must have had perfectly genuine miraculous powers. I saw a dervish bilocate once in Sind, mind you, but that man could only keep it up for minutes at a time. He was a remarkable fellow, actually—'

'We will come to the demonstration in a moment, Major,' said Holmes sternly. 'For now, I have two observations to make. Firstly, Frederick Garforth supposedly arrived at Parapluvium House that night only at eleven-thirty, an hour and a half after the shift you shared with Talbot Rhyne. By then, Greendale had of course been released from Experiment Room A and repaired to the summerhouse, where Rhyne had left the elements of his Garforth disguise. It was doubtless also Rhyne who collected and disposed of Kellway's clothes later.

'And secondly, that in arranging the shift rotas for that night, Rhyne had taken pains to pair himself with an observer who he knew could not be relied upon. Oh, I do not say that you were complicit in the deception, Major,' Holmes added as Bradbury began spluttering in indignation, 'merely that he could guarantee that your presence during your shift would not be constant. Rhyne and Greendale could be certain of a few moments, at least, during which the former could free the latter and release him into the grounds.'

'But Kellway was still in the room!' Gideon Beech objected, increasingly enraged by Holmes's refusal to address this point. 'We all saw him there for hours afterwards!'

His anger was nothing, however, compared with Major Bradbury's towering fury. 'How dare you, sir!' he blustered. 'I'll have you know I've faced down Dacoits and Thuggees, Mahdis and Mullahs, and none of those I've served with have ever questioned my resolve! Why, I stood watch for eight hours over my injured men during the Burmese campaign and—'

'You were a younger man then, Major,' Holmes said, 'and the unfortunate habits you have picked up out in the East were doubtless held in check. These days you are incapable of staying a room for an hour at a time, and when confined for a similar period in a cab with Watson and myself, you left us most precipitately, to vanish into Hyde Park on an unknown mission. I of all people recognise the symptoms of addiction, Major, and I know that you consorted with all kinds of local medicine men in India, when under the corrupting influence of Colonel Sebastian Moran. I do not know to what drug it is that you have become so enthralled, whether hashish or opium or some other substance with a similar—'

The Major was staring at Holmes, quite aghast, and frankly so was I. 'Holmes,' I said forcibly, 'might I have a word?'

He frowned. 'Watson, I am merely observing that the Major has acquired a debilitating habit which he hides in a way which makes it quite clear he considers it shameful, and that the unreliability this habit has engendered made him the perfect choice for Rhyne's—'

'Outside, Holmes, please.' I took him by the elbow and guided him out into the hallway, to a clamour of indignant protest from those left behind in the room. I glanced around to make sure that there were no servants there to overhear us, and told him quite firmly, 'Holmes, Major Bradbury is not an addict.'

Haughtily, he said, 'Watson, I rather think that I am better placed than you to identify—'

'Better placed than a doctor? I'm afraid you overreach yourself, old man. In most areas I defer to your expertise, but in this you must bow to mine. You are allowing your own unfortunate history, and perhaps the memory of the Moran affair, to cloud your judgement. Major Bradbury shows no signs of addiction that I can see.'

'The man can't sit still for the length of a meal!' Holmes expostulated. 'He leaves and returns with the regularity of a cuckoo popping out to announce the hour. And he does it so furtively! The man has a shameful secret, that much is quite clear, and if it is not an addiction, then—'

'Holmes!' I snapped, and then sighed. My friend's profession had made him so eager to find a criminal explanation that he had missed a very simple medical one – one that my own professional experience made quite obvious to me. 'My dear fellow, you and I are still relatively young men, and healthy, thank heavens. Older men sometimes experience... lapses... in bodily functions that you and I are fortunate enough to take quite for granted. Some of these, like an infirmity of the sight or limbs, may be discussed in polite company, whereas others may well make the sufferer feel ashamed or embarrassed – though quite irrationally so. It is assuredly no fault of Major Bradbury's if nature makes certain calls on him more often these days than it did when he stood watch over those men in Burma. A man doesn't vanish among the trees in Hyde Park to smoke hashish, Holmes.'

By now comprehension dawned on Holmes's face – and with it some embarrassment of his own. 'I see. Yes indeed, old fellow, I do see. I suppose we should give the poor man the benefit of the doubt. That... explanation... would certainly fit the facts.'

'And is not one that Major Bradbury would be pleased to have made public,' I reminded him.

'Well, no. Although as you say, somewhat irrationally so. Still... I owe the Major an apology,' he reflected.

'Perhaps it would be best to avoid the subject for the moment,' I suggested.

'Very well,' agreed Holmes. 'Perhaps it is time for my demonstration.'

We re-entered the room, to find Major Bradbury still fuming and everybody else bemused. Grandly, Holmes announced, 'I am afraid that we have allowed ourselves to be distracted by a peripheral issue. If we assume, as it seems we must, that Major Bradbury was forgivably absent from the Experimental Annexe for a short period during his watch, there is a far greater question to be answered. If, during that brief lapse, Rhyne did indeed release Theodore Greendale – or, as you called him at the time, Thomas Kellway – from Experiment Room A, then who was in there, under clear observation, for the remainder of the night, and what happened to that person between five o'clock and five minutes past five?'

'Damned right,' snapped Bradbury. 'If the fellow was let out, it wasn't during my watch.'

'As far as I can see, Holmes, none of this is any more explicable than it was at the start,' said Sir Newnham. 'Whoever Kellway really was, to vanish from that room yet seem to be still there is just as impossible as vanishing altogether, isn't it?'

I said, 'I fear Sir Newnham's right, Holmes. As we discovered, every theory that could explain the facts must entail some impossibility, and that's what we come back to. We've heard your theory, but the impossibility is still just as much there.'

He favoured us all with one of his most superior smiles. 'I must beg your indulgence – Miss Casimir, gentlemen. Pray follow me to the Experimental Annexe, and all will shortly become clear.'

We found the Annexe anteroom already lit, with Anderton in attendance. Next to him on the low round table lay the cane that Holmes had brought with him. Solemnly, Holmes picked it up and told us, 'We must replicate the conditions of the night in question, as far as possible. As you know I am already wearing the jacket that Theodore Greendale affected as Kellway. His Kellway cane is still in my rooms at Baker Street, but this one, which he used as Garforth, will suffice for our purposes. We know that Greendale had an accomplice to let him out of the room, and Major Bradbury would have left Rhyne alone there for merely a minute or two. May I ask you, Sir Newnham, to give your room keys to Anderton, and then that you all retire as a body to the chemistry laboratory for two minutes?'

I felt a little hurt that Holmes had taken the butler into his confidence in preference to myself, but I knew his penchant for the theatrical, and also how much he enjoyed seeing me respond to it as part of his audience. If he really had solved the riddle of Kellway's disappearance, I supposed that I could not begrudge him that.

'But we can all see that Rhyne *could* have let Kellway out, if he had a key,' Bradbury protested – tacitly accepting, I noticed, that he had indeed been absent from the room for a time. 'It's what came after that's the mystery.'

'The mystery,' Holmes promised, 'will be clear very soon.'

He stepped into Experiment Room A. By now the sky outside was dark, and the lighting was very similar to that which Holmes and I had observed with Skinner present, on the night of the dinner. Room B was lit up as before, and the table with its box still stood in its place – the billiard ball that was the nominal focus of the experiment still, I assumed, lying undisturbed within. 'Anderton,' he said, 'for form's sake, please lock the door.'

Anderton swung the door to and locked it, then stepped back to stand beside the table. We all peered in turn through the glass panel. Though the room was murky as before, we could all see Holmes sitting in the lotus position, just as he had been two nights previously – and just as I had seen him, albeit in better light, in our rooms that afternoon. This time, however, he was facing me. He looked up at me and winked.

When we had all had a chance to observe the subject, Anderton said, 'If you wouldn't mind stepping outside, miss and sirs?'

We did so, and kicked our heels impatiently in Sir Newnham's chemical laboratory. I peered at the flasks and bottles on their racks, and tried to remember the labels I had seen on the collection Holmes had been keeping in our bathtub.

'I don't know who he thinks he is,' Gideon Beech snapped after a few moments. 'Showing off like this. Such a sense of self-importance the man has.'

'It's justified, I think,' said Constantine Skinner, rather surprisingly. 'I think he may be a genius.' Miss Casimir made a dismissive sound.

'I just wonder what it is he plans to do,' Sir Newnham said gloomily. 'I almost feel as if I'll be paying out that reward after all.'

After the stipulated two minutes we trooped back into the antechamber. Anderton gestured in the direction of Room A, where we once again took turns to look through the glass panel at Holmes, still sitting in his meditative pose.

This time he had no wink for me. I thought there was something different about his position, too – were his legs the other way round from how they had been before? If I had had his powers of observation I would never have needed to ask the question – I would have noted and memorised his previous posture automatically – but having just my own, I struggled to remember.

We all finished our inspection. 'Well?' Beech demanded. 'What in the name of perdition is this supposed to prove? The man hasn't moved an inch, whereas from what he insists on having the gall to tell us, Kellway—'

'Kellway had left the room in the interim, and was already in the process of changing to become Garforth,' Holmes's voice confirmed.

It had not come from Room A.

We turned to gape as one, as Holmes opened the door of Room B and walked out of it, tossing the billiard ball idly in one hand.

Dumbfounded, I turned to look back at the glass panel. Holmes sat, his meditations serenely undisturbed, on the floor of Room A. I saw, in a sudden jolt of confusion, that *that* Holmes was wearing his own jacket and shoes.

'Does this feat of bilocation match the one you saw in Sind, Major?' the Holmes in the antechamber asked idly. He was still wearing Kellway's shoes and jacket, and the cane was tucked under his arm. 'Is it sufficient revelation for you to marvel at, Mr Floke? And Sir Newnham – does it qualify for your ten-thousand-pound reward?'

Excerpt from *The Inter-Planetary Columbus: A Novel* (1896), by Graeme M. Harcourt

At the moment that Professor Weltraum's machine rendered me incorporeal, I felt myself seized as if by a giant hand and taken up bodily into the sky. I saw the laboratory recede beneath me, and the wing of the house, and then the whole of Asphodel Manor, laid out like a living plan upon a table. In the space of a few breaths – though I had no need for breath in my insubstantial state – I beheld the whole of England's coastline as I had seen it in maps, obscured here and there by cloud but quite distinct, as the sun came into view beyond a horizon that I now saw quite clearly was curved, like the edge of a marble.

A moment later, the whole globe was a diminishing sphere, from which I was plummeting at immense speed. It became a disc, and then a mere point in the sky, distinguished from the stars by the bluish tinge of its oceans.

Though lacking eyes or head I found that I was able to direct my attention at will, and so I turned my gaze ahead to see where I was being taken. Ahead of me, a white star was expanding just as our Earth had contracted, growing from a point to a circle and then filling out to become a sphere, a pale globe such as might be held by the marble statue of some eminent explorer, swathed in pearly stuff that I soon understood to be cloud. With a shock I recognised the planet Venus.

Still at the same reckless speed, I found myself plunged into that cloud and towards the ground beneath. I thought I would be dashed to pieces upon the alien earth, forgetting for the moment my bodiless state, but instead I was set down as gently as a kitten in its mother's jaws, and finally the invisible grip on me relaxed.

I resumed my accustomed physical frame, not through any act of volition, but as an object no longer held aloft will tumble to the ground. I discovered myself to be in a landscape shrouded with mist, yet not shadowed by it, for the mist itself glowed with a warm yellow light, illuminating all around me, although further away objects became hazy as they faded into the light.

I stood on a grassy plain next to a grove of trees of an unknown kind, each bearing golden fruit that glowed with its own internal light. In the tree sat a bird, of about the size of a dove, and it too gleamed with a luminescence of its own that was wonderful to see.

I found that I was terribly hungry and thirsty after my earlier labours and the rigours of my interplanetary journey, and so faint I was like to fall down dead. Yet I was cautious to pluck the fruit, strange as it was to me. I hesitated, fearing for my life if I ate yet also if I did not, and then I heard a voice say to me, 'Eat of the fruit and be easy, for there is nothing in this world that can do harm to you.' And I realised that it was the bird that had spoken.

Encouraged by the bird I therefore plucked the fruit and ate it, and found it wonderfully satisfying, like eating the rays of the sun itself. And as I finished I looked up and saw, standing beside me, three beings of light, each shaped like a man yet shining so intently within that I could scarcely bear to look at them.

I would later learn that such self-illumination is the natural state of most of that world's organisms, bathed as they are in the mist that forms the greater part of the planet's atmosphere. Unlike our earthly mist it is a conducting and permeating medium, collecting the light of the sun that falls on the surface and distributing it around that globe so that there is no part of its surface that is not suffused by its luminous nimbus. Thus is the life-giving power of the sun diffused across the whole of that world, until it becomes incorporated into its food, its water and thus its very flora and fauna.

Under its influence the life of that planet has evolved far beyond the sophistication of our own world's life forms, and many of the animals and indeed the plants have reached a level of sapience not unlike some of our less developed human races. The intelligence of the Venusians themselves is far beyond anything one could encounter, except in the most exceptionally evolved specimens of our race.

Transcribed from a copy of the novel held by Camden public library, acquired by them in May 1896. — S.H.

CHAPTER EIGHTEEN

'Holmes,' I said, looking from the figure in Room A to the man who stood before me, 'If ever I have said before that your powers were miraculous, I take it back. All those occasions were, as you assured me at the time, mere trifles. *This* is a miracle.'

He gave an amused smile, acknowledging the double-edged compliment. 'And yet, I fear, once the trick of it is clear you will find it quite as mundane as my other feats.'

He said, 'As every one of you has now, I think, pointed out, it would have done no good for Rhyne to obtain a duplicate key and release Greendale during Major Bradbury's absence, unless there was some further scheme to make it appear that the room was still occupied. The Major, at least, would have realised at once what had happened, and regardless of his own embarrassment could never have been expected to go along with the deception. Had he done so, the suspicion that would have fallen upon him and Rhyne would then have been insupportable. No, the apparent moment of Kellway's dissolution had to happen in the presence of a witness whose testimony Sir Newnham, at least, would find utterly unimpeachable. Hence, as well as ensuring that his own shift was shared with the Major, Rhyne ensured that Garforth's shift – that is to say Theodore Greendale's, now attired and guised as his other personality – was paired with that of William Anderton.

'Fortunately, they had a trick in mind – and it is so singular that I believe it must have been the kernel of the entire plan, around which all the rest of the conspiracy was built.'

Holmes crossed now to Room A, where his counterpart still sat meditating, and bent towards the floor. 'Observe,' he said, indicating a near-invisible strand of twine that emerged from beneath the door. 'And perhaps one or two of you might observe the room? Major Bradbury, Miss Casimir, if you would be so kind—?'

The Major and the young woman leaned together to stare through the panel as Holmes gave the twine a sharp tug.

'Good God!' the Major declared, and Miss Casimir cried out too.

'He just crumpled and disappeared!' she said, and I noticed that her German accent suddenly sounded distinctly more Londonish. 'I say, though,' she added, looking more closely. 'There *is* something down at the bottom there. You can hardly see it with the way this glass squashes everything.'

'The trick relies on you, or rather on Anderton, failing to notice that fact in your general astonishment,' Holmes confirmed. 'What I have just done is, of course, what Greendale did a little after five a.m. on Tuesday, while you yourself, Major, were in conversation with Anderton.

'Had Greendale and Anderton been alone, Anderton's love of reading would have sufficed to take his attention away for long enough. Greendale must have been quite alarmed when you turned up, Major, the first of those unexpected arrivals that would in the end so thoroughly derail his plans. If there was no opportunity to execute this final stage of the trick, it would be easily discovered and could never have been repeated.

'In this instance, though you and Anderton fell into conversation, and a little reflection must have revealed to Greendale that it could be pulled off nevertheless.

'As I say, Greendale – or Garforth, if you prefer – did just what I have done, and caused the apparition of Kellway to vanish. Once you had all observed the room and seen it empty, he sent Anderton to fetch Sir Newnham at once. I imagine that in the excitement, Major, you may have felt the need to step outside again, just for a moment?'

Bradbury cleared his throat. 'Can't say I didn't. Whole thing was a bit of a shock.'

'Quite,' said Holmes, with a smile he probably intended to be apologetic. 'While briefly alone in the room, then, Greendale did this.'

This time he pulled more gently and steadily at the twine, drawing it through the large gap under the door. It brought after it a strange shape made of flimsy bamboo sticks, wire and cloth, connected with a mechanism that looked more than a little like that of a Speight's Super-Collapsible Pocket Umbrella.

'Upon my soul!' declared the Major as Holmes unfolded the structure, spreading it out on the table.

It was a life-sized, unbelievably lifelike image of Holmes, executed in blacks, whites and greys. Sitting before me on the table, it was quite clearly flat as well as colourless – and yet I could see how, erected in the twilit Experiment Room, and twisted by the panoramic distortions of Sir Newnham's patent glass, it could have passed muster as the real thing.

'A photograph,' Miss Casimir said, her accent recovered by now. 'The shape has been cut out from a photograph, surely. But it is so large! How is it possible?'

'Using a pinhole camera,' Holmes said. 'A less sophisticated version of the camera obscura you keep in the roof, Sir

Newnham. Greendale had set one up in Garforth's studio. He had less time than he had hoped to destroy it, and I have been able to reconstruct it from the remains.'

'A pinhole camera projects an inverted image onto the wall of the inner chamber,' Dr Kingsley observed.

I said, 'An inverted image! That's why the legs were the wrong way round!'

'Quite so, Watson,' said Holmes. 'A detail which it seems slipped Greendale's mind when it came to recreating his pose in the Experiment Room. With a large enough area of a photographic medium – let us say a linen sheet, impregnated with sufficient quantities of silver salts – one can capture a pinhole camera's image permanently, just as one would with a conventional camera. Of course there follows the reversal of the original negative image to create a positive one, not to mention a laborious chemical process of developing and fixing, which requires among other things a chemical bath of considerable size. Greendale used an actual bathtub for the process, as did I. We had both best avoid taking a bath at home until it has been emptied and cleaned, Watson.'

Who would do that, I wondered, with Mrs Hudson gone? It was not a task I would care to trust to the Irregulars.

'Cutting out my image and fixing its shape with wire was child's play in comparison,' he went on. I could see that in fact Holmes had cut out a larger outline around his own figure, then folded it back over the wire and sewn it in place. 'You will understand that I was obliged to follow precisely the method Greendale used, employing the same equipment as far as was practical, or I could not have known for certain that it was possible at all. As it is, I was fortunate that this morning was a bright one – without sufficient light I could never have created an image clear enough to pass muster. Greendale, of course, had been sure to rent a studio space with very adequate windows for the purpose.

'In summary, by the time Greendale was finished he had an image of himself as Kellway which was as large and, under the right circumstances, quite as convincing as the one you see before you now – all thanks to modern photographical processes. Not so much an Evolved Man, perhaps, as a Developed one.'

Holmes then showed us how the photograph was stiffened at the edges with a loop of wire, exactly like the one we had found among the burned cloth and wood in Garforth's bathtub. With practice the arrangement of bamboo canes which held it upright took only a moment to set up, and could be collapsed with a single twitch of the twine attached to their central rod.

He then unclipped the unnervingly large photograph from the frame and with a quick twist of his wrists folded it up into a flat shape a third of its previous size, which he passed to me. Removing from his back the jacket that Theodore Greendale had worn as Kellway, he showed us how this triple loop could be slipped through the long tear in the lining, to sit snugly against the wearer's back without noticeably distorting the garment's fit.

'This is how Kellway smuggled it into the room,' Holmes said. 'Garforth's jacket, which Theodore successfully destroyed before Simon arrived, must have had a similar tear in the lining so he could conceal it after he removed it. As for the framework...' He gave it a shake and it folded neatly into a bundle of bamboo sticks, which again he passed to me. He then unscrewed the top of the cane, revealing the filed-off stump of the blade, and I slipped the bundle into the body of the walking stick, which he then screwed shut.

'As I have said, this is Theodore Greendale's Garforth cane,' he said, 'which he was clubbed to death with.' Beech flinched again at the reminder, while Small looked quite fascinated. 'I fancy that the blade of his Kellway cane was broken by sheer accident some time ago, and this one was modified recently to match its useful deficiency. This specimen was almost the last piece of evidence Theodore had left to destroy, regrettably for him. At that point it still contained the frame, which he had concealed there after its use in the disappearing trick.

'It was only after Simon Greendale spoke to Talbot Rhyne that he came to realise its significance, and by then he had abandoned it at the scene of the crime. That is how this mechanism came to fall into my hands. I fancy that it is of Rhyne's own design.'

'I've heard back from my men at Victoria,' said Lestrade, who had just stepped outside to speak to a policeman. 'The valise was already gone – picked up by a lady, the porters said. We'll keep a look out for this Rhyne, but I don't think we're going to find him,' he finished gloomily.

And so it proved. Although Simon Greendale was found guilty of the manslaughter of his uncle, of the assault of the two footmen and of conspiracy to defraud, and still serves a life sentence for the first of these, Talbot Rhyne evaded justice and has not been seen since.

For Sherlock Holmes, though, the case had never been about punishing a criminal. As he had made clear to Sir Newnham at their first meeting, his interest lay in explaining the inexplicable, and he could pride himself that once again he had eliminated the impossible from the realm of the admissible. Though the work of the Society for the Scientific Investigation of Psychical Phenomena continues as rigorously as ever under Sir Newnham Speight, Holmes takes occasional satisfaction in noting that the ten-thousand-pound reward for demonstrating such phenomena remains unclaimed.

I have not reminded him of Constantine Skinner's words when he examined the scene of Kellway's disappearance.

Skinner's overwrought description of a 'hollow, flapping image' collapsing and being drawn away through a void seemed fanciful to us both at the time. Its similarity to the true facts of the case sits too uneasily with me to make light of it, yet I know that Holmes would dismiss the coincidence at once.

'And yet it could have been otherwise,' he said to me on one occasion when the subject of Sir Newnham's Society had arisen. We were once again in our sitting room, drinking tea from a pot supplied by the redoubtable Mrs Hudson – who had, after much pleading from myself, a large and apologetic bouquet from Holmes and a small fortune paid to an agency for domestics to come and clean up the depredations of the Irregulars, eventually consented to forgive us and return home.

He explained, 'Talbot Rhyne and Theodore Greendale devised a conjuring trick that fooled some very keen observers. We cannot be sure that Kellway's reappearance would have been handled as flawlessly as his vanishing, but it is quite possible that, had Simon Greendale not so inconveniently intervened in their scheme, the affair of the Interplanetary Man would have gone down in scientific history.'

'They didn't care about the science, though,' I pointed out. 'They were only after the money.'

'Of course,' said Holmes. 'Rhyne was a skilled inventor, but no scientist. Science is the progressive discovery of the truth, and a deception can never be part of that. The experiment would have proven irreplicable, and the matter would in the end have been entered into the annals as an example of a famous, perhaps an inexplicable, hoax. But it was the work of an exceptional criminal mind nonetheless.'

'Theodore Greendale?' I said. 'I hadn't thought of him as such, after he got himself killed in such an ignominious way.'

'And yet the more I consider the matter,' said Holmes, 'the

more I doubt whether Greendale was its prime instigator. Rhyne
was an excellent engineer; the collapsing framework was based
on his own modification of his employer's design, and I can only
suppose that the pinhole camera scheme was also his, inspired by
Parapluvium House's camera obscura and dark rooms. Nothing in
Theodore Greendale's prior career suggests a comparable degree of
technical knowledge. No, I would not be altogether surprised if his
contribution were merely the skill in disguise and impersonation,
and Rhyne were the true architect of the enterprise.'

'I thought your view was that Rhyne was coerced into
cooperating with Theodore as he was with Simon,' I said.
'Though I was never quite sure how.'

'I said that partly to spare Sir Newnham's feelings,' Holmes
admitted. 'It was clear that Rhyne's betrayal had hit him hard,
for certainly he was a charismatic young person. It may indeed
be that he joined Sir Newnham's service with the intention of
robbing him – it might even be the true reason for the loss of
the summerhouse key, and that unusual depth of clearance
beneath the Experiment Room doors – but if so he was playing a
long game. Indeed, he must have been motivated by something
other than greed, as there would surely be easier ways for a
millionaire's trusted intimate to extort ten thousand pounds, or
even more. Was he seeking pure entertainment, or revenge for
some imagined wrong? I fear we will never know.

'And yet, if he was the scheme's chief mover, then he is one of
the most promising young criminals I have yet encountered, and
certainly one of the most ingenious. And not, I think, without
his own abilities at disguise.'

'Really?' I was surprised. 'I would have thought there were
quite enough disguises in that whole affair already. I mean, with
Theodore posing as Garforth and both Greendales pretending
to be Kellway.'

'Perhaps, Watson, perhaps. And yet… we never did find out, did we, who the young woman was who Mrs Rust saw visiting Kellway, and who claimed to be his niece? Nor did we identify the lady who collected Rhyne's luggage from Victoria, nor she who the footman mistook for the ghost of Anne Heybourne, haunting the stair to Sir Newnham's study. That would have been around the time that Rhyne was borrowing the keys for copying. He would not have wanted to run the risk of being seen to do so – or of being recognised, at least.'

'You're suggesting that Rhyne was some kind of female impersonator?' I was astonished. 'Well, I suppose he could have if he'd wanted to. He had quite a feminine sort of face, as I recall. And his hands were very delicate.'

Holmes gave me an unreadable smile. 'Dear Watson,' he said fondly. 'I do believe that it has never occurred to you how difficult it is for a vast proportion of our population to find a fulfilling outlet for their intellectual capabilities.'

I frowned. 'Well, whatever his disadvantages, Rhyne fell on his feet with Sir Newnham. Which makes his betrayal all the more unconscionable.'

'Indeed. Well,' he added, crossing to the window, and looking out at the throngs passing along Baker Street, 'perhaps we have seen the last of Talbot Rhyne, and perhaps we have not. Yet there is more than one way for a man to vanish, even in this city of millions.'

And I fear that he is right. For all that Sherlock Holmes or I have been able to discover, Talbot Rhyne might as well be on the surface of a distant planet.

Letter from Mrs Charlotte Webster (née Haborn)
to Mrs Amelia Meadows (née North)

King's Shelton
19th September 1896

My dearest Amy,

I write to you in haste, for much of my attention is required here – not simply for poor Johnny, who has the chicken pox and for whose sake I came to stay with Mama and Papa in the country while Maurice trains with his regiment – oh, but I am muddling myself up, and must begin again.

Leaving Johnny aside (for in truth his nurse is more than capable of handling such a straightforward ailment), I have momentous news, which I must beg you to keep quiet for now until the family decide upon how we are to let the world know of it: *for Letty has come back to us!*

You will scarcely credit it, I know, after so long, but it is true. She arrived yesterday, just as she left – utterly unexpectedly, on a trap from the station, with a suitcase in hand. Papa is quite overjoyed, and Mama, though cold and unforgiving in her presence, has privately broken down in tears and confessed to me her relief.

For her part Letty has been moody and unpredictable, and she stubbornly refuses to say where she has been or what she has been doing these three-and-a-half years. We had quite given her up, presuming her to be married to some wastrel at best – but perhaps more likely dead, or mad like poor Great-Uncle Jeremiah Haborn of whom she was so fond, and who used to encourage her so.

For my part, I am ready to forgive, not merely the

anguish she inflicted on us that April and during the years since, but even all the things she put us through in her childhood – her experiments and inventions, her madcap schemes, her daring lies – merely for the pleasure of having her home with us once more. After such a long time that I had almost forgotten her dear face, it is so good to see it again – even though her hair has been shorn so short that, I swear, she looks just like a boy.

I am, though in haste,
Ever your loving friend,
Charlotte

ABOUT THE AUTHOR

Philip Purser-Hallard is the author of the trilogy of urban fantasy thrillers beginning with *The Pendragon Protocol*, and the editor of a series of anthologies about the City of the Saved. As well as writing various other books and short stories, Phil edits *The Black Archive*, a series of monographs about individual Doctor Who stories published by Obverse Books.

SHERLOCK HOLMES
CRY OF THE INNOCENTS
Cavan Scott

It is 1891, and a Catholic priest arrives at 221B Baker Street, only to utter the words "*il corpe*" before suddenly dropping dead.

Though the man's death is attributed to cholera, when news of another dead priest reaches Holmes, he becomes convinced that the men have been poisoned. He and Watson learn that the victims were on a mission from the Vatican to investigate a miracle; it is said that the body of eighteenth-century philanthropist and slave trader Edwyn Warwick has not decomposed. But should the Pope canonise a man who made his fortune through slavery? And when Warwick's body is stolen, it becomes clear that the priests' mission has attracted the attention of a deadly conspiracy...

PRAISE FOR CAVAN SCOTT
"Many memorable moments... excellent."
Starburst

"Utterly charming, comprehensively Sherlockian, and possessed of a wry narrator." **Criminal Element**

"Memorable and enjoyable... One of the best stories I've ever read."
Wondrous Reads

TITANBOOKS.COM

SHERLOCK HOLMES
THE PATCHWORK DEVIL
Cavan Scott

It is 1919, and while the world celebrates the signing of the Treaty of Versailles, Holmes and Watson are called to a grisly discovery.

A severed hand has been found on the bank of the Thames, a hand belonging to a soldier who supposedly died in the trenches two years ago. But the hand is fresh, and shows signs that it was recently amputated. So how has it ended up back in London two years after its owner was killed in France? Warned by Sherlock's brother Mycroft to cease their investigation, and only barely surviving an attack by a superhuman creature, Holmes and Watson begin to suspect a conspiracy at the very heart of the British government…

"Scott poses an intriguing puzzle for an older Holmes and Watson to tackle." *Publishers Weekly*

"Interesting and exciting in ways that few Holmes stories are these days." *San Francisco Book Review*

"A thrilling tale for Scott's debut in the Sherlock Holmes world."
Sci-Fi Bulletin

SHERLOCK HOLMES
LABYRINTH OF DEATH
James Lovegrove

It is 1895, and Sherlock Holmes's new client is a high court judge, whose free-spirited daughter has disappeared without a trace.

Holmes and Watson discover that the missing woman – Hannah Woolfson – was herself on the trail of a missing person, her close friend Sophia. Sophia was recruited to a group known as the Elysians, a quasi-religious sect obsessed with Ancient Greek myths and rituals, run by the charismatic Sir Philip Buchanan. Hannah has joined the Elysians under an assumed name, convinced that her friend has been murdered. Holmes agrees that she should continue as his agent within the secretive yet seemingly harmless cult, yet Watson is convinced Hannah is in terrible danger. For Sir Philip has dreams of improving humanity through classical ideals, and at any cost…

"A writer of real authority and one worthy of taking the reader back to the dangerous streets of Victorian London in the company of the Great Detective." **Crime Time**

"Lovegrove does a convincing job of capturing Watson's voice."
Publishers Weekly

TITANBOOKS.COM

SHERLOCK HOLMES
THE THINKING ENGINE
James Lovegrove

It is 1895, and Sherlock Holmes is settling back into life as a consulting detective at 221B Baker Street, when he and Watson learn of strange goings-on amidst the dreaming spires of Oxford.

A Professor Quantock has built a wondrous computational device, which he claims is capable of analytical thought to rival the cleverest men alive. Naturally Sherlock Holmes cannot ignore this challenge. He and Watson travel to Oxford, where a battle of wits ensues between the great detective and his mechanical counterpart as they compete to see which of them can be first to solve a series of crimes, from a bloody murder to a missing athlete. But as man and machine vie for supremacy, it becomes clear that the Thinking Engine has its own agenda…

"The plot, like the device, is ingenious, with a chilling twist… an entertaining, intelligent and pacy read."
The Sherlock Holmes Journal

"Lovegrove knows his Holmes trivia and delivers a great mystery that will fans will enjoy, with plenty of winks and nods to the canon."
Geek Dad

"Brilliance itself." **The Book Bag**

SHERLOCK HOLMES
GODS OF WAR
James Lovegrove

It is 1913, and Dr Watson is visiting Sherlock Holmes at his retirement cottage near Eastbourne when tragedy strikes: the body of a young man, Patrick Mallinson, is found under the cliffs of Beachy Head.

The dead man's father, a wealthy businessman, engages Holmes to prove that his son committed suicide, the result of a failed love affair with an older woman. Yet the woman in question insists that there is more to Patrick's death. She has seen mysterious symbols drawn on his body, and fears that he was under the influence of a malevolent cult. When an attempt is made on Watson's life, it seems that she may be proved right. The threat of war hangs over England, and there is no telling what sinister forces are at work…

"Lovegrove has once again packed his novel with incident and suspense." **Fantasy Book Review**

"An atmospheric mystery which shows just why Lovegrove has become a force to be reckoned with in genre fiction. More, please." *Starburst*

"A very entertaining read with a fast-moving, intriguing plot." **The Consulting Detective**

TITANBOOKS.COM

SHERLOCK HOLMES
THE STUFF OF NIGHTMARES
James Lovegrove

A spate of bombings has hit London, causing untold damage and loss of life. Meanwhile a strangely garbed figure has been spied haunting the rooftops and grimy back alleys of the capital.

Sherlock Holmes believes this strange masked man may hold the key to the attacks. He moves with the extraordinary agility of a latter-day Spring-Heeled Jack. He possesses weaponry and armour of unprecedented sophistication. He is known only by the name Baron Cauchemar, and he appears to be a scourge of crime and villainy. But is he all that he seems? Holmes and his faithful companion Dr Watson are about to embark on one of their strangest and most exhilarating adventures yet.

"[A] tremendously accomplished thriller which leaves the reader in no doubt that they are in the hands of a confident and skilful craftsman."
Starburst

"Dramatic, gripping, exciting and respectful to its source material, I thoroughly enjoyed every surprise and twist as the story unfolded."
Fantasy Book Review

"This is delicious stuff, marrying the standard notions of Holmesiana with the kind of imagination we expect from Lovegrove."
Crime Time

TITANBOOKS.COM

For more fantastic fiction, author events, competitions,
limited editions and more

VISIT OUR WEBSITE
titanbooks.com

LIKE US ON FACEBOOK
facebook.com/titanbooks

FOLLOW US ON TWITTER
@TitanBooks

EMAIL US
readerfeedback@titanemail.com